CORR SYL THE WARRIOR

Garry Rogers

The characters in this book are not real.
They live only in our thoughts.
[There is a complete list of characters
and places in the appendix.]

Cover:
Anya Kelleye and Garry Rogers.

Map:
T. J. Vandel and Garry Rogers.

Editors:
Kate Robinson, Tara Fort, Harvey Stanbrough

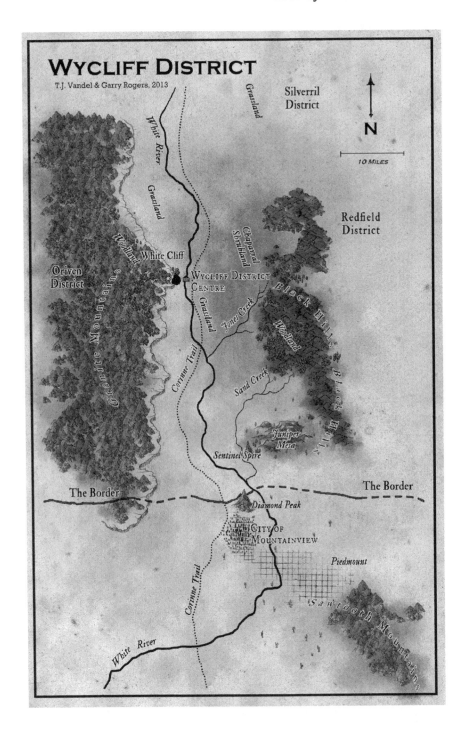

For
Denise

Contents

FOREWORD

Some of the characters in this story are Human, but most of them are intelligent animals that resemble Humans. Animals became intelligent early in Earth's history, and though many species came and went, intelligence remained and grew.

Intelligent animals solved many of the riddles of nature. They learned to transform energy and matter, they learned to prevent disease and senescence, and they learned to alter their genes and change their shape.

Most terrestrial animals have human form but they usually keep their species' original skin covering. Mammals have fur, lizards have scales, and birds and fish retain their wings and fins. The animals call themselves Tsaeb (silent T, long A—sābe). See Appendix A for more about the development of intelligent animals and the Tsaeb civilization.

Part One: Corr Syl

The Tsaeb Warriors. In the peaceful Tsaeb civilization, few warriors remain to preserve the ancient knowledge of combat and war. It is good that warriors persist, for like unworthy thoughts, dangerous individuals and species appear from time to time, and civilization needs its defenders.

History of the Tsaeb. The Warriors.
Morgan Silverleaf, Librarian of Wycliff District

Corr Syl

The warrior, a youthful, five-foot tall descendent of an ancient rabbit lineage, wiggled his four furry toes, scratched an ear, and thought about singing with Ralph and dancing with Allysen last night. He grinned and rolled out of bed. As he reached for his jar of dried fruit and nuts, he began an imaginary practice attack. He dropped to the floor.

The assassin moved across the smooth stone with quick, light steps, slashing with his gleaming blade down from right to left.

The warrior had dropped to his right beneath the cut. He drew a short sword from its scabbard on the wall and turned to block the whirling assassin's rising cut. As the assassin recoiled from the block, the warrior drew his long sword and attacked in Two Heavens form, the rapidly rotating blades beating down the defenses of the backing assassin. In seconds the warrior stopped, his short sword holding the enemy blade, the edge of his long sword pressing against the imaginary assassin's neck.

Corr Syl, the youngest fully trained warrior of Wycliff District, liked the direct block and the power of Two Heavens, but if he drew both swords, his long sword could end the encounter almost instantly. He grinned, and his long gray whiskers twitched when he thought about the damage the edge-to-edge block by his almost indestructible drahsalleh sword would do to a metal blade. He added the attack to the collection of tactics in the battle kingdom of his memory world and pulled on his weapons harness.

As he turned toward the door, one of his six thoughtstreams, like a mocking child, produced a conclusion: *Rhya Bright doesn't like me.* Corr severed the stream and gave the freed capacity to a new botheration.

The day before, as Corr had strolled toward the river enjoying the warm sun on his fur, Arden Aquila, the Chairman of the District Council, had swooped to a landing and made a befuddling announcement. "Corr, the council has appointed you its volunteer agent; we need to have at least one warrior present at all meetings."

In the glare of the old golden eagle's intense gaze, Corr had slowly lowered his hands from the sword hilts projecting above his shoulders, his wrinkled brow and squinted eyes signifying a mental vacuum from which questions might arise.

Aquila hadn't waited for questions. "The council meets at 9:00 a.m. tomorrow. Address any questions to Counselor Korhonen." And generating a dusty blast of leaves and twigs that left Corr's eyes watering, Aquila had flown away.

Corr had stared. *What? Why would the council choose me for its agent? And what is an agent of the council?*

Corr's seven years of training followed by a five-year internship had gone well, but he had no experience. Nineteen of the District's 21 warriors had fought real battles. Corr's given name came from a warrior who had died in battle, but many warriors had died in battle. The council had already given him one undeserved and unwanted duty. *Now another? Who decided I needed something to do?*

Corr's plan did not include attending all council meetings. Long ago, he had decided he would complete his training and internship, serve the community for one year, and then become a traveler. He wanted to sail the great oceans, and walk the deserts, the jungles, the frozen polar seas. His training and internship had ended a year ago, and he was still here. But no more delays—next month he would leave, and everyone knew it.

He wondered whether his becoming the agent of the council might impress Rhya, but he doubted it; nothing he did seemed to impress her. Rhya Bright would make a perfect traveling companion, but the painful rebuffs lying scattered about like trampled daisies in his memory world's Rhya Meadow included so many ignores and dismissals that Corr sometimes wanted to purge the whole thing.

He sagged at the thought of attending every council meeting. The council made decisions about food storage, birth planning, celebrations and, amidst bursts of laughter, passed resolutions on everything from Agave Day to Week's Worst Joke (Corr had two of those), and on and on and on. *No need for me to attend. As long as I'm in the District or even in North America, a two-second call will get my total support. I don't need to sit through production forecasts and lectures on new storage techniques in order to serve.*

He decided to refuse the council appointment. He would assure the council that they could depend on him, but because of his imminent departure, they would have to choose another warrior as their agent.

* * *

It was time to go out and begin his daily routine. At the entry to his flat Corr reached for his climbing pegs but paused, his long, pale gray whiskers twitching. He gently redirected a tip of the ivy covering the interior of his wall and always trying to cover the window.

Corr took the climbing pegs out into a pale dawn that illuminated an enormous vista. He stepped to the brink of the ledge that passed his door and stared at the amazing view. He was high on the side of a pale gray cliff covered by shrubs and vines. White Cliff was the eastern face of a promontory jutting out from the mountains that formed the western boundary of Wycliff District. Ledges crisscrossing the cliff provided access to the apartments of residents of the District Center. The ledges sloped back to gutters filled with soil, organisms, and roots. Corr's view included plains to the north and a dark line of silent volcanos 25 miles east across White River Valley.

For a moment, he relaxed conscious control over his senses. With the unique abilities of the Tsaeb warrior, he listened to the quick, insistent beat of ultrasound and the slow, haunting throb of infrasound; he sampled the rich clouds of fragrance; and he sensed the dancing energy of countless electrons in the air and in the stolid rocks embedded in the valley's sea of twinkling soil. The concentrated messages of life flared amidst it all: softly glowing plants, twinkling sparks of distant minds, bright lights of nearer minds, and the clear emotions and intentions of beings in the woods below.

Not far from the foot of the cliff, White River ran through scattered cottonwoods and willow thickets, passing around the far side of the huge granite mound that contained the carved halls and rooms of the Wycliff District Center. The Center provided emergency shelter and storage for food reserves. It also served as the district museum, council chambers, communications center, and the District's heart, the tavern.

Corr scanned the scene for signs of discord or danger. He focused his senses across the valley on the eastern mountains, drew the scan in across the valley floor to the White River Bridge, and combed through the small forest surrounding the Center. As his scan approached the cliff, his automatic tactical system reacted to something unfamiliar in the woods below. His skin quivered, his fur shifted its reflectivity to match his background, and he reached for his swords. Nothing of Corr remained visible except his gray harness, auburn eyes, and the gray sword hilts above his shoulders.

After a fruitless search for strange thoughts or scents, he shrugged and glanced up at the stubby trail of a jet passing high overhead. Frowning, he shifted his gaze south toward the glow of Mountainview, the Human city south of Wycliff District, and considered devoting a thoughtstream to the Humans. Then he looked down at the two cylindrical climbing pegs and remembered the pipe his friend Allon Trofeld had carried as a pretend weapon when they were children and only wonder filled the world.

A small grass sparrow peeped as it streaked past on the way to awaken his friend. Corr smiled as his gaze followed the sparrow's flight.

Rhya appeared two ledges below. She looked up, nodded, and started down. She would cross the river and go for a run on the east bank. She never ran with Corr, and she ignored him if he joined her.

As he used his climbing pegs to ascend the cliff, Corr replayed memories of Allon. Corr had met Allon almost 21 years earlier while standing in front of his new home in Nursery Canyon, immersed in a sea of unfamiliar sound, scent, and vision. A small, tawny creature with white spots had staggered out of a nearby doorway and Corr had jerked back a step when a huge creature had lunged out of the doorway and snatched up the small one. The captive had issued a piercing scream, struggling and squalling as its captor carried it inside. Corr had hurried through his own doorway, and his mother had explained that a mountain lion family had come to live next door. Corr had witnessed the attempted escape of two-month-old Allon Trofeld, the only other child in Nursery Canyon. For several years, the two children roamed about the canyon together, but after their families had moved apart, the boys had not remained close. Corr recently learned that Allon was in trouble, and he had become concerned, but it had been nothing like the foreboding he felt this morning.

Three Deaths

The messenger streaked through the trees toward the base of White Cliff. There, on a flat granite shelf, a raucous group of variously furry, feathery, and scaly creatures was crowded around an intense rock-paper-scissors contest. The contest was between perennial loser Corr Syl, and perennial winner Alexander Maypole. Today, a library trainee had joined the contest. Corr had a rare lead over Maypole and total dominion over the young librarian.

The starter raised his hands. Corr swiveled an eye toward each of his opponents. The crowd leaned in—and the messenger thumped to a swaying landing on Corr's shoulder.

Corr snapped, "*What?*"

The crowd froze, all eyes on the small bird.

The bird tweeted, "Councilor Korhonen needs you."

The crowd groaned.

As she leapt into the air, the little Vireo trilled, "Did you know you look stupefied with your eyes walled like that?"

The librarian laughed.

"Ah, too bad, boy," said Alex. "Perhaps you can try again tomorrow. Now, go get ready for your new job."

Corr dug out the sense of relief he had felt earlier when he'd decided to refuse the agent business. "Tomorrow, squirrel." Then he smiled at the little librarian. "I'm sorry, but I have to go," and away trotted the soon-to-be former agent of the council.

* * *

Councilor Korhonen zealously conducted his daily dialogue on life, the universe, and current affairs (Human dominated) in an outdoor amphitheater near the entrance to the District Center.

The Center rose above the surrounding trees two hundred yards east of the rock-paper-scissors alcove. The mammoth facility extended deep into bedrock, its many chambers filled with preserved food and a huge collection of art as well as inventions and curiosities accumulated over a very long history.

White River, Wycliff Valley's principal stream, meandered from a few miles north of the Center to the district border sixty miles south. Intersected by numerous tributaries along its course through the high-desert valley, the river finally entered a deep gorge cut into basalt-capped mesas. Below that, the river crossed the border into Human land and died in a reservoir that supplied the Human City of Mountainview.

Some mornings Rhya Bright sat with Counselor Korhonen. As Corr trotted along the familiar path, he tried out various interesting remarks he might make if he encountered her: *How unusually fine is the morning! Isn't the air brilliantly clear? Aren't the mint green colors of spring wonderful!* and— *Aaargh! She'll just ignore me as usual!*

Corr's communicator beeped as he neared the Center and another messenger flew alongside. "About an hour after sunrise, an armed platoon of Human troops crossed the border east of Diamond Peak. They're following the survey route."

Corr sped up. Athol Shorel and the six members of the district's main battle group were only a few miles west of Diamond Peak. By now, they would be racing to meet the platoon. Corr made a quick series of calls to alert his battle group.

"Sorry to interrupt the match, Corr," Korhonen said over the heads of his company. "The council needs you to investigate a death that occurred this morning." The great elk was communicating in Tsaeb Standard, Earth's common language of interwoven motions, chemical signals, sensory net flickers, and sounds. If Humans needed to join the conversation, Korhonen would use English, the local Human language.

"Who died?" Corr asked while noting Rhya's absence.

"I don't know, but the report is disturbing. The death occurred in the Black Hills on the left bank of Jones Creek just below the upper falls."

"Okay, but something else is going on too."

Korhonen nodded. "I heard. Shorel will let us know if he needs anything. The council meets tomorrow morning at 9:00 a.m. We need to have a report on the death." The great elk's large dark gaze held the small warrior for a moment. "Take Allysen."

* * *

Corr waited for Allysen on the White River Bridge, a stone arch built with ivory, tan, and brown sandstone blocks and protected with a layer of drahsalleh. Allysen looked thoughtful when he described the assignment, but she said nothing, so Corr turned and set a fast pace across the bridge toward the dark eastern hills.

When Corr and Allysen neared the site, they slowed to a walk, checked their recorders, and began describing the scene. As Corr eased through the oak brush, the scent of blood and other fluids assailed him. He was listening to the murmuring of observers as a body came into view. Descending into a small clearing in the rocky debris covering the slope, he noted that the soft soil of the clearing would simplify the analysis. But then he recognized the tracks surrounding the body and stopped.

To the Tsaeb at the edge of the clearing, Allysen said, "Did anyone see what happened?" Her gaze followed Corr.

"Not all of it," said a blue jay from his perch in an oak shrub. "I saw Allon Trofeld kneeling beside what I first thought was a bush. He didn't speak, but he was blazing with tension. Pretty soon he stood and trotted up the slope."

Other witnesses nodded.

Corr looked around. The hollow held only the body, pebbles, twigs, leaves, and lion tracks. Nevertheless, he studied everything before beginning on the body. He looked at the beautiful young face for a moment, then began a minute examination. *This was not an accidental death.* Deep cuts on the back of the deer's head matched the spacing of a mountain lion's claws. Whatever had caused the linear depression in the skull to the left of the cuts almost certainly had caused the death.

Corr opened a pouch on the deer's waist belt. It contained a letter, a ribbon, grooming items, and a purple petunia blossom. Addressed to Lisa Roman, the letter invited her to visit a friend across the valley. The Roman family lived near the spring at the head of Jones Creek. *Ah, Lisa....* Corr rose, his eyes moist, his sensory webs blazing.

Spreading tendrils of doubt drained the emotions. Tsaeb rarely killed, and only in self-defense. The murder taboo formed part of the core of Equivalency and was a cornerstone of Immediacy, the guiding ethos of Tsaeb civilization. Allon had no need to kill. Carnivores had modified their metabolism to eliminate the need for meat long ago. *Perhaps Lisa fell and Allon went for help.*

Lisa's mother and father arrived, identified the body, and asked to take it home.

As Corr and Allysen left, Corr's com unit beeped. As he answered, a falcon swooped to a landing.

"Corr, the soldiers in the platoon that crossed the border this morning fired their rifles at a Tsaeb greeting party. Tsaeb attacked a few minutes later. Four soldiers are down."

Corr and Allysen looked at one another. Corr said, "They'll probably retreat rather than hold for reinforcements."

"Right," Allysen said. "Let's alert the group and then swing south anyway."

During a council meeting after Corr had finished his internship, the council had voted to form a new battle group and asked Corr to serve as leader. As Corr had digested the inexplicable request and started composing a refusal, Allysen had stood and said she wanted to join the group. Before Corr could add that twist to his refusal, the chair of the council had thanked him and Allysen and moved on to another issue.

Five other warriors had joined the group within days. All had fought in the border war, and some of them in earlier conflicts. Corr had decided that doing a little scheduling in return for getting to travel about the district with a band of warriors wouldn't be too bad.

One battle group had served the district during the 100 years since the border war. The group toured the district and the southern border, and Corr had toured with it during the five years of his internship. He had enjoyed that time, even though the group did nothing but train. There weren't any conflicts, and Corr had seen no reason to form a second group. Now he wasn't so sure.

* * *

The Human military did not return that day. Late in the afternoon Corr and Allysen reached White River and turned north toward the Center. After a fast trip along the river's left bank, they stopped on the bridge to catch their breath.

Sitting on the bridge railing, Corr raised his foot and inspected the sole. "Do your feet ever get hot?"

Allysen burst out laughing. "I wondered if you noticed. It's the stepping stones through the grassland. Some genius decided textured drahsalleh would make them safer."

"They applied a second layer?"

She nodded. "To the tops, mixed with fibers. The fibers add friction. If you run very far on them, they cause the soles of your feet to get hot. I decided to turn the stones over, but I've put it off too many times. Maybe you can help me get motivated again."

Corr felt his hot foot. "Glad to."

After a few minutes, they trotted across the bridge into

the woods surrounding the District Center. Corr stopped beneath a cottonwood tree on the north side of the Center. Allysen continued toward the cliff to join her friend, another warrior named Ankolla Siran.

In the dusk of a bizarre day, invisible against the broad silver-gray tree trunk, Corr felt safe at home. He relaxed his fur as a smile tugged at the corners of his mouth and became an involuntary grin. Tonight he would see his friends, share the news of the Human border incursion, and resume his efforts to make a breakthrough with Rhya Bright. But first, the Entry.

The Tavern

To the left of the main entrance to the center, a noisy crowd of creatures was sitting near a long stone counter. Most were sitting on the floor around low stone tables rising from the native rock. Others were seated on carved benches or perched on assorted sculptures. Suddenly, a warrior broadcasting weary confusion stumbled through the doorway. Primed by rumors of the day's events, the crowd froze. All heads snapped toward the disheveled Corr Syl.

Now, Corr thought. He stretched to his full five feet, shifted his fur into a shimmering corona, vaulted onto the counter, and raised his right hand. "Never fear, never fear! The fact is, I just need a beer!" Standing there, fur shining, face uplifted, whiskers twitching, the warrior looked spectacular. With embarrassed chuckles, patient sighs, and a few invectives, the crowd returned to their conversations.

"Should stick to kicks!" chirped one patron.

"Death of a swordsman," intoned another.

From his prominent position, Corr saw Rhya. A huge feather rose from something on her head. In fact, the entire crowd looked odd.

Friends and visitors with comments and questions surrounded Corr when he jumped down from the counter. Corr finally stepped onto a stone mound carved into the shape of a crescent moon and called for attention. "There were three deaths today. Allon Trofeld was involved in one of them, but the cause of that death is uncertain. I will report its details to the council. The others who died were Human soldiers." He looked around the hall. *Big crowd tonight. All the district's attorneys, their spouses, and their friends must have come for Allon's trial. But everyone looks odd and— Oh right! It's hat night!* Corr remembered the inaugural occasion of hat night, one of the latest council resolutions. Rhya was wearing a turban. Corr whipped out his Robin Hood cap.

"Who did Allon kill?" asked a muskrat wearing a navy

blue yellow-fringed 19th century Human tricorner.

"Lisa Roman died, but we have to wait for the council to determine the cause of death. There is another issue. This morning a platoon of Human soldiers crossed the border carrying weapons in open violation of the treaty. The platoon followed the route of the recent survey. Lots of Tsaeb saw them. Four local leaders approached, but the soldiers formed a line and started shooting."

"Anyone hit?"

"No."

"The soldiers continued along the survey route, but they didn't get far before two children watching from a boulder dropped onto one of the soldier's packs, opened the pack, removed the pin from a grenade, and fled. Apparently, several grenades detonated. Shrapnel hit most of the soldiers, and the retreating platoon left four of its members behind. Our healers saved two."

"I think Morgan Silverleaf is those kids' uncle," a small character wearing a black ski mask said.

"Any idea what the soldiers were up to?" asked a rock dove wearing a cowboy hat and a Lone Ranger mask.

"No," Corr said.

Someone said, "I think those soldiers are the first casualties in 133 years."

"The only ones on our border," said a kestrel wearing a beanie with a propeller. "Last winter I heard about one in the Atacama Desert."

A packrat wearing a hat with a brim broader than her height said, "It's been 143 years, not 133."

"No," a warrior said. "You're thinking of the Diamond Peak battle. There was a small skirmish ten years later. I saw it. Allysen Olykden knocked a Human soldier off his horse, and he struck a rock and broke his neck."

As the room filled with other comments and speculations, Corr stole a glance at Rhya. She was sitting at a table with the possum from the RPS match, some birds, and a big jackrabbit wearing a tall top hat. Corr didn't know the jackrabbit. He was probably a lawyer here for Allon's trial.

After ten years of training, Rhya Bright had come to the Center to study with a specialist in Human psychology. She would soon continue her training as an intern in one of the battle groups. The group led by Athol Shorel needed a replacement for a member who had decided to travel. Corr was disappointed, but having Rhya in his group might create a barrier of formality. He didn't want that.

Rhya looked his way.

Corr nodded and turned away, wishing for a moment she would hurry up and go join Shorel.

While waiting for more questions, Corr received a report from Shorel, reviewed his story about the warrior that defeated Ankalagon, followed conversations about Human activities, and listened for new jokes.

Every creature in the room was following several streams of thought. Most divided their thoughts and senses into two or three streams, and some four or five, but of the hundreds of creatures present in the Tavern, only Corr, Rhya, and old Alex Maypole could follow six.

After a few minutes, Counselor Tau Korhonen stood and spoke from beneath a broad set of fake antlers. "Corr's news highlights the growing need to resolve the Human problem. The council will discuss the topic tomorrow morning."

"Aren't you going to do something about Allon Trofeld?" asked a horned lizard sitting at the bar.

"The council will deliver a final verdict on Trofeld."

A finch perched in Korhonen's antlers said, "Hooray! The Wycliff council can actually make a decision!"

Tau rolled his eyes upward, and then looked down at Corr. "Anything more?"

The phrase *final verdict* echoed in Corr's mind. He looked at Korhonen for a moment, then turned to the bar. "One other issue. Is any of last year's beer left?"

A few patrons chuckled, and a deer mouse swaying

beneath a gay sombrero squeaked a cheer. The District brew master had retired, and his apprentice had immediately become the subject of jokes and impossible suggestions. Then the poor beast's perfectly flat first batch of beer provided inspiration for the longest run of comic insults and rude remarks heard in Wycliff in decades. It wasn't fair, of course, since the position of brew master, like all Tsaeb occupations, was voluntary. Everyone felt sympathy, but in Tsaeb communities no one ignored a chance to inspire laughter.

Chatting with friends, Corr reflected on his successful quip about the beer and puzzled over his frequent failure to get a laugh. Confident that he would improve, he saw Rhya joining a group dancing to a Human hip-hop melody. Within a few minutes, almost everyone in the Tavern got attitude. Corr danced near Rhya, intensely aware that while dancing, she was painfully beautiful.

"You're a good dancer," Corr said when the music stopped.

"Thanks," Rhya said with a slight smile as she turned toward her table.

Corr soon said goodnight. He took a wide loop through the dark woods listening to the quiet rustling and murmurings of all the endings and beginnings before climbing the steps to his flat. Inside, he hung his harness and flopped on the bed. Normally, he would have gone to sleep quickly with only his automatic tactical senses alert, but for a few minutes he remembered some of his first adventures with Allon.

Doubts and Melancholy

Morning came and Corr awoke feeling gloomy and tired. On the ledge outside his apartment he experienced a rare blank moment.

He ran in the uplands again, and afterward paused at the top of the cliff and looked down at trees he had climbed and grassy glades in which he had sprawled in those years he spent studying with Halbert Sims. He remembered waking up every morning eager for the challenges and possible adventures the day might bring. His melancholy mood was blurring a growing alarm from his tactical senses.

Corr jerked his foot back when, inches from his toes, the grinning face of Wycliff's other battle rabbit popped above the edge of the cliff. Rhya Bright sprang over the brink, brushed past Corr, and sailed away up the path.

After a blank second, relief flooded through him. No one would see his red face glowing through his fur. Then he succeeded in resisting the urge to turn and watch Rhya's beautiful back as she ran up the path. She had climbed quietly and shielded her sensory fields. *She played with me!* Corr leaned down, placed his pins in the first set of holes, swung out wide over the edge of the cliff, and streaked down with a buzz of clicking pins. Just enough time remained to beat the squirrel before the council meeting.

But Corr's mentor, Halbert Sims, intercepted him before he could go to the morning's rock-paper-scissors match.

Corr grinned. "What's up?"

Sims spread his shield and explained. When finished, he said, "Rhya Bright's interest in Human psychology will be useful. It's time for her to join Shorel anyway. Ask her to go with you to the conference and then on to the border."

Corr grinned now and then as he trotted toward the Center for his first day of agent duty.

Council Meeting

At 8:55 a.m. Corr entered the Center. He walked past the empty tavern to the council area across the hall. Corr walked to the front row and scanned the audience. Halbert Sims was near the center of the crowd, and Rhya was sitting near the back.

From his position in the center of the row of counselors sitting on a carved ledge, Arden Aquila called the meeting to order at 9:00 a.m. "Most of you probably know about the Human surveyors who crossed the border two weeks ago. Well, there has been another border incursion. Corr Syl will describe what happened, and then we will have an open discussion."

Corr repeated the description he had provided the night before, and Aquila asked for comments.

One of the council members said, "This might be related to the Mountainview City Manager's plan to build a road across the border."

This will take a while, Corr thought. *There's time to try Halbert.* Then he began a deception that only one other person in the room could accomplish. He used his sensory webs to reinforce his image within the minds of nearby Tsaeb. Then he adjusted his fur to blend with his surroundings, concealed his thoughts, and slipped away while continuing to reinforce his image. He came within striking distance of his teacher before Sims' tactical senses responded. "Huh! That's damned good Corr."

Rhya had been looking at Corr when he began the deception and had seen him reappear beside Sims. *That's astonishing*, she thought. Jonas had said cloaked action was a Sims strength. Obviously he had passed the trick on to his student.

The discussion produced no explanation for the border crossing, but it aroused interest in the Mountainview City Manager Ivan Johns.

As comments wound down, Aquila stretched his wings. "We need more information. I suggest we ask Ambassador

Farr to hold a meeting to discuss the incursions."

The council agreed and decided to have the meeting on Juniper Mesa in two days.

"Just a moment, please," said Korhonen. "We are worrying about a brown leaf as a snowstorm approaches. Shouldn't we at least begin discussing general options for dealing with the Humans?"

Aquila reflected for a moment. "Tau, no Tsaeb community has taken action against the Humans for more than a hundred years. Our basic preparations will enable us to react if they send other forces across the border."

The head of the Rock Squirrel Caucus stood. "We need to do something about the Humans. Combustion wastes in the air damage the plants and trap heat. All kinds of crap winds up in the water. Every week the gleaner assembly says it's approaching the limits of their ability to keep up."

Another audience member stood and said, "The problems are building up everywhere, but it's worse along the southern border near Mountainview."

Councilors and others throughout the crowd nodded.

Aquila said, "Fine. I'll ask Librarian Silverleaf to assemble a report on the methods used to deal with troublesome species."

Korhonen frowned. "Weren't you involved in the last one?"

Aquila's eyes flashed and Corr felt a tingle in his tactical system. Aquila said, "Tau, everyone knows that Ambassador Farr is working on solutions. We need him present if we are going to discuss specific actions. The Tuesday meeting with Farr will focus on the border issue, but it can include a discussion of the general Human problem as well." He looked at Corr. "Corr, you will accompany Ambassador Farr to Mountainview after that meeting. Try to learn what the Humans are planning. Take your battle group." He looked around the room. "Council will recess until 10:00 a.m. Representatives of Allon Trofeld should be present at that time."

* * *

At 10:00 a.m. Aquila's voice filled the hall. "The council will now consider the case of Allon Trofeld. Previous evidence presented to the council established that Trofeld murdered two district residents. Today we will review additional information, and we might pass a sentence. Will Trofeld's representatives please stand and state their names?"

He sighed as all 35 of the district's attorneys and their students stood.

When the procedure ended, Aquila said, "Corr Syl, please present the new information."

Corr stood. "Yesterday Allysen Olykden and I investigated a death on Jones Creek in the Gray Hills. We found a deer's remains surrounded by large footprints. The cause of death is uncertain, but several residents saw Allon Trofeld beside the deer. One witness is present."

"Were you able to identify the deer?"

"Yes. Items in harness pouch bore the name Lisa Roman. Lisa's father recognized a birthmark and confirmed a gene marker as Lisa's."

"Thank you."

Corr sat down.

Aquila called the witness forward. "Did you see Allon Trofeld kill the deer?"

"No."

"Do you know what caused the death?"

"No."

Aquila called for questions and, after a moment of jostling, a Trofeld attorney asked, "Was the deer's blood fresh?"

"It smelled fresh."

Another attorney asked, "Did you see any injuries or blood on Trofeld?"

"No."

"Did you see any sources for the blood other than the deer?"

"No."

Another asked, "How far from Trofeld were you?"

"Thirty feet."

"What time was it?"

"8:00 in the morning."

The questioner, a lynx, held up his hand. "What is the distance between us right now, and how many claws have I extended?"

"About 25 feet. Two claws."

None of the lawyers found reasons to doubt that Trofeld had been in the clearing with Lisa.

Aquila asked whether anyone had heard from Allon— no one had—and then called for other comments.

Corr stood. "One thing is puzzling. Zuberi Taxus and Bataar Lee pieced together Allon's movements over the past year. He spent most of his time along our eastern and southern borders. He may have crossed the border, but there is no indication he went into neighboring Tsaeb districts to the east or west. My battle group interviewed Tsaeb living along Allon's path. We didn't find anyone who knew where he slept or where he got food. Can anyone suggest what he might have been eating?"

The warrior Ankolla Siran stood. "Maybe he ate Humans."

Uproar filled the court. Despite doubts and questions, several healers agreed that Allon could have been metabolizing meat.

Aquila shook his head. "We would have heard something if Humans were disappearing."

One of the lawyers said, "He probably just gathered food as he moved about."

Corr didn't think Allon could have collected enough food without local gleaners noticing. He and Ankolla had discussed the Human idea, but it had seemed too weird to be probable. However, some Humans homes near the border had no close neighbors. Perhaps Allon had friends there.

When other comments ended, Aquila said, "We know without doubt that Allon Trofeld killed two Tsaeb deliberately and without provocation. The penalty for such acts is death. Now we have circumstantial evidence from Lisa Roman's death that suggests Allon killed her as well. It is certain that he did not report the incident. We now know that Allon has remained in the District and remains a threat to our residents."

Before a silent crowd, Aquila obtained a motion to execute Trofeld. He called for discussion, but the hall remained silent. The council voted unanimously for execution.

Aquila said, "It is the decision of this council that Allon Trofeld must be executed. Corr Syl, you are the agent of the council. Will you accept this task?"

Corr stood. He had been worried about Allon, but this was an impossible request. The Trofeld and Syl families were friends. In the years since their time together in the nursery, Corr and Allon's friendship had faded, but Corr still felt Allon was his friend. *Could I kill him?* He thought he could, but as he prepared to answer the question, the room seemed to grow dim. Not only was Allon his friend, but Corr had never knowingly killed any being, sapient or otherwise. Throughout his years of training and patrolling the border, he had assumed the necessity to kill would come only during a desperate struggle with strangers. Nonetheless, Allon's actions appalled Corr and he guessed that at least part of Allon must be in agony. Corr looked up at Aquila. "I will find him."

Aquila studied Corr for a moment, then said, "If there are no objections, this meeting is adjourned. Corr, I need to speak to you."

After Corr left, Halbert Sims spoke privately to Aquila. Aquila said, "Are you sure?"

"Yes," replied Sims. "Corr is capable of more. I am sorry

about Trofeld, but I think it's something he has to deal with. Aquila, we need this. Trouble is coming."

* * *

As Corr left the Center, he spotted two members of his battle group, Zuberi Taxus and Bataar Lee. As usual, the two were engaged in debate, this time about the shape of tree crowns.

Taller and broader than Corr, Zuberi Taxus was a stolid, soft-spoken badger descendent from a family of warriors. He had gray fur, white cheeks, and a black spot in front of each ear. A white stripe ran from his nose over his head and beneath his pack. In contrast, Bataar Lee was a brash, outspoken collared lizard with no warriors in his family history. Well under four feet, he had a large head, black lines around his neck, and a rainbow of granular scales covering his body.

As he came near, Corr could feel the two warriors' tactical senses and remembered the shock he'd had when his training had included the first combat demonstration by two warriors. Now he knew that his life could end within seconds if he tried to attack. Corr's training and talent were among the best, and his daily practice enabled him to continue to improve, but all warriors continued improving. In a real battle with two older warriors, Corr would last no longer than a candle flame in a hurricane.

Corr said, "So… feel like a trip south?"

Lee asked, "Do we have to sing all the way?"

"There will be singing. Ralph and his brother have surely been composing, but there is a task that will keep you from traveling with Ralph."

Lee said, "You know, Corr, they're teaching that poor Human kid to sing. How's that going to be?"

Corr grinned. Lee had adopted the name William Wild and had begun responding to Wild Bill or just Bill. "Bill, signal Allysen, Ankolla, and Quin to meet us here at noon, ready to travel. Rhya Bright is going with us, so I need to get her."

As he trotted toward the cliff, his fellow warriors wriggled the skin of their orbital ridges at one another.

Rhya had gone home after the meeting. She was standing on the ledge outside her door watching Corr approach. As usual, she carefully concealed her interest. Corr had completed his training five years ago and had risen to prominence. He hadn't done anything very important, but Rhya felt far behind. Besides, danger was stirring, and she wanted to investigate the cause, not begin a romance.

Corr asked, "How was your run?"

"Good. Thanks for leveling that stone. What's up?"

"Would you like to go to the Juniper Mesa meeting with my battle group? Afterward, we'll meet Athol at the border."

"Sure. When do we leave?"

"After lunch."

"Be right back."

Rhya went into her flat. While he waited, Corr admired his good luck. He would have days with Rhya. He also reviewed the results of his battle simulations. The forces with the most symmetry at the start of combat usually won. A symmetrical beginning provided more options for responding to the enemy. He considered what he would say to Allon, and he thought about the meeting on Juniper Mesa. He couldn't really see any need for a meeting, and he definitely didn't see any need for him to be there. He would resign his agent position as soon as he got back to the Center.

Rhya came out and they started down. Corr felt as if he was leaving something behind, but he couldn't think of anything. His window was closed and the ivy would be fine. Water reached it automatically. *Besides, I won't be gone long.*

* * *

As they walked toward the Center to meet Bataar and Zuberi and the others, Rhya said, "I like your bow, Corr. Whoever engraved the pattern for the face took his time."

"Yes, he did."

Corr released his bow and almost struck Rhya on the head as he swung it into his left hand.

Rhya dipped sideways and stepped into a freshly watered section of the trough at the back of the ledge.

"Oh... sorry," Corr said as Rhya lurched out of the trough with mud up to her ankle.

Corr pointed at the engraved design on the bow. "The upper limb depicts the life of a battle rabbit, born at the knock and maturing to the arrow rest. On the lower limb, he fights battles, stands with friends, and appears to have a family as he fades into the distant future."

They strolled along, serene on the surface, each shielding emotions whirling like berries in a blender.

Corr finally said, "Sims had my bow made in Silverril. Did Miller get yours there, too?"

"Yes," Rhya said, turning Corr's hand so she could follow the story on the bow. "Finally. I used bows from his collection until the last year."

Rhya's warm fingertips on his hand caused Corr to pause for a second before he replied. "Same for me. Your bow is more elegant than mine."

"It looks delicate, but you know how drahsalleh is. Yours is heavier, but I can still hit targets at 300 yards."

"I know." Corr peered at Rhya's bow, still clipped to her pack. "What are those images?"

"They show the life cycle of an insect."

"Insect?"

"Yes. Well, it's a butterfly, a black swallowtail."

Corr sensed Rhya's hesitancy and stored the fact for future investigation.

As they walked on, Rhya's memory replayed some of

her experiences in Nursery Canyon....

When her family moved to the canyon, no other children were present. Between lessons, Rhya dug in the sand beside the canyon stream and poked about in the shrubs below the canyon walls. One morning she was basking on a rock when a black swallowtail butterfly floated by, flashing its bright rows of yellow spots.

"Hi," Rhya said, and held out her hand.

The butterfly circled, then settled on her finger.

"What's your name?"

The butterfly didn't reply, but Rhya could feel its interest. She directed more questions to the small creature. It studied her with its large sparkling eyes, but it did not reply. After a while, it flew to a biscuit-root plant and began probing the blossoms.

The butterfly came every day. Sometimes it perched on Rhya's nose. It tickled and Rhya giggled, but she didn't mind. With the butterfly so close, she could fully wrap it in her small sensory fields, and she could feel its emotions more clearly.

The tiny rabbit girl was sitting with the butterfly on her nose when her mother first saw the insect. She smiled at the unlikely friends and felt sad for her daughter.

One day Rhya noticed one of the butterfly's tails had disappeared. It was still missing the next day.

"Are you going to regrow your tail? Rhya asked.

The butterfly broadcast nothing but its usual interest. Rhya began to notice scales were missing and there seemed to be more small rips in the butterfly's wings every day. After a few days, the other tail disappeared. Rhya became alarmed.

"You need to fix your wings right now!" But her demand only added a trace of confusion to the small creature's usual interest and friendly feelings.

The rips became worse, and Rhya begged the butterfly to fix itself. Finally, she decided it couldn't. She tried to use what she had learned about sensory fields to heal the butterfly's wings, but she couldn't make its cells respond.

Rhya went to her mother, but she didn't like her mother's answer.

"Many small species are not able to heal themselves. They do not develop star cells, and without those, no one can repair problems for them."

Whole sections of the wings disappeared, and one day the butterfly didn't come. Rhya searched until after dark, but she couldn't find her friend. She told her mother what had happened and asked whether the butterfly would come back.

"Rhya, think about the happy times you spent with your friend," her mother said.

Rhya did, but sometimes her chest hurt and she squeezed her fists hard.

Other families came to the canyon, and though Rhya made friends, she always remembered the butterfly....

"These bows probably came from the forge in Silverril," Corr said. "Did you ever meet anyone from there or the other northern communities?"

She nodded. "When I was five, my family went to a spring equinox party in the north borderland. What a night! Hundreds of rabbits came from both districts. I still exchange letters with some of them. Another time, a band of travelers from Silverril camped near my home. A drought had cut into Silverril's productivity, and the travelers were looking for a new home. I guess we couldn't add them, and after a two-day stop, they went west. I heard they found a place in a district on the coast."

"Did they say anything about the drahsalleh forge?"

"One friend's father works there. He says there are hundreds of projects underway, but I don't know much about them. That's where Allon studied engineering, isn't it?"

"Yes."

* * *

After obtaining travel rations at the Center, the two went outside to await the others. They watched a group of young Tsaeb darting about, playing and laughing while inspecting soil crusts and new shoots, and they listened to the fast-paced buzz of a flock of finches inspecting branches and buds overhead.

Two youths, a Human and a gray wolf, stopped to say hello.

"Where are you boys headed?" Rhya asked.

"The river," the wolf said.

Rhya addressed the Human boy in the local Human language. "Duncan, how is your English?"

"Uh, it is becoming good."

"I am leaving for the border today. Perhaps I can pick up some of the latest slang."

The boy grinned. "Cool."

Watching the pair trot away, Corr wondered what specialty the Human boy would choose. "Isn't it odd that the Humans are so hairless?"

"Hmm... well, lizards are even balder."

"Yes, but they have scales."

Zuberi and Bill arrived, followed by the red-tailed Hawk, Quin Achiptre, Counselor Tau Korhonen, Allysen, and Allysen's roommate, the antelope Ankolla Siran.

Corr beckoned them close. All shields went up.

"We must attend a meeting on Juniper Mesa. There are tasks here for Bill and Zuberi, but they can leave for the mesa in the morning. Sims says something is out of place here, and we've all noticed that Zuberi has been more fretful than usual."

Everyone grinned.

"You mean Jumpy might be right this time?" asked Bill.

Zuberi nodded.

"Sims wants Bill to help him find the source of the problem. Zuberi, stick with Aquila. He's going to contact the Continental Center. If you're alone, have him ask about spies."

Bill said, "Uh, excuse me, but I have a hard time thinking of anything a spy could learn that isn't common knowledge even among the Humans. What's the point in spying?"

"If there are spies, there is an enemy," Zuberi said. "Perhaps the Humans are planning something serious."

They all looked at Korhonen.

"Everyone knows how I feel about the Humans," he said, "but I haven't even considered that they might do more than accidentally kill us with pesticides."

"Why does Sims think we have spies here at the Center?" Zuberi asked.

"He isn't sure we do. He's hoping that his and Bill's senses combined will be strong enough to catch any hidden hostility that is present among the visitors or staff."

"Quin, Allysen, and Ankolla can leave now," Corr said, then looked at those three. "Rhya and Tau are going with you. Pick up Ralph. Ellan Marin says strange Tsaeb have been seen around Mountainview military headquarters. She says Ambassador Farr thinks they might be foreign agents. Take time to warn local leaders along the trail. I will meet you at Traveler's Notch at dusk tomorrow evening."

The group trotted through the woods and across the bridge, then turned south. Corr went east alone.

* * *

Corr planned to go to the site of Lisa Roman's murder and try to follow Allon from there.

Beyond the strip of grassland beside the river, Corr's path rose steadily through chaparral-covered hills and arroyos to juniper-piñon woodlands on the esplanade below the steeper slopes leading to the summits along the district border. The chaparral varied from dense thickets on north-facing slopes to scattered shrubs on ridge tops and open sod grass with scattered acacia on south slopes.

Dry ravines divided the slopes.

The best paths through the chaparral followed the ridges and washes. The sandy-floored washes were the easiest and the most private. Corr followed neither path. He chose a course that led him across as many ravines as possible, in hopes of finding Allon's trail.

Besides visually scanning for signs, Corr used his sensory webs. The lion could cloak his presence somewhat, so Corr probably would not detect him beyond a few hundred yards, but he had the help of several small birds from the Center's messenger pool.

As he trotted through the chaparral, he detached a stream of awareness to watch for unusual plant forms and the shadows they cast. Local residents often pruned and trained the branches to create recognizable shapes. Sims said that once he had seen the noontime shadow of a creature with tall ears and a bushy tail, cast by the branches of an old live oak. He saw it along one of the washes Corr would cross, but the shadow might last for only a few minutes if the branches that cast it were very far apart. It wasn't worth a special search, but Corr always looked for it.

Corr moved through clouds of sensory fields, chemical signals, sounds, and sights of local creatures. No one stopped him to chat. News of Allon's sentence had spread, and no one wanted to interfere. Almost no one.

Late in the day, Corr sensed two small rodents waiting behind a boulder on the path ahead. As he drew near, he sprang forward, twisting to land facing the boulder from its far side.

Two white-footed brush mice dove left and right into the shrubs with surprised squeaks. In a moment, they peered out at Corr. One of them asked, "How did you know?"

"Your thoughts held me and yourselves, not the boulder and the ground. My name is Corr Syl. What are your names?"

The mouse that had spoken before said, "I am John Peromys."

"I am Nia Peromys," the second mouse said.

John asked, "Are you after Allon Trofeld?"

"Yes. Which of you saw me coming?"

"I did," Nia said, "but John wanted to surprise you." She glanced sidelong at her brother.

Corr smiled. "It's good to practice stealth."

"Is Allon your friend?" John asked.

"Yes."

"Are you going to capture him?"

"I don't know. I have to find him first."

Nia dragged out a large bag. "Do you want these seeds and grass? Our father said we should always help warriors."

Corr took the bag as expected. "Thank you. Please give my greetings to your mother and father. Goodbye, John and Nia."

"Goodbye."

That night as he ate from the bag, Corr thought about how quickly things changed. He knew John and Nia's parents. Both had studied African Human culture. They had often visited the Center library before their children were born. The last time he'd seen them, they were expecting twins. Now, only a few years later, the children were thoughtful, generous, and brave. Corr felt concern for their safety and began a stream of thoughts about spies.

* * *

On Monday, dawn found Corr trotting southeast through a juniper and piñon woodland. City lights glowed through the dense haze surrounding Mountainview, and he could sense the bright mass of Human thought and activity. The city always felt wrong, but he sensed a new dissonance. He followed his instincts and allowed a small sharpening of his tactical senses and a faint increase in his energy level.

In another hour, he reached the foot of the mountains and turned south. Looking west, he slowed and stopped. The early morning sun illuminated the branching lines of bright yellow-green willow leaves mixed with the ruddy haze of Cottonwood flowers on trees lining the washes and streams feeding the White River. Corr thought of his recorder, but decided that an image could not capture the feeling of the cool clear air and the width and depth of the scene.

At midday, he shifted course toward Sentinel Spire. Continuing to angle across washes, he began moving downslope. Desert grassland with scattered shrubs gradually replaced the woodland. Around 3:00 p.m., beneath a thickening layer of clouds, Corr crossed a rocky ridge and abruptly sensed Trofeld. The lion was crouching in an oak thicket about a quarter of a mile down the wash below.

The direct path lay across the completely exposed, dry, south-facing slope. Corr could slip back over the slope and come nearer Trofeld before moving into the open, but he decided on a fast, direct approach. He shielded his scent and thoughts and began running with a random pattern of light steps. Just as he started, one of his scouts glided in, probably to report sighting Allon. Corr detected alarm; Trofeld had bolted. Corr could catch him, but it would take hours.

Corr looked south toward Juniper Mesa. He had kept his word and found Allon. He called in his flight of helpers and arranged for a surveillance team. Finding Trofeld would never again be difficult, and there would be no more victims. An image of the Peromys twins came unbidden. Corr would find and confront Allon after his visit to the Mountainview Embassy.

Part Two: Lactella

Evil peers out with shining eyes when pleasure merges with hunger and fear.

Arden Aquila, Chairman
Wycliff District Council

The Spider and the City Manager

Ivan Johns, the new Mountainview City Manager, had one eccentricity. He cut his own hair in an uncommon style: short on the sides and long in the back. No one, not even his family, knew the secret it hid. Beneath the long hair, like a fat tick, a huge black widow spider clung to Johns' neck. The spider's claws and webs and the powerful chelicerae bracketing her mouth held her fast. Her hollow fangs reached deep into the City Manager's flesh. In public, Johns appeared calm and relaxed. In private, the spider liked to make him beg and scream.

* * *

The strange pairing had been the result of a misfortunate accident. Intelligent spiders are rare among the Tsaeb, and those who exist tend to keep the shape and some of the instinctive behaviors of their progenitors. Black widow spider hatchlings still spin the tiny web strands that originally serve as sails and carry the spiderlings to new, and hopefully richer, habitats. Intelligent black widows snip those first webs and prevent the spiderlings from floating away. On rare occasions, they fail to snip in time, and the spiderlings are lost.

On a stormy summer day, a spider egg hatched unattended. Wind caught the baby spider's web and carried her far from her family home. Such waifs rarely survive to become adults. The small spider survived because of luck, and because of her unusually high intelligence. Deposited in the heart of a large city, she grew while locked in a daily struggle to survive alone.

The spider's quick mind kept her alive, but she did not learn the body and mind controls that a normal Tsaeb family life would have given her. She received none of the great store of Tsaeb experience and wisdom. Instead, she learned only how to avoid threats and satisfy hunger.

The spider found that other creatures broadcast

sensory images. When she inserted her fangs into them, her inherited mental powers enabled her to sense the electromagnetic fluxes surrounding their muscles and nerves. She soon learned to replace or guide the impulses with her own, and she finally began to gain control over the muscles and senses of her victims. Her power became so complete that she could keep an animal conscious and calm while she fed. As her size and ability increased, she learned to use larger creatures for transport.

* * *

When Lactella's latest host's malnutrition made it too weak to serve, Lactella abandoned it and entered the nearest house through a rip in a window screen. There she found the sleeping form of Ivanstor Johns.

She sank her fangs into Johns' thigh, immobilized him, and began taking control. For two days she kept Johns in bed pretending illness while she mastered his conscious mind and his speech and movements. Preparing for action, she shifted her point of attachment to the back of Johns' neck, concealing herself under a scarf worn to "prevent a return of the chill."

The City Manager's mind opened the universe to Lactella. She had known nothing of Human society or technology. She soon began to grasp the nature of power and security on a breathtaking scale. She also learned that controlling Johns took much more effort than controlling smaller creatures.

She started thinking of ways to extend her control to Johns' family. She explored her new home and decided the City Manager's armpit would make an excellent hatchery. As her spiderlings hatched, she softened Johns' skin and numbed his nerves. She had such control over his nervous system that the burrowing and gorging of young spiders caused no visible reaction.

But Lactella didn't have total control. Sometimes Johns

made noises and movements that surprised her. Most annoying, a finger twitch started whenever other people were present. Lactella could control everything else Johns did, but the finger twitch persisted. Johns played piano, and Lactella assumed that his finger control came from that. She could stop the twitch by freezing Johns with her venom, but that could be disastrous if other people were present. Discovery could mean death.

Some of Lactella's hosts had suffered injuries and had become septic before Lactella understood the problem. With knowledge she'd gained from Johns', she learned to control the spread of bacteria. She became a willful commensalist, the ecologist's term for a parasite that benefits from, but causes no harm to, its host. Of course, the term applied not at all to Johns' poor mind.

As her offspring grew and developed their own venom, Lactella sought to teach them the chemistry and methods of control. But while she slept, Johns managed to douse his armpit with rubbing alcohol and none of her children survived. That was the last independent act beyond finger twitching that Johns ever achieved.

Lactella wanted minions and would continue until she got them. She laid more eggs and resumed her vigilance.

As she spent more time with Johns' wife and children, she learned she could use criticism to cause pain. She also learned she could use Johns to inflict physical pain. After a few months, almost anything Johns' children did or said could be cause for a beating. Johns' wife begged him to spare the children and offered herself as a substitute for their punishment. Before long, she developed a permanent limp and her right eye would not focus.

Lactella explored Johns' memory and learned a great deal about Human society. Johns held an important position in Mountainview, the capital of the Human State of Normount. Acting through him, corporations guided the development and administration of public policy. Before Lactella had taken him, Johns had considered himself the prince of the city.

Lactella learned that the corporations had partial control over the Federation armed forces. The military used public funds to procure equipment and services from corporations. The corporations used some of their profits to reward military procurement staff, and some to reward elected officials for maintaining high military budgets.

The corporations also used some of their profits to support elected officials that protected their other interests. In the end, almost all lawmakers, judges, and law enforcers in Mountainview served the corporations first and the citizens second. Humans in leadership positions in Mountainview and every other city eagerly used their power over others for personal enrichment.

Lactella also learned about the Tsaeb. Searching Johns' mind, Lactella determined the Tsaeb were defenseless neighbors that she could use for labor and food.

A few weeks after Johns returned to work, the young City Planner, Albert Morton, came to talk about a problem. "We are holding several subdivision applications for 500 or more homes. Changing the zoning requirements won't be a problem, but water will. We have begun rationing, but Engineering predicts that within 15 to 20 years we will have to find new sources. If we approve these subdivisions, we will need more water sooner."

"Can't we use the land and water north of the city?" Lactella asked through Johns.

Morton shook his head. "There isn't much to develop there before we bump into the Tsaeb border. Actually, I don't see why we can't annex some of the Tsaeb land. There's nothing there. If we get some housing going, there'll be roads and power, stores, a school or two, and maybe even a hospital. That will be good for the Tsaeb, and we'll have water for more growth."

Lactella had Johns arrange meetings with corporate and military leaders to discuss accessing the Tsaeb lands. The worst that could happen would be an armed conflict, and that would justify increased investment in military equipment and weapons. The military leaders feigned reluctance, but the corporate leaders openly agreed with the idea.

"Your fellow there, Albert Morton, has it right," a local banker said. "Anything we do on Tsaeb land is going to improve things for them. It might take some convincing, but in the end they will thank us."

Johns and the corporate representatives asked the regional military commander to take a proposal to the central military command. Almost overnight, they received approval to conduct a few small tests of Tsaeb response. For the first test, military engineers disguised as civilians would survey a short road into Tsaeb lands.

Johns and Morton publicized the survey as an act of friendship. The road would enable more Human citizens of Mountainview to view the scenery and become acquainted with the Tsaeb. The press release attracted very little attention.

The survey teams encountered Tsaeb but met no opposition. For the next step, the military command sent a tactical patrol with visible weapons to follow the surveyors' route. Their orders included explicit instructions to kill or capture any Tsaeb that showed signs of hostility. Two Tsaeb children caused an incident that killed two soldiers and wounded several others. The commander in charge of the operation attributed the deaths to mindless mischief and wanted to return with a strike force to administer punishment.

The description of the incident struck Lactella as odd, but she could see no reason to slow her efforts to advance the move on Tsaeb lands. Wishing she had more influence over the military, she spent all the time she could spare studying and testing her offspring.

Lactella's early life revolved around fear and food. Food had become less important after she'd learned to control large mammals—their vascular systems provided constant nourishment—but she hungered for power: power for security, power for pleasure, power forever. She began to imagine a vast hierarchy of living creatures serving her. As her ambitions filled her with excitement, she wriggled her claws, sending streaks of pain through Johns.

While taking over Johns' life, Lactella had matured. She tried to enjoy Human art and theatre, but tormenting Johns and exercising his power were her principal sources of entertainment. She had come to define all other creatures as either resources or threats. If they did not help Johns feed her, protect her, or entertain her, they had no value. With earlier hosts, she had learned to enjoy giving pain. With Johns, she learned to give pain to others. And she wanted to do more.

Sentinel Spire

After the near miss with Allon, Corr headed directly for Sentinel Spire, but he took time to visit with local gleaners. He answered questions about council activities, Humans, and Trofeld. He asked about travelers and unusual events. He tried a few jokes.

He learned that the gleaners had seen at least two unfamiliar Tsaeb traveling north toward the Center. Why hadn't he known this before? He alerted his battle group and Halbert Sims.

Corr approached Sentinel Spire at dusk under heavy cloud cover. The tall basalt-capped column was a short distance from the western escarpment of Juniper Mesa. In the deepening gloom, it appeared dark and quiet, but it was ablaze with the thoughts and actions of its inhabitants.

Council Chair Aquila's ancient family nest occupied the top of the spire. Numerous bird nests and a bat cave occupied the upper and middle heights. Smaller mammals and reptiles lived here and there on the lower half of the spire. Caves at and near the base housed a mountain lion family (not Trofeld's), a ringtail family, a swallow colony, and a band of bighorn sheep.

Allysen, Ankolla, Quin, Ralph, and Rhya had arrived and settled into Travelers' Notch, a sandy-floored alcove at the base of the spire. The warriors and numerous local residents had gathered around a glowing bulb on the floor of the alcove. Rhya was sitting between two rabbits and had a small owl on her shoulder. She glanced across the group at Corr.

Ralph Mäkinen, a large gray wolf descendent and member of Corr's battle group, was tuning a small stringed instrument and chuckling at someone's joke. Corr's teacher had told him that in extreme circumstances, Mäkinen could produce the greatest speed and power he had ever seen. "In battle, Ralph can become a tornado. Don't stand too close."

Tonight, Ralph's easy-going banter and good humor

obscured his fearsome potential. The females of several species clustered near him certainly weren't afraid.

No space was available near Rhya, and Corr had to sit next to a porcupine. Why do they keep those quills on the backs of their heads? Now I have to hope she doesn't get excited and turn her head too fast. And they talk slow.

"Hello, Mr. Syl," the porcupine said. "I am Wilma Tarryton. Do you remember me?"

"Hi, Wilma. Call me Corr. Did we meet at your parents' home three years ago?"

"Yes."

"Have you started your apprenticeship yet?"

"Yes, Sir. I'm studying succulent plants."

"Well, that's good. Watch those quills."

Wilma had a pink ribbon with white dots tied around her quills. She smiled, and in response, the hard expression on Corr's face melted into a smile.

Corr pushed his troubles to the back of his mind and looked over the group. At least a dozen species had gathered. A few local leaders and elders had come, but young people like Wilma were more numerous. This was not the time and place to discuss Allon or the Human soldiers.

Apparently, Corr's battle group had learned nothing troubling. Ankolla watched, smiling, nodding, and making occasional comments. Allysen, like Rhya, was happily engaged in several conversations, at one point even jumping up to demonstrate a dance step. Ralph couldn't have been more relaxed, though Corr detected a slight stiffness, a pedagogic air probably brought on by all the attentive youngsters. Corr smiled again. Then an outburst of laughter caught his attention and he began sifting through stories and jokes he might try.

Bill and Zuberi arrived not long after Corr. As they found seats, Bill asked, "What, no singing? Is Ralph's throat sore?"

"We needed a molto soprano to arrive," said Ralph.

Later the group shared a meal and sang songs. At one point Zuberi stood and sang with such feeling and power that many streams of thought faded.

Then Bill joined in and the pair sang strange songs in minor keys they had learned while traveling in Asia.

When a storm broke, a gust of wind carried rain and snow into the alcove. Everyone jumped up, exchanged farewells, and left for home. The rabbits continued speaking with Rhya. One left, but the other rested a hand on Rhya's shoulder and leaned closer. Corr walked to the back of the alcove and yanked his blanket out of his pack.

As all became quiet and still, Ralph sang, "Good night, oh friends of miiiiiinne." Bill groaned as if in agony, and Rhya chuckled. With that small sound in his ears, Corr smiled, relaxed, and closed his eyes. He dreamed of strange eyes peering at him from the darkness and shivered as if he heard claws scraping across ice.

* * *

Invisible in deep shadow, the line of warriors followed a trail up a cleft in the west escarpment of Juniper Mesa. On a ledge at the base of the basalt layer capping the mesa, they paused and looked across fog-filled Wycliff Valley. The light and texture of the cloudy sky merged perfectly with the fog. They might be looking over the edge of the world.

At the top of the cleft, Corr motioned the group together. "Look for strangers. Quin, check anyone holding in the air above the mesa. Let's catch any spies that have come."

Ivan Johns' Conspiracy Builds

Human military leaders in blue and tan uniforms glinting with gold braid, shining stars, and shimmering ribbons were gathered around a gray table in a pale green room. The men leaned forward in their chairs, eyes and teeth flashing, the astringent odor of aftershave rising from heated skin. Dusty flags and a projector screen stood in a corner. Two 8x10 photos of the Federation President and Armed Forces Chief of Staff hanging on a wall did little to alleviate the barrenness of the room. Outside in the hall, men in gray suits, brilliant ties, gleaming rings and subtle aftershave sat on the edges of gray steel benches awaiting the start of the meeting.

The Chairman of the Western War Command, Lt. General Alston Marbellet, opened the meeting. "Okay, gentlemen, today we're going to turn talk into action. The SecDef and the JC Chairman likes the proposal by the city boys. After Ivan got the city council's approval and the resolution from the Normount State Legislature, they decided we had a strategic opportunity here. It's time to stop the damned Tsaeb invasion. We're going to show the rest of the Federation what we can do. Hell, the whole world's going to see." He held up a sheet of paper. "I got orders this morning. The JC's worry about public opinion. They don't think people see any danger in the Tsaeb. The cute little bastards are more like cuddly pets than invading enemies. The JCs wants us to find a way to show people that we have to get firm with the Tsaeb."

General Sampson Howell spoke up. "For those of us who must choose the manner in which we carry out the wishes of our wise leaders, it seems prudent to ring the bell before we break down the door. We should address our concerns to the Tsaeb Ambassador, Whistol Farr. If his response isn't acceptable, we can proceed with other actions."

"Sam, we've been over this and over this," Marbellet said. "Farr ain't gonna change anything."

"Sir, this is a matter of national importance. The Tsaeb defeated us the last time there was a conflict. Do we risk a major conflict now? If we aren't going to speak to Farr, shouldn't we ask our leaders to join with our President to begin negotiating a new treaty with the Tsaeb?"

Marbellet and the other military staff at the table

glared at Howell. Marbellet said, "You can trust that people at the highest level reviewed this before they said to go. They like the civilian connection. Mountainview's need for Tsaeb land for development and progress justifies the action. Command wants to see how the Tsaeb react. And if things go south, we have a scapegoat. Everything gets blamed on Mountainview civilians, not the Federation."

"Besides, we're just going to shift the border a little ways north. It's not a national conflict. Nobody loses their homes or anything, and Mountainview will get the water and land it needs for its progress. The Tsaeb may not even notice. If the annexation goes well, we can expand the effort and maybe even set up a new treaty."

Howell frowned. How could such a dimwit rise to a leadership position?

After aides retrieved Johns and the others, Marbellet said, "Ivan, the Joint Chiefs like your proposal and want to provide support. Tell us what you want."

"Thank you, Sir. General Miller and I discussed this and decided we should begin a publicity campaign to turn public opinion against the Tsaeb."

"What kind of publicity? You mean to tell everybody how they're invading Mountainview?" Marbellet asked.

"Well, that's probably too complicated. We think we can put out a little news about problems with the Tsaeb. Some editorials and a little help from some of our church leaders will get things started," Johns said.

"Why would the churches help? The Tsaeb don't do anything to them, do they?" Marbellet asked.

"Tsaeb don't criticize the churches, but religious scholars say that the Tsaeb believe in something called Immediacy. They think of spiritual belief as a mental aberration. A recent article in *Spiritual Times* warned that Immediacy could undermine religious authority. Let me read you a bit from the article."

Johns dug through a stack of folders, extracted a stapled document, and began to read: "The Tsaeb civilization accepts a central ethos that encompasses metaphysics, epistemology, and ethics. This is expressed in the behavior of individuals and collectively in the—" "

"Hold it, Ivan. Any more of that and we'll need a nap break. What's the bottom line?"

"If Immediacy spreads, faith-based groups will shrink."

"Okay, so the churches will help, but how?"

"Simple. The church leaders mention the Tsaeb problems when they speak to their congregations. This will stir up doubts and let us claim the Tsaeb forced us to take action."

"Hmm. I guess you should email us that article."

A distant air conditioner thumped and a rush of air began producing a thin whistle as it flowed into the room.

"Sure. Send me a request for the Normount *Spiritual Times* article and I'll attach it to a reply."

"What's your address, Ivan?"

"Uh, the city system is upgrading. Send it to IvanstorJohns@gmail.com."

Howell watched Johns' index fingers tapping on the table and thought how odd the man was. Aware of the general's gaze, Lactella moved Johns' hands into his lap and decided she would look for a chance to discredit Howell.

Stephen Miller, the Army General in command of the Mountainview military installations, turned to Marbellet and wrinkled his forehead.

Marbellet nodded.

"This may interest you," Miller said. "We are planning to move the local army base closer to the border. Al helped us pick a site just south of Diamond Peak that had only one house in the way. It isn't far from the old Corinne Trail that runs north past the west side of the Peak." He paused to look around the room. "In addition, General Marbellet has given me permission to conduct a reconnaissance tour to test the Tsaeb. They appear to have nothing but bows, knives, and a few pistols, but it won't hurt to verify that.

"I am sending a company to scout the environs of the new base. They will set up and garrison a small post midway along the route that we just surveyed. The commander has orders to kill or capture any Tsaeb that interfere with their movement. If needed, we can use prisoners to break resistance to our presence."

"How can we justify this?" General Howell asked.

"It's a routine security patrol for the new base."

"You just tried the same thing, didn't you?" Howell asked.

"That was only a platoon and a single accident forced them to withdraw," Miller said.

"When would you begin?" Johns asked.

"Tomorrow. I'll have engineers and builders follow on the heels of an infantry battalion to the site of the new base. One company will continue on to a campsite across the border. On Thursday they will tour the trail, detach the garrison north of the peak, and return to the new base."

Marbellet looked at Miller. "Steve, this has to go smoothly. Any real trouble and you pull back. No screw ups."

"Bring back some rabbits or squirrels," said the Vice President of Seastate Oil. "My grandfather used to say we should eat the critters, not live with them."

"I'll see what we can do," Miller said.

General Howell stood, looked around the table, and strode toward the door.

"Sam, wait. It's a joke," Miller said.

"Let him go," Marbellet said. "He'll get over it."

Johns' eyes followed Howell as he left.

* * *

Marbellet said, "There is one more thing—Ivan, we have some Tsaeb spies."

Lactella leaned Johns forward. "Spies?"

"Yes. There used to be Tsaeb everywhere before we

created the border and ran them out. Most of 'em moved to their side of the border, but there are exceptions. One is a troublesome little bunch occupying the Sawtooth Mountains southeast of the city."

With a languishing sigh, the air conditioner stopped and the whistle trailed off.

"A few months ago we hauled in a gang from Piedmont, their name for the Sawtooth area. They claimed some sort of nonsense about farms in the area causing a food shortage. We jailed 'em, and convinced some of them to work for us." Marbellet held out a folder. Here is a summary of their reports."

"Very interesting," Johns said. "Thank you."

Agreeing to move quickly to complete a plan, the group scheduled a meeting on Thursday to review the PR campaign.

Back in Johns' office, Lactella immediately began reading the spy reports. She learned the Wycliff Tsaeb had only two tiny military groups that occasionally patrolled the border. The Tsaeb had a plan for dealing with armed invaders, but the response options amounted to rock throwing, bows and arrows and hand-to-hand combat using knives. The little military groups had some sort of powered hand weapons as well, but Lactella assumed they must not work well because no one had ever seen them used.

The Tsaeb really had no way to resist a trained and well-armed military force. As Lactella had first believed, taking Tsaeb lands would be ridiculously easy.

When Morton got home that evening, he shouted, "I'm home."

His wife rushed out of the kitchen and found a grinning and posturing Morton.

"We're moving up, Honey. I'm going to expand my department!"

She smiled. "What happened?"

Morton described the meeting and said, "With the

army behind the plan, things will start happening. Look out, Tsaeb! Here we come!"

Juniper Mesa

Encircled by tumbled basalt boulders, Whistol Farr was sitting on a stone resting his feet in dry grass and forbs. Around him were representatives from neighboring Tsaeb communities. Two of Farr's aides—the raven, Ellan Marin, and the merlin, Sakura James—had perched on the bear's shoulders. As Corr's group approached, Farr greeted them in his deep rumbling voice and introduced everyone.

Corr moved close, cloaked Farr and guests with his sensory fields, and reported what Sims had said and what he had learned on his way south.

"We shouldn't discuss new strategy for dealing with Humans. The purpose of this meeting should shift to catching spies."

"Damn," said Farr. "Is Halbert sure?"

"I guess it's just a feeling, but others have also noticed something."

"You're not talking about Zuberi, are you?"

Corr smiled and shook his head.

"Crap. Excuse me." Farr turned and spoke quietly to a badger who was wearing the crossed swords of a warrior. Others excused themselves to pass Corr's warning to their traveling companions.

In a moment, Farr turned back to Corr. "Safe topics will frustrate some of our attendees."

A kingbird appeared and hovered before Farr. "The near approaches to the mesa are clear."

"Thank you," Farr said, then stood and raised his arms. With a booming voice, he called out, "Greetings. It is time to open the meeting. If no one objects I will act as meeting Chair."

"No objection. You have great talent for visibility!" a chipmunk shouted.

Farr frowned, then continued. "After the incident four days ago in which two young squirrels terminated a Human incursion, the council asked for this meeting to discuss the border situation." He nodded toward Corr.

"Corr, you lead off."

Corr said the young squirrels had been lucky to be unharmed. He spoke briefly about the recent survey and the long absence of any border concerns.

"Who wants to review the basic protocol followed when meeting Humans?" asked Farr.

"I'm happy to," said a stout raven from atop a nearby boulder. At a nod from Farr, the raven seemed to swell. "Human prospectors, hunters, and settlers often killed other species. First, we set up the border. Then, we set up rules for dealing with Humans who crossed it. Over the years those rules have changed very little. These days, all Tsaeb children are taught the history of the border, and they receive basic combat instructions. This is clearly effective. In the recent incident, the young squirrels recognized that the soldiers posed a threat, and they knew what to do when they found a grenade.

"The border treaty does not permit Humans to carry weapons into Tsaeb land. The appropriate response to armed trespassers is to give them a warning and order them to leave. An aggressive response is appropriate if the warning is ignored or if the trespassers attempt to do harm."

A member of the group asked, "Couldn't we have assembled a fighter group and captured the soldiers? We might have learned something of their mission."

"The youths were hasty," the raven said, "but we must recognize that they may have prevented the Humans from hurting someone or achieving a dangerous objective. They certainly taught those particular soldiers a lesson."

"Thank you," Farr said. "Of course, we treat unarmed Humans differently. We try to develop connections. In the past, this has led to friendships that have endured. Unfortunately, most Humans can become violent, and caution is always required.

"We always consider size. The ideal encounter for small Tsaeb is with children. With adult Humans, particularly adult males, it is important that only Tsaeb species of medium stature attempt to make contact. Large Tsaeb are likely to be considered dangerous. Small Tsaeb, no matter how boldly or impudently they speak, are not respected."

Everyone but the chipmunk grinned.

"It has always seemed too simple," a member of the crowd said. "Is it likely that Human children will ever be alone? Do we expect to meet Hansel and Gretel? And why don't we immediately arrest any armed Humans that cross the border?"

At this, numerous conversations began.

Scanning the attendees, Corr detected something odd about a pair of raccoons near the back of the group. They were cloaking their thoughts. One did so poorly; the other very well.

Corr strolled out into the scattered juniper and signaled his group. "Two raccoons near the southwest margin of the assembly seem odd." He described what he had seen. "Let's try to corner them in the alcove at the base of the cliff northeast of where Farr is standing. I'll have Farr invite the group there for lunch. Allysen and Rhya, check the alcove for back exits. Do any of you know any of the other raccoons?"

"I do," Ankolla said.

"Ask them to engage the suspect pair in some sort of lunch-time entertainment to draw them into the alcove."

During a moment while two members of the assembly were arguing a point, Corr spoke to Farr. "Whistol, know the alcove by those rocks? It would be a nice spot for lunch."

Farr said, "Okay. We'll wrap this up in a minute."

As the argument ended, Farr stood. "It seems most of you feel our current preparations are fine. Clearly, we need to remind everyone to be cautious. I'll send a reminder through the leadership. Let's take a lunch break. There's a nice spot nearby. We can discuss topics for this afternoon while we eat." No one objected, and Farr said, "Corr, lead the way."

Corr turned and moved off. As he approached the alcove, he sensed the suspect raccoons moving along with everyone else.

Rhya approached and leaned close. "There is a crevice at the back of the alcove that opens into a blister cave. There's no way out."

For a moment, Corr was aware only of Rhya's sweet warm breath on his ear.

As everyone settled down and opened their packs, Ralph began strumming the cords of a familiar ballad.

"Please," Bill said. "We are trying to eat."

When Ralph finished, the raccoons Ankolla knew started whistling, clapping, and dancing. Ralph began picking up the rhythm and others began humming.

As they danced, the raccoons capered over to the suspects, took them by the hands, and drew them into the dance. The two halfheartedly danced along. As the dance adjusted to the movements of the newcomers, it became a simple polka. The joyful steps of most of the raccoons appealed to everyone, and other members of the crowd joined in.

The raccoons drifted past Ralph and danced into the alcove. Corr's battle group coalesced into an arc across the opening. Backed by Whistol Farr and others, the arc tightened. The three known raccoons slipped through the arc, leaving the suspects behind.

One of the raccoons growled, "What are you doing?"

Corr stepped forward and the raccoons backed to the crevice at the back of the alcove. One entered the crevice, but the other hesitated for a moment before his comrade yanked him inside.

"Ralph, hold this position while I speak to our captives."

Ralph said, "Wait, Corr," but he was too late.

* * *

Corr expanded his pupils, focused his awareness fields, and stepped through the crevice. As he entered, he snapped forward and heard the clink of a missed sword thrust. In the dim light entering the cave, Corr saw that one of the raccoons was only a few feet away with empty hands. Corr dropped to the sandy floor as a sword swished overhead.

Jackknifing and leaping toward the sword-wielding raccoon, Corr pulled himself upright using the raccoon's clothing. He pinched a nerve in the raccoon's sword arm, flung his arms around the raccoon's head, wrapped his legs around the raccoon's, and thrust a shoulder into the raccoon's throat.

The raccoon began twisting and writhing, and finally lunged forward.

Oh no you don't, Corr thought as he flexed his knees and twisted. On the way down, he felt something strike his opponent. Corr rolled aside and stood, sword in hand.

The raccoon got to his feet, and coiled to make another thrust.

Corr snapped a kick at the raccoon's chest, but the raccoon lurched forward and the kick struck his throat.

The other raccoon faced Corr across his former companion.

"Thanks," Corr said. Then he dropped to his knees beside the fallen raccoon. "Let's see if we can save this critter."

The standing raccoon joined Corr and helped probe the downed spy. The bump Corr felt had come from a blow to the raccoon's back. The lurch that caused Corr's kick to strike the throat had come from another blow. Corr's kick had crushed the larynx. Corr and the other raccoon concentrated their sensory fields on the injury, but they could not get the star cells to respond. The fallen raccoon resisted their aid, and in moments all its consciousness was gone.

So, that's how it is. I only wanted to end the fight. There were voices outside the cave, but inside everything was quiet. Corr detached a stream of thought to consider the event and decide what he should have done. *I could have talked with them before I entered the bubble.* Corr looked closely at the surviving raccoon. He was very young, wearing a plain vest over a waistband with one shoulder strap. He had a worried look, but Corr could sense no fear. "I know you observe for the Humans. Who are you and why are you spying?"

"I'm Arthur... Arthur Tummel. My family... well a group of families... left home three months ago. We traveled west from Piedmont and passed just south of Mountainview. The Federation army arrested and imprisoned us. They demanded that some of us serve as spies or they would execute our families." He nodded toward the inert form on the floor. "I think this raccoon was a real spy. He wasn't from Piedmont. He and I sleep in a cave south of here and travel around asking questions. He sends reports back to Mountainview. I've not known what to do. Can you help me?"

"Are there other spies?"

"Yes. Members of our group and other Tsaeb like this raccoon are in other districts."

"What do the Humans want?"

"So far they have only asked us to report on military activities. Of course, there haven't been any."

"What have you told them?"

"Not much," Arthur said. "They know about the two battle groups, and they understand your border alert and response plan. But I don't think they know much about Tsaeb warriors."

"Why was your group traveling?"

"It's a long story, but basically we're running out of food."

"Why? What happened?"

"Our community has had an unfortunate history. We have become an island surrounded by desert and Human farms," Tummel began. "Piedmont originally occupied 700 square miles, but it has been squeezed down to less than 300."

"Hold on a moment," Corr said. He went to the opening and asked Ralph to tell everyone that things were under control, and that he was interviewing a captured spy. "Ask everyone to finish lunch and continue the meeting. I'll provide some details shortly." Returning to Arthur, he asked, "Was Piedmont's border defined in the border treaty?"

"No. In those days, we had a good working relationship with the few Human farmers in the area. We were running cooperative farms with shared produce. We received permission from the North American council to remain in Human territory. No one foresaw how the growing Human population would change things. The farms became quite large and spread into our area. The new farm owners knew nothing of the original understandings, and they ignored our complaints.

"The large farms used so much of the ground water that the depth became too great for farming to continue. The farms began shrinking and we believed things would get back to normal. But about thirty years ago, housing subdivisions began filling the vacant farmlands. Our central mountain range, the Sawtooths, and its surrounding slopes are not suitable for irrigated agriculture, and that protected us from the expanding farms. But now, Human houses are edging up the alluvial fans toward the slopes."

"Are there any warriors in Piedmont?" Corr asked.

"No."

"Why didn't you do something sooner?"

"We discussed the problem with Human farmers and officials on numerous occasions. We never achieved more than a temporary halt to the encroachment. Two years ago, we spoke to Whistol Farr, and he and his staff began talking to the Humans."

"How do you think this will end?"

"We've been rationing, but we're almost out of emergency stores. Productivity isn't enough to support our population. We've decided that at least half of us must migrate. We know there probably isn't room anywhere, but we have no choice. Our group was the first to leave. The place the Humans are keeping us isn't very strong, and we could escape. We just don't know where to go. We don't want to fight a running battle, and we can't go back to Piedmont."

Corr sat very still. Learning that the Humans held numerous Tsaeb prisoners erased his initial pleasure with having a double agent drop into his lap. The existence of the prisoners was, in turn, a small problem compared to the plight of the whole Piedmont community. And where had the other spies, the ones with real spy skills, come from? Corr had a strange sensation and all his thoughtstreams seemed to fuse and flow forward to a shimmering scene. As he tried to understand the scene, it faded like a dream.

After a moment, he said, "Arthur, I think you should go to the Embassy in Mountainview. For now, I want you to pretend to be my prisoner. Extend your hands... and you will have to wear this." Corr took a thin silver band from a pouch on his harness and laid it across Arthur's wrists. The ends of the band coiled around each wrist.

Outside the cave, Corr led Arthur to the meeting site. He announced that the raccoons were indeed spies, and that during the fight inside the cave, one was killed.

The crowd clamored for explanations.

"I'm sending the captive to the Embassy in Mountainview. I'll send a report as soon as I understand what the raccoons wanted and who sent them," Corr said. "I can't say more now. Let's finish the meeting."

"Yes. That was quite a lunchtime show," Farr said.

"Let's get back to work."

Quietly Corr explained the situation to his battle group. "Zuberi and Bill, I want you to take Arthur to the Embassy. Drop him off and meet me tomorrow evening where the Corinne Trail crosses the border. Arthur, please stay out of sight inside the Embassy until I arrive."

Corr had the spy's body picked up for recycling, asked his battle group to continue studying the crowd, and focused every free neuron on the problems brought out by the captured raccoon.

When even the most garrulous had nothing left to say about border interactions, Farr invited everyone to visit the Embassy and then he bid them farewell.

Corr joined in farewells, but most of his thoughts were focused on the problems. The Mountainview military might learn about the capture of their spies, but even if they didn't, the lack of reports would let them know something was wrong. The Piedmont prisoners had to be rescued soon.

Lactella Questions a Captive

Lactella asked General Miller for permission to question a prisoner. She did not expect a Tsaeb from Piedmont to have much useful information. However, she wanted to know how Tsaeb differed from Humans.

On Wednesday, two soldiers arrived with a raccoon. Lactella had the soldiers tie the Tsaeb in a chair and leave.

"What is your name?" asked Lactella.

"Marion Tummel."

"What did you do in Piedmont?"

"Teach."

"What did you teach?"

"Human languages and literature."

"Did you have many students?"

"No."

"Did you have another job?"

"No."

This is pointless, Lactella thought. *I don't know what I can learn from this raccoon.* She warned the conscious remnant of Johns' mind, *I'll be back.* Then she released a paralyzing jolt of venom that stiffened muscles and dissolved thoughts, giving Johns an unintended respite from his anguish. Lactella slowly and stiffly withdrew her fangs and claws from the back of Johns' neck. As she crawled onto Johns' shoulder, Marion's eyes widened.

"Never seen a spider before?" she asked in a creaky voice.

"You are the largest black widow," replied Marion. She focused all her senses on Lactella. The spider's mind was powerful, but its abilities were unfocused, resembling those of a precocious child.

Lactella felt Marion's sensory fields, but assumed they were a fear response and ignored them. It did not occur to her the fields were under Marion's control. She crawled down Johns' arm onto his desk and across to the seated and bound Marion. She abruptly leapt for Marion's neck, but her atrophied muscles propelled her only to Marion's chest. Nevertheless, Lactella enjoyed the surprised flinch. Wasting no time, Lactella crawled up onto Marion's shoulder and stabbed her claws and fangs into the helpless raccoon's neck, questing first for the carotid artery and then for a nerve bundle.

Marion felt burning pain as the spider's venom entered her system. The venom included a familiar neurotoxin mixed with unfamiliar compounds. Marion's star cells, her responsive and versatile versions of white cells, immediately neutralized the toxin and isolated the compounds. She began an analysis of their chemistry and returned the rest of her attention to the spider.

Within seconds, impulses like static began flooding her mind. The spider had somehow connected with her nervous system. She decided to play along and study the spider's abilities and goals. She first built a dense barrier around her analysis of the compounds. Then she carefully attenuated her controls over her mind and body, leaving just enough to monitor what happened. The static increased. She began to stiffen her muscles to simulate ataxia, an appropriate response to the neurotoxin.

Lactella began stimulating Marion's memories. This was much faster than verbal interrogation. Lactella's principal source of knowledge about intelligence, Ivan Johns, had not prepared her for the higher intelligence and refined capabilities of a mature Tsaeb. She did not know how completely she was exposing herself. Something was wrong, however. Normally, her victims' initial responses were comprised of a virtual storm of confused thoughts and impulses. *What's keeping this raccoon so calm?* She began a series of personal questions while watching for a fear response. "Tell me about your family."

"My mother and father are Viola and Wilson Marston. My father's mother and father are Angela and Frank Marston. My grandmother's mother and father—"

"Stop!" Lactella said. "Do you have offspring?"

"Yes."

"Where are they?"

"I do not know where my son is."

"Why did you leave Piedmont?"

"There is not enough food. We decided to try to find a new home."

Lactella paused. *This is pointless.* She could think of nothing important the raccoon could tell her. Well, it was good to know her venom worked on Tsaeb as well as it did on Humans. The raccoon's lack of fear suggested the Tsaeb were even more susceptible than Humans. She decided to return to Johns, but before she withdrew, she gave Marion a powerful jolt of neurotoxin sufficient to cause serious nerve injury, even death. As the raccoon's eyes rolled back and her muscles began quivering, Lactella left her victim and returned to her familiar place on the back of Johns' neck. Then she awakened Johns and had him call for the soldiers.

"This raccoon is sick," Johns said. "Take it away."

One of the soldiers untied the bindings holding Marion in the chair and slung her across his shoulder. As they returned to the jail, Marion continued her analysis of the compounds Lactella had injected along with the neurotoxin. She had first neutralized the compounds by directing her star cells to flood them with cations. *The compounds must reduce resistance to Lactella's control,* she thought. *If Johns' behavior is typical, they must be very effective on Humans.*

Marion also thought about Lactella. She concluded the spider had tremendous natural talent, but the real danger came from the spider's ability to motivate Humans. In control of an influential Human such as Johns, the spider could cause widespread problems. Marion wondered whether there were others like Lactella. *Do spiders control Human society?*

* * *

After lunch on Wednesday afternoon, Johns and two staff members drove to the military headquarters to clarify a few details with General Marbellet.

General Howell met them. "Hello, Ivan. Marbellet just called. He's inspecting the new post. He'll arrive in about 15 minutes. Have you had coffee?"

"I have. Say, if we have a minute, could you tell me more about the Tsaeb prisoners?"

"Glad to. Would you like to see them?"

"Yes."

Howell led the way through a side entrance and across a small courtyard to a large, windowless structure.

"This was originally built for munitions storage, but as the city enveloped the area we moved everything out west of the city."

Entering an unmarked doorway, they came to a table backed by a seated security guard. Recognizing the general, the guard stood and saluted. Howell asked for visitor tags, and gave them to Johns and his assistants.

"Come this way," Howell said. "We can see the entire group in an open storage yard." Howell led the way through a door and down a corridor to a long, narrow window overlooking a courtyard surrounded by high walls topped by steel bars and razor wire.

"We keep the prisoners in this area most of the day."

Johns looked down into the area. Tsaeb were running about, apparently randomly.

"What are they doing?" asked Johns.

"I think it is a game. They do it every day." Howell pointed. "There is the Tsaeb you interrogated this morning."

"Where?"

"She's running... right there." He pointed again.

As Johns watched, a raccoon completed a run to the center of the courtyard.

"But... that raccoon was ill. Are you sure?"

"Yes. See the collar? We placed it on her this morning

before we took her to your office."

Through Johns' eyes, Lactella stared. The venom she had injected should have left Marion incapable of movement for at least a day, and yet here she was, vigorously active only an hour after receiving the venom. Lactella realized this was important and began reviewing the interview.

On the Way to Mountainview

As clumps and streams of Tsaeb left the mesa, Corr's group paused again to look at the valley. South, a cloud of brown haze hid Mountainview. West, only faint haze obscured silhouettes of the mountains. The valley itself held long shadows cast by the late afternoon sun.

Cradled by inactive volcanic mountain ranges and never glaciated, the floor of the high, structural valley bore only the incisions of small, intermittent desert streams. The warriors stared at the valley. Had it been capable, the land would have smiled at its small band of defenders.

Ralph pointed northwest. "There's White Cliff. That gray mound is the District Center. When it's clear, you can also see our Embassy in Mountainview from here."

"Is Mountainview always so hazy?" Rhya asked.

Farr said, "Wind sometimes clears the air, but if it blows very hard it can pick up dust that's as bad as the haze."

"Is the haze toxic?"

"A little. Many of the Humans develop chronic coughs and headaches whenever it's at its worst. Many of their children have asthma."

As they descended to the dry riverbed, Quin and Farr's feathered assistants spiraled upward.

Pausing after descending from the mesa, Corr motioned the group together and asked Farr to call in his assistants. Ellan and Sakura immediately landed on Farr's shoulders. Corr described the Piedmont situation, concluding, "Thirty-five peaceful travelers are imprisoned. We have to do something."

Farr looked at him. "Like what?"

"Whistol, explain things to Sam Whortin. Ask him to begin investigating the prisoners' situation."

"Okay." Farr looked at his assistants. "Ellan, call Sam. Sakura, catch up with the representatives from our neighbors and repeat what Corr just told us." He glanced at Corr again. "Corr, anything else?"

"I think there are secrets we need to uncover," Corr said. "We'll meet Shorel at the Corinne trail crossing tomorrow evening as planned, and I'll go to Mountainview with you. It seems probable that we'll need some fighters. In the morning we should split up and alert leaders as we head for the border."

Korhonen said, "Corr, I think Rhya should go to the Embassy too."

As they stopped for the night, Allysen asked, "Corr, any reason I can't travel with Ankolla tomorrow?"

"No, that's fine."

Ralph spoke up. "Corr, I suggest Quin and I head west to Periwinkle Canyon and then angle back toward the crossing. I can see my nephew's new pup, and we can visit with some of the western leaders. Sakura can reach us in minutes if something comes up."

"Fine," Corr said. "I'll go with Tau and Whistol, and Rhya should go with us if she wishes."

"Sounds good," Tau said with a wide-eyed innocent look mirrored by the battle group and accompanied by a barely audible snort from Ankolla.

The group camped in a sandy stretch of stream channel and were joined by local residents who gathered to visit and exchange news. The spy capture was by far the most interesting news in many years.

In the morning, Corr's band followed the riverbed as it wound south. They stopped occasionally to speak to residents.

Rhya asked, "Corr, have Zuberi and Bill lived at the Center very long?"

"No. They returned from traveling while I was studying with Halbert Sims."

"Had they traveled very far?"

"Yes. They left long before the border wars. Bill says they were in Africa when Humans and Tsaeb signed the border treaty. They came home across Asia."

"They're so different. How did they get to be such good

friends?"

"They were in the nursery together. After training they interned together and just continued from there."

"What's with Bill?"

The others grinned at Rhya. "Bill is a rare second child, about six months younger than his older sister. He's unusually egocentric. He would risk his life for any of us, but he would complain while doing it."

Rhya had a more interesting question. "Whistol, I've met two young Humans living with Tsaeb families. A boy named Duncan lives with the Mäkinens, and Lila Bright lives with my uncle's family. My aunt said you could tell me more about her."

"Sure. Seven years ago, we adopted three Human babies. The Mäkinen family took Duncan, and your father's grandparents took Lila. The other child lives with a deer family in the mountains near the western border."

"Is Lila normal?"

"Oh, she's healthy," Farr replied.

"Why wouldn't my aunt say more?"

"The children are orphans. We took them out of kindness, but also because we wanted to try an experiment. We wanted to know whether proper education would give them normal intelligence. The project wasn't advertised so the Humans wouldn't misinterpret what we were doing."

"What happened to her Human parents?"

"Let's see... I think Lila's mother died in some kind of accident. I'm not sure about her father."

"The training seems to have worked," Rhya said. "What are their levels?"

"They have passed level two and continue to improve. Humans mature slowly. We're not sure what to expect, but they may reach level five."

"Amazing. There aren't any Humans above two are there?"

"Not that I know of. We tried to teach simultaneous

thinking to volunteer college students. None rose above two. Children raised in a Human home get their limits imprinted early.

"We might be able to teach Human parents to raise their children properly, but they would need training and probably a Tsaeb to assist. We would never find enough Tsaeb volunteers for that. Plus, all the Human institutions, their government, churches, and corporations would resist.

Corr asked, "Why? Seems like they would appreciate our help."

Rhya said, "No. It would threaten their leaders' power. Besides, many of the leaders use us as a threat to keep their groups together. The groups do what their leaders ask because they are told they have to defend themselves from us and other groups."

"The leaders want followers for power?"

"Yep. Power, wealth, and reproduction."

"We have tried to break through by being friendly and helpful," Farr said. "Our best program is in education. We have volunteers teaching courses in most Human schools. The volunteers try to build connections with their students."

"Is that working?"

"Somewhat, but it's too slow. The Human population is growing too fast. We aren't reaching enough of them."

Tau Korhonen snorted. "Whistol, I can't help wondering if you and your staff don't have better things to do."

"Humans might never overcome their terrible handicap."

The four walked on in silence. At mid-morning, they reached an easterly bend in the stream. The channel widened into a sandy floodplain bordered by an extensive stand of mesquite and scattered cottonwood and willows. Corr stopped beneath a cottonwood tree near a low cliff on the stream's right bank.

"Rhya, this bend in Sand River is the eastern gathering

point for groups of 294 fighters and higher. You are familiar?"

"Yes. We assembled a Force-Five group of 100,842 fighters here when the Human War started. Do you know why only one F-5 group? Wycliff District could form four F-5 groups."

Corr looked up. "Just a moment."

Seconds later Sakura landed on Farr's shoulder and a messenger landed beside Corr. "Corr, the entire Mountainview military detachment is moving."

Corr made a face, his thoughts racing. First the survey, then the armed platoon, and now this.

"Alert the air defense. Set up surveillance teams over the troops and the airport and keep me advised," Corr said. "Rhya, anything else?"

Rhya shook her head.

Corr said, "Whistol, do you have someone who can speak with the military command to ask what's going on?"

"Yes. Well, I usually speak to a General Marbellet, but he doesn't tell me much. Sakura, ask Petra to arrange a meeting with her military contact. Perhaps a backchannel approach will give us some answers."

Late in the afternoon, Corr scanned ahead and sensed the other members of his battle group converging on the meeting place. Athol Shorel's battle group was approaching from the west. Quin glided over, and shortly afterward, Allysen appeared.

The group stopped to watch Allysen's graceful approach. She ran so smoothly she seemed to float toward them.

Corr asked Allysen, "Everybody arriving soon?"

"Ankolla and Ralph are at the border crossing, and Zuberi and Bataar will be there in minutes," Allysen said, refusing to use the lizard's adopted name. "Quin will be there in 15 seconds, here in 30 seconds, there in 45 seconds, here in—Well, you catch my drift."

"Thank you," Corr said.

As the group approached the border, Wild Bill was sitting atop a boulder, and Zuberi, Ankolla and Ralph were sitting in its shade. A moment later, Quin landed beside Bill.

Rhya sensed a strong bond linking the seven warriors.

Corr asked, "Zuberi, did Arthur tell you more about Piedmont?"

"Yes. Apparently it's a sad place. After the last ice age, the community built gardens on the upper valley slopes north and west of the Sawtooth Mountains. With small water diversions and springs, they could easily produce surplus food. A few Humans lived nearby and helped with the gardens like any other Tsaeb. 200 years ago a wave of Human migrants replaced the aborigines. They built a small town out by the river, and a few settled near Piedmont. At first they were hostile, but soon they began helping with the gardens just as their predecessors had. The border commission decided to leave things alone. You know the rest."

Bill spoke up. "There are other problems. Humans view the Sawtooth Mountains as suitable only for recreation. As the Mountainview population has grown, visits by hikers and small vehicles have increased. They spread weeds, cause fires, and disturb soil surfaces. The Tsaeb can't keep up with repairs, and the productivity of the mountain slopes is declining."

Rhya said, "That sounds like typical Human behavior. You have to remember that the people moving into the houses or hiking in the mountains don't realize the damage they cause. Unfortunately, their leaders proclaim housing developments and recreation to be desirable."

"Ah, the insights of a student," Bill quipped.

Rhya's nose twitched and she shifted her balance.

Bill jumped backward, laughing. "Whoa there! Studying is good."

"They finally asked for help," Farr said. "Two years ago they asked us to intervene. We're trying, but the Human leaders aren't interested. Since there is no real boundary, and since Tsaeb don't bother with land ownership records, there is no legal way under current laws to prevent Human use of Piedmont lands. We can't convince the Humans to legislate new laws. I am sorry to say that I did not know how bad things had become. We knew nothing of the capture and imprisonment of the travelers."

Corr turned to Farr. "Whistol, Shorel will be here in an hour. I'll review the situation with him and then go to the Embassy." Then he looked at Mäkinen. "Ralph, you want to go with Whistol? Work with Embassy security to learn what you can about the Piedmont captives. I'll arrive tomorrow."

"Sure," Ralph said.

"I will go with them too," Korhonen said.

Corr nodded. "Whistol, something is beginning. I recommend you alert your staff and keep everyone as close to the Embassy as you can."

"That seems excessive."

"Please."

Farr hesitated, then shrugged. "Okay. Off we go."

Ralph began humming a marching tune and the group trotted away.

Corr watched them go, wishing Farr would call now and not be so obstinate. He addressed his group. "Let's take rations from the Center Cache while we wait for Shorel."

As Corr and the others trotted toward the cache, Rhya asked, "Corr, were these southern caches built because of the border?"

"I think so. Shorel said Jonas Miller and Halbert Sims chose their locations."

"Jonas didn't mention that."

"Halbert didn't either. Shorel said Jonas and Halbert were central figures in the border development. He can tell you all about them. You probably know about the Diamond Peak battle. I'll bet you didn't know that among the fighters were Whistol Farr, Jonas Miller, Halbert Sims, Quin Achiptre, and Ralph Mäkinen's father."

"What a small world. That was 1870... 143 years ago."

"That isn't all. Whistol Farr became the principal authority for establishing the North American border. Halbert Sims became the chief coordinator for laying it out. I think Jonas helped him. After completing the border, the three of them eventually returned to Wycliff District: Farr to head our local Embassy and Sims to form our first battle group. I think Jonas sat on the council."

"Jonas mentioned that he worked on the border and then served on our council."

"Sims spent almost 30 years at the Continental Center at Brushy Mountain north of the Arkansas River. Whistol and Jonas were probably there most of the time too."

As they trotted along the trail, Rhya overheard what at first sounded like an intense argument between Zuberi and Bill.

"Seventh Collegiate, you toady!" Zuberi said

"I am not your deuteragonist!" Bill retorted.

"No, but you are a deuteranope!"

"I see colors perfectly. You, however, are quite diarthrotic."

"Buzzt! Spell it."

"D-i-a-r-t-h-r-o-t-i-c!"

"Call!'

"Spell, please."

"D-i-a-r-t-h-r-o-s-i-c!"

"Challenge!"

"Okay, 80 to 78, you dudgeon."

"Catachresis!"

"Ah ha! You aren't sharp?"

"Oh. Oops."

"Eighty-one to 78. Webster's New World, First edition, samiel."

"You are the windy one, you...."

Corr said to Rhya, "Let's let them get ahead."

Zuberi and Bill grinned. As they trotted on, the exchange began again.

Rhya said, "That was Human English. What were they talking about?"

"They invented a dictionary game. Points accrue when an error is made in spelling, usage, or interpretation."

"What does 'Seventh Collegiate' mean?"

"It's a particular dictionary edition that is the authority until an error occurs, after which the winner can choose a new dictionary."

"Can't they just use one dictionary?"

"The versions aren't identical. They can't use words or meanings that aren't in the one called."

"So they have to memorize all Human dictionaries? What a waste!"

"Right. But they finally agreed to limit the number to a dozen and use each one for at least seven continuous rounds. When they started, they tried to keep hundreds active. They had to form so many new storage places, retrieval actually bogged down. Apart from tactical abilities, they could do hardly anything. In the midst of this, I asked Bill to spell his name, and it took him about a minute."

The two rabbits looked at each other. Rhya noted that the long whiskers just below Corr's nose were twitching.

Then they learned about the Human army approaching the border.

The Human Foray

As the warriors neared the cache, Corr received a call from Quin. "Corr, it appears the Mountainview detachment of the Federation army is setting up a new base south of Diamond Peak. Of immediate concern, however, is an infantry company leading the way. They're geared up for an assault."

Consternation. "Company strength?"

"Approximately 120 troops."

"Does Shorel know?"

"He should by now."

Ideas swirled. Corr's thoughtstreams merged and a blurry image formed. This time he caught some of the details, and he made a decision. "Bill, ask local leaders to build a Force-2 fighter group at Sand River Bend and another at Boulder Court. I'll ask Athol to manage the Boulder Court group. Bill and Zuberi, take charge of the Sand River group. Allysen and Ankolla may join you later." Then he spoke into his communicator. "Quin, call for air sentries. Set up a regular monitoring schedule with hourly reports to you and me. It will be dark soon. If the Human company crosses the border, they may follow the route they surveyed two weeks ago. Have someone check along the route for likely campsites and station surveillance there." He turned his attention to Ankolla. "Ankolla, go to the cache and get us extra ration packs."

Then Corr and the two strategists extended their awareness nets and began discussing the situation. Bill concentrated on calling local commanders to request that they gather their units and go to their assembly points. Zuberi paced.

As they talked, inquiries and reports came from the Wycliff council, Halbert Sims, neighboring districts, and Sam Whortin, the Mountainview Embassy security chief.

Quin returned, and after conferring with Corr, flew south toward Mountainview.

Corr said, "Allysen, can we assemble the resources

required to contain the Human army while we rescue the Piedmont captives?"

"Yes. We could stop the advancing company within minutes. The only delay would be delivery of sleeping gas from the Center or the Embassy. If we didn't use gas, we could destroy the company in an hour. I think we could overcome the total Mountainview garrison in 12 hours. Things might get messy if the Humans send aircraft from other states."

"The rescue needs are trivial," Allysen continued. "Human military and police would be unable to hold the captives if they wished to leave. Sam Whortin may already have the necessary details, but if not, he and Ralph can probably acquire them by the time our forces reach the Embassy, say in one hour. The weapons at the Embassy and the District Center are sufficient for any special needs."

"Thank you," Corr said. "Rhya, any thoughts?"

"Rescuing the Piedmont prisoners could get the full North American Federation Army involved. The Federation's central military command might not defend so small a force as a company that's clearly violating the treaty, but they might retaliate if we take action across the border."

Corr asked, "Can we repeat the approach we took to obtain the border agreements?"

"No," Allysen replied. "The total suppression of all Human military forces was simple and casualties were light. In the hundred years since the treaty, the Human population has exploded, and their military capabilities have grown. Suppressing them today will produce many casualties."

"How long would it take us to prepare a continent-wide attack?"

"Umm, let's see... we would want to make many simultaneous attacks. Fighters from 30 or 40 districts would be involved. We'd have to use our high-powered weapons. I'd say about seven days: four or five to convince everyone, and two to assemble the forces and weapons. Of course, other Human nations might come to the Federation's aid."

"Right. We would have to work through the other Continental councils to coordinate preparations with overseas districts. So add a week to prepare."

Allysen nodded. "But Corr, as Rhya said, it's typical of Humans that the Piedmont problems are due to actions by a small group of individuals that have attained power. Can't we find a way to control the local leaders?"

Rhya looked thoughtful. Human decisions usually came from the top down, the opposite of the Tsaeb. It would be possible to identify all the leaders.

"Yes," Corr said. "Some of us have to go to the Embassy and work this out. Now, let's consider what to do with the company about to cross the border. Allysen?"

"We can discourage the advance without confrontation. Ankolla and I can take charge of that. We'll each need three fighter groups. We'll set up enough accidents and mechanical failures to keep them up all night. They will be more than ready to return to base in the morning."

Corr grinned. It would be a hard night for the Human troops.

When Athol Shorel arrived, Corr described the plan.

Shorel said, "Corr, I agree we should begin assembling fighter groups, but what comes next? We can rescue the captives, but I don't see how we can help the Piedmont community. We need a new border around Piedmont. If the Humans refuse to remove their encroaching farmers, we will have to use force. We can destroy the Human military in Mountainview, but that would surely lead to full-scale war with the Federation. Other Human countries might come to their aid. Helping Piedmont could start a global war."

"Perhaps Whistol has developed strong enough support among the people of Mountainview that the

Human government could be forced to negotiate."

Shorel shook his head. "I just can't see the Mountainview leaders giving up anything unless forced."

Corr doubted it too, but if a war started, many Tsaeb would want to decimate and subjugate the entire Human species. Corr slumped. *Could it come to that?*

It began to grow dark, and the soft songs of insects began to fill the cool evening air. Shorel said, "As for the advancing company, I like confusing them better than killing them, but it will not deter them from coming again."

"But it won't risk escalation," Corr said, "and it doesn't prepare them for future encounters." He paused, then said, "Allysen, after you finish with the company, assess the new base. Learn what defenses they are setting up."

Rhya softly said, "Shorel, Korhonen asked me to accompany Corr to the Embassy."

"Good," Shorel said. "This is all coming out of Mountainview. It all seems very strange, like nothing else the Humans have done. Maybe they are getting dumber." Then he stepped aside to take a call before loping on to the cache.

He's enjoying this, Corr thought. We all are.

When Ankolla returned with supplies, Corr signaled Quin and started back toward the border.

Rhya matched pace with Allysen and began asking about the Human military. Corr smiled and listened.

Before reaching the border Allysen, Ankolla, Bill, and Zuberi turned toward the river.

Corr said, "Allysen, be careful. There is an unknown element in all this. Rhya and I will remain at the border tonight and go on to the Embassy in the morning. Call if things get out of hand."

At the border, Corr and Rhya ate together in moonlight, and then slept until dawn.

During the night, while the Human company floundered, Tsaeb fighters quietly assembled.

In the morning, Corr and Rhya ate while laughing at

the humorous observations of a hoary bat that dropped in to report on the high points of Allysen and Ankolla's work on the advancing Human company. Confused, frustrated, and with a flood of curses, the colonel in charge had ordered withdrawal at daybreak. Quinn saw to it that the colonel's helmet bore a large white splat.

Faced with a grave situation and with the potential for global death and destruction, the two young warriors began loping south toward Mountainview. As they ran, they discussed situations that might arise and listened to reports from the battle group and from Quin's sentinels. They also called each other's attention to interesting plants, the fine color of the blue sky, and the delightful warmth of the rising sun.

The Humans Advance and Retreat

The company separated from the main army and moved north around 7:00 p.m. In command was a Human colonel who, like Corr and Rhya, was excited to see his first action. The troops sang marching songs filled with energy and spirit. What energized every step the most, however, was the live ammunition and the call for full tactical alert. Not a man in the company had ever fired a weapon at an enemy.

Excited and armed to the teeth, the company of Human soldiers plowed through beautiful cactus desert on their way to what they hoped would be a chance to kill something. Around 8:00 p.m., they crossed the border and, under a bright, silvery moon, began having accidents.

As the evening progressed, Allysen, Ankolla and the fighter groups caused stumbles, flat tires, and sputtering engines.

The Human soldiers suffered numerous injuries and two fatalities. One enterprising scout fell out of a cottonwood tree and struck a narrow boulder protruding from the sandy bank of the river. The other death occurred when a jack placed on sand dropped the hub of a truck wheel on the neck of a careless soldier.

The company did not make camp. They spent the night making repairs and tending minor injuries. At sunrise, with half his vehicles stalled, the frustrated and irritable colonel ordered a return to the site of the new base. They hadn't seen any Tsaeb.

* * *

Thursday morning Marbellet opened the meeting and called for progress reports.

Johns asked, "Is General Miller coming?"

"No, he's not joining us today," Marbellet said.

"Did he say how the invasion went?"

"It didn't go so good. They didn't find any Tsaeb."

Howell suppressed a grin. "Why not?"

"Apparently, our guys weren't ready for an advance across rough terrain. I've never seen such a list of screw-ups," Marbellet said, thinking of the line of limping troops and trucks towing other trucks. Miller was going to catch hell for this.

The group discussed, revised, and agreed upon plans for the anti-Tsaeb campaign. During the next month, the Tsaeb would start becoming unpopular. In the end, they would be depicted as villains, selfishly hoarding much more land and water than they needed.

In Eastern Asia

A man in silk robes sitting beside a tall window turned and beckoned a young woman standing in the shadows across the room. "Send for Halen, have a jet prepared, and send in Ya."

Aaron Li, the most powerful individual in Taoso, the oldest and largest Human nation on Earth, had watched events unfold in Mountainview and wondered whether the long-awaited moment had arrived. If the foolish invasions across the border catalyzed a Tsaeb action against Humans, Li would strike.

During the battles that preceded formation of the border, the Tsaeb had utterly defeated Li's father, his country's most renowned general. The loss of face devastated the man. He resigned, but insisted that his government maintain what it could of its army. Afterward, the general began scheming with others to build an anti-Tsaeb organization. He spent the remainder of his life aching for revenge.

The former general's first wife had borne him daughters and had died during the war. Following the war, Li devoted himself to studying the Tsaeb. After developing a reputation as a historian of the Tsaeb and Human conflicts, General Li married a young university professor. The general's ambitions grew when his second wife bore him a son.

When first the old general held his new son, Aaron, he felt renewed energy to continue his plans. As Aaron grew, he became a receptacle for his father's military knowledge and hatred for the Tsaeb. Aaron loved his father, and as the old man lay dying, he vowed to avenge his life and destroy the power of the Tsaeb.

Aaron Li continued the obsession with the Tsaeb. He became the head of his father's underground organization and expanded its potential. He spent a long life preparing all the forces and weapons his brilliant mind could conceive.

Li soon became his country's de facto executive head of state. He advanced Taoso's military might and built strong treaty alliances with other nations.

Ya Zhōu, the son of one of Li's older sisters, became Li's principal confidant and ally. Through Li's influence, Zhōu became Taoso's Plenipotentiary of Foreign Affairs. Directors of corporations controlling democracies, and the military, theological, and ideological dictators controlling other countries, all became uncomfortably familiar with the cold-faced Zhōu. Using the power of Taoso's advanced military, Zhōu forced other nations to join the International Coalition for Peace (ICP), an organization invented and controlled by Li. The ICP required a contributed military force of sufficient strength to prevent conflicts among its members. It also required that each of its members develop and maintain a strong army.

Taoso's legations to countries great and small included assassins and spies. Zhōu used the assassins to control Human leaders that opposed military buildup and other treaty obligations. Those leaders often lost family members and, if that did not bring them into line, they disappeared.

Because of ICP, the Human civilization invested a large portion of its resources in its military. Every capitol city hosted fleets of combat aircraft, heavy bombers, and troop transports. Every major city in countries and states bordering Tsaeb lands hosted military enclaves. All Human universities offered military courses and training. In all Human countries, the military became an independent partner of the dictators, theocracies, and ruling corporations. The Human people paid for it all. Never before had a peaceful civilization made such vast preparations for war.

Li and Zhōu were aware of the irony that their preparations for war created universal peace among Human nations, but only Zhōu found it humorous.

The ICP's local delegacies monitored everything

related to war readiness. They recorded and analyzed public health, economic development, and environmental conditions. Li, Zhōu, and most Human leaders began to see decay nibbling away at Human civilization. The past century's rapid improvement in Human health and economic conditions had slowed. Cities, industries, and the worldwide system of roads, education, and medical services were deteriorating. The leaders could see poverty spreading and wealth concentrating. The obvious cause was the exploding Human population. Natural resources and productivity of Human lands could no longer sustain the Humans.

Some Humans blamed their troubles on the Tsaeb. Li did not make that mistake, but he acknowledged that access to the vast area of fertile Tsaeb land might give his species time to resolve its problems and find true peace. The Human decline worried Li, but he kept his focus on avenging his father.

There, in his silent shadowy room, Li reached out to the vast power of his global war machine. He smiled. He stood, tall and strong, ready to strike.

PART THREE: MOUNTAINVIEW

Rhya's lips parted and she gripped Corr's arm as the bus drove trailing its cloud of dust and exhaust toward a cluster of tall buildings. Yards shrank, trees and shrubs dwindled, and building size increased. Finally, only large buildings and paved lots, some with a few parked cars, lined the street. The normal background radiance of life was gone. They had reached the heart of the Human abattoir.

Entering Mountainview

As Corr and Rhya approached Mountainview, the landscape changed. Soil surfaces became bare, their protective crust of microorganisms gone. A carpet of springtime weeds obscured the almost continuous cover of vehicle tracks. A few shrubs remained, but no native grasses. Exposed roots beneath the shrubs told of the loss of topsoil to wind and water. The lack of ant mounds indicated the severity of the Human impacts.

Rhya grew silent. She paused when they reached pavement. Walking stiffly, she followed Corr to the sidewalk, then stopped and stared at the smooth concrete and asphalt surfaces, the tall palm and eucalyptus trees, coriander shrubs, and lawns—all like heavy makeup on a corpse. Tears filled her eyes. She looked so desolate that Corr wanted to hug her.

"Have you been to a Human town before?" he asked.

"No. Sorry. I read about this, but these streets and those plants are—"

"Yes. You will adapt. Tell me what you know about the city."

"This is a young city as Human cities go. It began as an agricultural center and changed into a residential center. The street layout is rectangular. I memorized a street map, so I know how addresses are assigned, and I know where the government offices and major corporate headquarters are."

"Have you spent much time talking with Humans?" Corr asked.

"Only a little. I've met a few visitors, and I know Duncan and Lila, of course, but I also know they aren't typical. My internship with Shorel is supposed to enable me to meet more Humans. Corr, I know a great deal about Humans. I understand why they build these streets, but I know little about their daily lives and how they interact. I hope you don't mind coaching me."

"Sure. Right now, we should move on though. We will

walk. Most Humans move slowly when they are not using a vehicle."

"How do they greet each other?"

"That's easy. Strangers in this city usually don't greet each other. A glance and nod, perhaps a short statement such as 'Hello' or 'Good morning' will cover about everything."

Rhya reviewed what she had learned of Human social psychology. Suddenly she wasn't eager to see the real thing.

The Thomases

As Rhya and Corr walked along, a woman and small child came out of a house. The woman did not acknowledge the two Tsaeb, perhaps because she hadn't seen them, but the child stared. Rhya slowed and stared back. It occurred to Corr that he needed to speak with these people. He laid a hand on Rhya's arm.

"Hello," he said.

The woman looked up and said in a faintly quizzical tone, "Hello."

"We are going to the Tsaeb Embassy. Do you know if this street will take us there?"

Just then, a small boy ran out of the house, stopped abruptly and stared at the two gray-furred rabbit descendants.

"The Embassy is on Martin Avenue. Martin crosses this street about a mile from here," the woman said.

A man came out of the house and walked toward the van.

"These Tsaeb asked for directions to the Embassy," the woman said.

"Hello," the man said. "The Embassy isn't far from here. We're driving right by it. Can we offer you a lift?"

"That would be great. My name is Corr Syl and this is Rhya Bright."

"Hello," Rhya said, looking up at the tall Human.

"I'm Howard Thomas. This is my wife, Marcie, and our children, Willie and Charlotte."

He slid the door open on the side of a vehicle parked in the driveway, beckoning Corr and Rhya. "Hop in." He reddened slightly. "Sorry, I meant no offense."

Rhya smiled and Corr chuckled. "None taken," Corr said as he and Rhya entered the van. *Interesting,* Corr thought. *He recognized our original species.*

"Willie, get in the back. Charlotte, sit beside Rhya." Howard and Marcie slid in front and Howard backed the van out of the driveway.

Rhya inhaled the soapy scents and sweet breath rising from Charlotte and barely resisted an urge to put an arm around the little girl wriggling into the seat beside her.

As Howard drove down the street, Marcie turned to Rhya. "Is this your first time to Mountainview?"

"Corr has been here before," Rhya said, "but this is my first visit."

"How do you like it so far?"

"It's impressive. Do you travel through the city often?"

"Five days a week. Howard and I take the kids to school and then we go to work."

"Why are you all furry?" Willie asked.

"Lots of reasons. It's our kind of clothes," Rhya said. "But we never have to change."

"Can you jump rope?" Charlotte asked, holding up a multi-colored jumping rope.

Willie stared at the hilts rising above Rhya's shoulders. "Are those swords?"

"Children!" Marcie said. "Be respectful."

"I don't mind,... I would like to try to jump rope, Charlotte. Yes, these are swords." Rhya tapped a hilt.

Several of Corr's thoughtstreams focused on Rhya's wonderfully musical and precise English.

"How old are you, Charlotte?" Rhya asked.

"I'm almost five, and I go to school."

"You are four!" Willie said.

"I said almost."

"How about you, Willie?"

"I'm six. I'm the oldest."

"How old are you?" Charlotte asked.

"Eighteen," Rhya replied.

"Where is your school?" Willie asked, assuming someone only a little taller than him must be a student.

"I just finished, and now I am starting my internship."

"What's intership?" asked Charlotte.

Howard interrupted. "There's the Embassy."

"Will you both be in Mountainview long?" asked

Marcie.

"Probably just a few days," Corr said.

Then Marcie glanced at Howard. "Would you like to have dinner with us while you are here?"

Corr turned to Rhya and raised his eyebrows. "Sure. I think our evenings are free."

"Yes," Rhya said, "that would be nice."

"Tomorrow is Friday. Howard, do you think your father would mind if we had extra guests?"

"No, he wouldn't."

"Howard's family is having dinner with us tomorrow evening. Would you like to come?" Marcie said.

During the exchange, Charlotte rested her hand on Rhya's and gently wiggled her fingers in Rhya's fur.

Rhya's eyes brightened. "Yes."

"What can we bring?" Corr asked.

"Oh, nothing, unless you have a favorite beverage," said Marcie. "Do you mainly eat nuts, fruits, and vegetables?"

"Yes," replied Rhya.

"Good Please come at 5:00. We will eat at 6:00."

"Here we are." Howard pulled over to the curb and handed Corr a card. "Call if you want a ride."

"Thank you," Corr said, stepping out of the van.

"Yes, thank you," Rhya said. "We will be there at 5:00."

The children called goodbye and waved as the van pulled away.

Corr sensed the meeting with the Thomases had excited Rhya, and he felt a need to pause and think for a minute as well. "Want to sit somewhere for a moment?"

"Yes," Rhya said. "That would be nice."

Corr motioned toward a broad gravel path. "There's a bench beside the Embassy gate."

As the two rabbits walked toward the bench, a small junco landed on Corr's shoulder and began speaking quietly.

Rhya listened in on the bird's report, then asked, "Corr, did you expect anything like this to happen?"

"No, I've met Humans in the Embassy and elsewhere, but I haven't been inside a Human home."

"Do you think the Thomases are unusual?" Rhya asked.

"Perhaps," replied Corr. "But the way they trusted us with their children seemed fine. Humans rarely operate more than one conscious stream of thought, but a lot goes on in their unconscious minds. I sensed interest and excitement. Did you get anything unusual?"

"No. The children are delightful."

Mountainview Embassy

Corr and Rhya entered the Embassy grounds through a broad gate in a high wall. They stopped and looked up at the rough, cracked surface of the massive rock containing the Embassy. Herbs, shrubs, and cacti grew in the crevices. Droning bees filled the airspace about masses of brilliant yellow Encelia blossoms. Walking up a sandy path, they passed through double doors into a winding corridor that opened into an immense circular chamber with a shiny chocolate-brown floor and a domed ceiling resting on a massive central column.

Rhya slowed, then stopped and stared. The great hall exceeded the size of the Wycliff District Center by a large margin. Moreover, although the District Center's walls and floor varied in color and texture according to the character of the native material, this hall appeared astonishingly uniform. The brown floor, creamy walls, and ceiling of the flattened hemispherical dome were perfectly symmetrical and uniform in color and texture. But most surprising, the hall's gleaming surfaces glowed softly from within, providing the light of day free of glare.

Thousands of carvings and paintings covered the walls. The central column itself appeared to be enormous scrimshaw. Sculpture, variously of stone, wood, water, and plants, dotted the floor. Numerous heavy stone benches were scattered about.

Many species, including some Humans, moved about the hall, some walking, and others talking or viewing the exhibits. Birds entered and exited on outstretched wings through openings in the dome. Light and energy filled the huge space.

For once, Corr openly watched Rhya, smiling to see her reaction.

Near the entrance was a life-sized sculpture of a Human and a ringtail extending their hands to one another. The body positions and facial expressions conveyed eager interest.

As the rabbits studied the figures, a lynx approached. The well-dressed cat reminded Corr of the literary figure Puss in Boots. He carried an epee and a dagger on his belt. The original character in Human literature had been an unscrupulous servant who used any means to serve his master. Something other than the cat's clothes nagged at Corr.

"Nice, huh? Corr Syl and Rhya Bright? I am Able... Able Remington."

"Hello," Corr said.

"Whistol asked me to watch for you," Able said.

Just then, Farr came out of a nearby doorway. "Corr and Rhya! Here you are, and you've met my chief assistant, the son I want when I have one."

Able snorted. "And whom, were that true, you would never know as I would have become a traveler long ago."

Corr asked, "Where are you from, Able?"

"I spent a few years at the Continental Center and then came here to learn about transforming Human society from the great Whistol Farr."

Farr grinned.

Corr smiled without moving his whiskers. During the exchange, he spread an awareness envelope across the great hall, focused a portion of his attention on the unfamiliar lynx, and sent a roving sensory field questing for Ralph. Something wasn't right.

"Ralph and Ellan went out for lunch," Farr said. "We expect them back in an hour or so. Refresh yourselves and join us in the Tea Room for lunch." He gestured toward an arched doorway across the room.

Like the great hall, the Tea Room surprised Rhya. The large, sunken oval, which they reached by steps and ramps, had an ivy-covered wall on the left beyond a series of counters and islands contained food and drinks. A forest of trees reached into misty heights on the right side of the room. Floating windows appeared like movie screens between the trees in the perfect 3-D forest. Scattered among the trees, many carved stone tables rose from the floor like mushrooms on their single pedestals. Hundreds of Tsaeb and a few Humans were walking among the food counters or sitting beneath the trees in the forest. Like the District Center, the only seating was on the floor. Rhya noticed that her immediate surroundings seemed better lit than the rest of the room. A beautiful, pure-white snowshoe hare and a tall snowy egret were standing with Farr and Remington.

"Rhya Bright, this is Petra Austin, an assistant to our security chief, Sam Whortin," Farr said, introducing the hare.

Rhya's nose twitched as she realized the white rabbit had changed her natural hair color.

"Hello, Rhya," Petra said. "Corr, it's good to see you again. Sam said he would find you a little later. He asked me to give you an update on the information you requested."

Petra was wearing silver rings, sparkling earrings, and a gleaming white harness with a beautiful red clasp.

Rhya's hand wandered toward her gray harness and she looked away.

Turning to the Egret, Farr said, "Corr Syl and Rhya Bright, this is Adisa Lin, a visitor and member of the Redfield District council. Adisa, Corr is the Agent of the Wycliff council and the leader of one of our two battle groups. Rhya is a battle strategist and Human specialist just beginning her field training. Corr, Adisa has just returned from Piedmont."

Corr said, "Adisa, I am pleased to meet you. How long were you in Piedmont?"

"Oh, only one day." The smooth white feathers covering Adisa's face terminated in little tufts and gave the impression of a mask through which gleamed the bird's intense yellow eyes.

As the group followed Farr to the serving area, with Corr walking beside Adisa, he said, "I need to know as much as you can tell me about conditions in Piedmont."

"Oh, yes. It's not much. I spent most of my time near a small lake on the west side of the mountain."

Farr led them along a counter that held fruit, vegetables, eggs, and cheese.

As they finished filling trays, Rhya asked, "Why did you go to Piedmont, Adisa?"

"Oh, I—"

"Let's eat in my office," Farr said. "I have a conference table we can use, and I want to show off my new window." He turned to his assistant. "Able, ask the section chiefs to stop in for introductions. They can give Corr and Rhya a summary of their work. Adisa, please join us for any or all of the meetings."

"Thank you."

As they left the Tea Room, Petra took Corr's arm and steered him aside.

Rhya looked after them, then turned to Farr. "Whistol, the Embassy is awesome. Nothing I read adequately described it. Why is it so... so museum-like?" she asked, motioning about the hall.

"The embassies serve multiple purposes. They are impregnable fortresses, and they are indeed museums, as well as libraries and cultural activity centers. The Continental council wanted the embassies to serve as valuable resources for our two civilizations."

"Are all the embassies like this one?"

"Yes. The seven in North America and 56 worldwide are quite similar, though some are cast concrete rather than natural stone. This Embassy was the first. Tsaeb engineers carved it within an outcrop of bedrock and coated everything with drahsalleh. The engineers even bored three shafts through the central column and filled them with drahsalleh."

"I didn't know we could make so much drahsalleh. The column is certainly beautiful."

"The scrimshaw is nice, but subtle. Some of the scenes

are brighter."

"It changes?"

"Yes. You know, we used a lot of drahsalleh. I wonder if the engineers found other uses for it after finishing the embassies."

As they entered Farr's office, Rhya gazed through a wide window at panorama of Mountainview's northern residential subdivisions, scattered homes in the desert, and Diamond Peak in the distance. The windowsill and jambs were quite narrow.

"Whistol, how can the walls be this thin?" Rhya asked as her tactical senses bristled.

"The walls are at least 40 feet thick."

"Ah, I see... the window is a screen."

"Right. Lenses on the roof capture and distribute images throughout the Embassy. The view can be controlled."

Farr stepped to the side of the window and twisted a knob. The view panned to the left. Farr clicked a second knob and the center of the scene grew closer. "We can zoom in and see individuals at a distance of about 20 miles.

"Nice," Rhya said.

One wall of Farr's office displayed stone tools, weapons, an old cavalry saddle, and numerous images of landscapes and people, mostly Humans. One image showed Farr and a group of unkempt Humans posed outside the mouth of a cave. The Humans were wearing coarse skirts and capes woven from strips of— *Is that bark?* Beneath the photo a small plaque read, *The Ordway family, the original residents of the Mountainview Embassy.*

"Whistol, tell me about this image."

"The Ordways?"

"Uh huh."

"The Ordways came in the first wave of Humans. During my history internship, I studied the species' migrations. I did field surveys, but I gradually became interested in social issues. I lived with the Ordways for a while."

"They've come a long way."

"Yes. It's incredible."

"Whistol, what does the security staff do?"

"Not much, really. They keep an eye on things. Now, Petra has had a real assignment lately. We have an information source within the local military. Petra is the contact for a colonel who works for General Howell. The information we get isn't detailed, but it appears to represent a genuine concern for maintaining good relations."

"When did this start?"

"About a year ago. We're not sure who should know about the colonel, so Petra is giving Corr the latest update privately."

"Corr and I had an interesting encounter on the way here." Rhya described the Thomases and their invitation.

Farr beamed. "Excellent! It's the friendly attitude we've been cultivating. Excuse me a moment."

Farr opened the door and admitted Corr and Remington.

Everyone took a seat at Farr's polished stone conference table.

"So, ah, Rhya," Adisa said, "for our council, I flew to Piedmont yesterday after learning about the spies on Juniper Mesa. We were already concerned about two travelers camping near our southern border. After realizing they might also be spies, we arranged a meeting. One would not speak, but the other's story resembled that of the raccoon on Juniper Mesa. I went to Piedmont to investigate."

"Piedmont is south of Redfield. Didn't migratory birds already know about the Piedmont situation?" Corr asked.

"Ah... so," Adisa replied, "but for years the number stopping in Piedmont had declined. They were hearing complaints, but no one asked for help. It is obvious now the encroachment is excessive. I am sure our district will be eager to help correct the problems."

Rhya stared at a perfect sequence of Crinoids down the center of what had to be a Permian-aged slab of polished limestone used as Farr's table. The structure of the Crinoids varied slightly. Then she realized the table was a vertical slice of rock showing an evolving series of fossils that probably spanned more than 100,000 years. *Wow!*

"Adisa," Corr said, "we have a three-part challenge. We need to free the Piedmont captives, restore the Piedmont community, and figure out why the Human military has begun making forays across the border. Our council has requested a plan for dealing with the situation. If you can wait a few days before returning home, we should have an outline you can take to your council."

Adisa said, "I heard we killed two soldiers. Has there been anything else?"

"Yes. Two days ago, a heavily armed company of approximately 120 troops crossed the border. We used improvised accidents and mishaps to stop them," Corr said.

"Shoop! What's going on?"

"The Embassy security staff is investigating. If we can figure it out, we may incorporate a response into our plan to resolve the Piedmont issues."

Corr said, "Whistol, we have to get the captives released and the Piedmont lands restored. We could ask the Human leaders, or we could move a battle group in and take control of Mountainview. Rhya and I need you and others on your staff to help us define the options and anticipate Human responses. Let's meet with your section chiefs."

"Able, what's the schedule?"

"The sequence will be Public Affairs and Education, State Coordination and Environmental Issues, and then Security," Able said, stepping toward the door.

"Just a minute," Farr said. "Corr, I have to say right now that I feel you are too anxious to start something violent. Keep in mind that the Embassy staff has worked for years to make ties with the Humans. We don't need to start talking about battle groups."

Remington opened the door, and Farr stood. "This is Wilson Smith, the head of our Public Affairs and Education Division. Wilson, this is Corr Syl and Rhya Bright."

Smith said, "It's good to see you again, Corr. Rhya, I see you are a battle rabbit like Corr. What are your specialties?"

"Battle strategy and Human psychology. I'm beginning my internship," Rhya said.

"Corr, I am sure you and Rhya understand the fundamentals of our work. I'll summarize our current progress and answer your questions." Smith described 40 years of gradual expansion of the Tsaeb education mission. "We now have a staff of more than 700 Tsaeb, and we receive support from Wycliff, Oriven, Redfield, and the Continental Center.

"As for results; there is a visible improvement in attitudes. Most young adult Humans in Mountainview know about Immediacy and Equivalency. Our courses are popular. If we can sustain the growth of the program, it could eventually replace the entire Human education system. Given enough time, a complete shift in Human culture might occur."

Rhya said, "Wilson, I have a question." She described the encounter with the Thomas family. "Do you believe this is a result of your education programs?"

"At least partially. Howard and Marcie Thomas took Tsaeb courses through their entire school careers. This sort of ready interaction with Tsaeb is becoming common."

Corr asked, "There's something else?"

"Last year Howard's father appeared in all the news media when he resigned in protest over police policies. The Police Department fired him for incompetence, but we found out that he had refused to follow an order to arrest a political opponent of the mayor. The incident might have given him and his family a broader perspective on things."

Corr said, "The children were completely comfortable with us. Do young Humans generally consider Tsaeb equals?"

"It depends. A large portion of the Human population belongs to various faith institutions. The institutions often criticize other groups. I'm afraid some families teach intolerance to their children."

Corr asked, "Don't they understand Equivalency?"

"They probably do, but they don't practice it. We've tested and studied thousands of students. Humans are imaginative and inventive, but they have limited conscious abilities. They have poor memories, and probably only one in a million is capable of concurrent thought. They simply do not have sufficient mental power to understand their surroundings and the long-term consequences of their actions.

"Even when they acknowledge the logic of Immediacy, Humans have trouble applying it. For almost all Humans, innate appetites and impulses rank higher in importance than the long-term consequences of their behavior. They easily become victims of ideologies, and leaders that feed their appetites and insecurities."

Rhya asked, "Is the reason for Human limits still a mystery? Anything new on causes?"

"No. There doesn't seem to be any physiological limits. It just seems to be something in the way they marshal their thoughts."

Adisa said, "Oh, Wilson, how have the Mountainview leaders responded to the education program?"

"Mixed. Most ignore it, but a few are opposed."

"Well," Farr said, "Corr, Rhya, anyone, more questions? No? Remi, is our liaison coming?"

"I am sure she is, Whiz," Remington replied.

Remington opened the door for a tall white individual with bright blue nubs of remnant horns.

"Hello, Elsa," Farr said. "I think you've met everyone here but Rhya Bright. Rhya, this is Elsa Loret, our principle liaison with the local government. Elisa interacts with Human leaders in a variety of ways. She also runs our environmental monitoring program."

"Hi, Elsa," Corr said. "Is Sam Jr. still around?"

"No, he went to the mountains to pursue his interest in elemental crystal forms. And he might do that, if he can settle down with just one ewe."

With a rumbling chuckle, Farr said, "Elsa, please give us a brief description of your work."

"Sure. My department strives to become a valuable resource for the Humans. We provide information and support for public health, civil engineering, and product development. We also try to place Tsaeb in important positions on committees and boards of community groups, government agencies, and private enterprises. The Humans are beginning to rely on us for help with all kinds of projects."

Corr asked, "Is it wise to give technology to Humans?"

"Definitely not," Elisa replied. "We provide only the most rudimentary technical suggestions. We try to prevent mistakes."

"Oh, why help them at all?" Adisa asked.

"The goal is similar to Wilson Smith's, but we are trying to influence the Humans from the top down rather than bottom up. We have worked with economists, planners, and public health workers to help them see the consequences of improper land use and waste generation. We try to show them how to apply what Wilson's teachers are saying in school. We've made a little progress. For instance, the crappy condition of the air and water are often mentioned in the daily news."

"What do you do with the political system?" Rhya asked.

"The greatest overall barrier to helping the Humans is that the Federation lacks a truly representative government. The Federation Constitution allows too much influence by private businesses, churches, and the military.

Members of the executive, congressional, and judiciary branches of government usually represent only their most powerful supporters.

"At first I provided an alternative source of support for politicians willing to behave sensibly. We have access to large quantities of gemstones and rare metals, so I began converting them to Human dollars that I used to form a Tsaeb lobby."

"Did any of the politicians accept the money?" Adisa asked. "They knew it was coming from the Tsaeb, right?"

"Oh, yes. We were very generous, and word spread rapidly. There was almost a line at the door. Some politicians requested office space in the Embassy."

"Ha! So how is it going?"

"After a few years I closed the lobby. Human corporations and the military turned to kidnapping and murder to regain control of the leaders I had preempted. When the mayor's wife disappeared, I knew we had to develop a major security system or give up. We don't have enough volunteers to guard all the leaders, so we gave up. Besides, the council never liked the lobby. Tau Korhonen and others argued that buying good behavior was not an effective long-term solution to the Human problems. They felt we were just reinforcing the weaknesses that are at the heart of the problem."

"How does the military influence the leaders?" Rhya asked.

"They provide money and prestige just like the corporations."

"Why do they do it?"

"The Human military invests in real estate, manufacturing, and equities. They aren't as wealthy as the corporations, and as things stand now, they generally take orders from the corporations."

Farr interrupted. "Let's order something to drink. You can catch Elisa later if you come up with more questions. Remington, see if Sam is ready."

Corr reflected on the way the Human groups worked. Too much came from the top down. He realized that this backward arrangement worked because of the limited intelligence of the Humans. It allowed brighter and more energetic individuals to become group leaders who could use their group for personal benefit.

As Remington exited, a stream of Tsaeb wearing aprons and hats came in carrying pitchers and platters of fruit and cheese. After arranging everything on side tables they filled cups and plates, and plopped down around the room.

Farr laughed. "Come and get what you can before the kitchen staff eats it all."

Sam Whortin, the Tsaeb Embassy Security Chief, presented a brief overview of the Embassy defenses, the local military capabilities, and the city police. Farr nodded to one of the kitchen staff and the group gathered empty dishes and left. Whortin then described the conditions of the imprisoned Piedmont captives, and said, "The Piedmont situation brings into focus the value of our efforts to help the Humans. We must continue Wilson Smith's work in education, and Elisa Loret's work with the political system."

Corr turned an unfocused gaze toward the window.

Farr asked, "Sam, anything new on our informant?"

"Yes. His value is increasing." Whortin looked around. "Last year we were contacted by Colonel Sean Phillips. About once a month he makes reports on Human military activities. The information he gives Petra is becoming more interesting."

"What is his position?" Rhya asked.

"He works in General Sampson Howell's office. Howell has publicly criticized the Tsaeb education program. We assume Phillips is acting independently."

At that moment Petra rushed in. "Hello, everyone. Phillips just called with some disturbing background on yesterday's border crossing. A group of Mountainview leaders is developing a plan to discredit the Tsaeb and invade Wycliff. Led by Johns, the city and state elected officials and the military and corporate leaders have committed to a forced annexation of Tsaeb land across the border."

Farr frowned, but did not speak.

Corr looked at Farr. "Whistol, can you arrange for Rhya and me to visit a school and meet Johns? Will it be possible to do that in the morning after our meeting, and can someone with local experience come along?"

"Yes," Farr said. "Able, ask Wilson and Elsa to set up appointments with the principal of the school across the street and the City Manager. Corr, do you want us to try for a police chief or general?"

"No, let's skip the police and military, and let's choose a school farther from the Embassy."

As everyone filed out, Corr signaled Rhya to wait. "Whistol, what response have you received about the Piedmont farms?"

"Nothing, really. We've gone through the usual government channels and planned to increase pressure. We haven't pushed hard. We didn't know about the prisoners."

* * *

As they exited the room, Farr turned to Rhya, "Let me show you something."

Farr led the way across the hall to an image etched in sandstone. "This is a replica of the remains of an etching made at least 50 million years ago. Battle rabbits have been with us for a long time."

"I know this image," Rhya said. "The records are in the Rocky Park library, one of our oldest. Other images in the collection show harness and weapons similar to what we use today. Some think the tail served as a counterbalance used in combat. Others think it was an expression of personal vanity."

"Yes," Farr said, "and some of our scientists believe the uncharacteristic tail is an indicator of the approximate time of the beginning of Tsaeb control of genetics."

Corr listened without comment. The image was the one that hung in his room, but this wasn't the time to bring up his story.

Farr turned and said, "Corr, you and Rhya can use rooms 13 and 14 above the Tea Room. Those rooms contain window viewers. If you would like to show Rhya the way, I will tend to a few matters and join you for dinner in two hours."

"Thank you. Rhya, let's tour the hall."

Rhya hesitated and then nodded. Like Corr, she devoted most of her attention to the Human and Piedmont Tsaeb problems, but she didn't know how much longer she and Corr would get to spend time together.

Corr pointed to three large bas-reliefs of the Earth carved into the wall. "These show North America in the lower Cenozoic Era when Tsaeb civilization had its beginning."

"Water still covered part of the Great Plains."

"Yes, but the climate was drying. By the end of the Age of War, the Plains were completely dry and many of our current species began appearing. Later, water covered central California, but the extent of the water was nothing like the inland sea that had filled the Great Plains."

As they continued, Rhya began feeling tense and started checking the surroundings.

Corr grinned. "It's the paintings."

Rhya paused a moment and then said, "Why are they so scary?"

"Look back. The series was designed to have a cumulative effect."

Corr also felt tense, but not because of the paintings. He began scanning the room, thinking of the spies on Juniper Mesa. "Shall we go to our rooms? We can look a little more before dinner."

* * *

Corr led the way across the hall to a broad opening with a well-lit tunnel going down on the left and a balcony going up on the right. Cut into the walls, the balcony spiraled up around the dome, soon becoming a tunnel and disappearing into the dome's ceiling. Doors along the balcony led to corridors with rows of rooms.

In her room, Rhya napped for a few minutes, groomed her fur, and went out onto the balcony. Corr appeared shortly.

For the next hour, the two sampled the sights, sounds, and scents their fellow creatures had produced to adorn the Embassy walls.

"Rhya, have you noticed how quiet it is?"

"Yes, now that you mention it, but I hadn't given it much thought."

"See the ripples and raised panels on the walls?"

"Yes, but even they couldn't dampen the echoes."

Corr spoke quietly. "The Embassy builders placed sound-dampening devices in the central column and molecular energy relays in the walls and ceiling. An antimatter generator in the basement powers everything."

Rhya stared at Corr. "I thought that except for our energy weapons, all such high-energy technology was abandoned millions of years ago."

"Most of it was, but the knowledge is preserved in the libraries. Antimatter generators are present in all the district centers and embassies. We have one in the Wycliff center basement."

Rhya began reviewing the technology.

"Do some of these pieces seem plain to Humans?" she said.

"Some do, but there is still much they can appreciate. Farr says some of them create multilevel effects that everyone can experience. When the hall opened, the decorators found that some of the pieces produced such a strong emotional response that they had to be removed. They are in a special gallery Humans may view only after being warned."

The two rabbits hadn't gone far when they met Whistol Farr, Able Remington, and Arthur Tummel, the Piedmont spy Corr had captured on Juniper Mesa.

"How about some dinner?" Farr asked.

After dinner, Corr asked Able if he would show them around the neighborhood. Corr knew the area well, but he wanted to meet more Humans, and he knew Rhya would be interested.

"Leave your swords and bows," Remington said. "We don't want to alarm the locals."

Able's wife, Melissa, joined the group for the neighborhood tour. Corr noticed the pair rarely touched and didn't seem to share many thoughts. Perhaps they were in the midst of an argument.

The Golden Court

Human developments encircled the 28-acre Embassy. A park lay across the street. A shudder ran through Rhya's frame. The walkways, ball courts, and alien plants filling the park covered once-healthy soil. She wished the Humans understood how many beings such developments killed.

North and east of the Embassy lay a residential district, and to the west lay a mixed-use residential and commercial area. The group walked west toward a row of restaurants and taverns. Some of the people they met on the street nodded or said hello, but no opportunities for conversation occurred.

Stopping at a black door with a shining gold drawing of a pitcher and the name *Golden Court—Drinks and Dancing*, Remington asked, "Shall we have a beer?"

"Sure."

Inside a large, dimly-lit room, they found a dance floor surrounded by tables. Youthful Humans occupied about a third of the tables and bar stools. Young women wearing metallic gold shirts and shorts hurried about with trays of drinks. As they watched, a band started playing, but no one danced.

"Let's sit," Able said.

The four Tsaeb found an empty table and ordered beer. Able asked Rhya, "Want to dance?"

"I think I would rather walk," Rhya said. Corr felt the same. The four abandoned their drinks, returned to the street, and began to walk back toward the Embassy.

"Sorry you didn't like the beer," Able said.

"The beer was fine, but the place was pretty empty," Rhya said.

"It will be busy tomorrow night," Remington said.

At the Embassy, they found the dimly lit great hall occupied by a few clusters of Tsaeb.

As Corr and Rhya approached their rooms, they paused and looked out across the hall. After a minute, Corr smiled, said "Good night," and entered his room.

Tea and the Human Military

Farr, the Embassy section chief, and a few other members of the Embassy staff gathered in the Tea Room for breakfast. Later they convened in a small conference room next door. The conversation floated between the border incursions and the Piedmont Tsaeb.

"I have never understood why the Human military even exists," Sam said. "They haven't had a battle in decades."

"Maybe they're still pissed about the border," Ralph said.

"That and the general need for power and security," Elisa said. "Whistol, is it like this everywhere? I know some Human nations have armies. Do they all?"

"As far as I know, they do. Zuberi, you and Bill were abroad after the war. Any impressions?"

"From north Africa through southern Europe and into western Asia, the armies were winding down, but in eastern Asia we encountered strong military remnants. The resentment of the Tsaeb was greater there than anywhere else."

"Yes," Bill said. "We passed through Taoso about 20 years after the border was formed. Zuberi swears he didn't sleep for three weeks. I know he did, but there was always a faint aura of danger."

"Rhya, what do the psychology texts say?"

"I don't recall any answers. One text concluded a section on Human social institutions this way." She recited the passage from memory:

"The universal presence and continued growth of military systems is an unexplained element of Human society. For most of their history, Human nations had armed conflicts. After the border war, conflicts declined. The last battle between Human states occurred in Africa 49 years after the treaty. But as I write this, 50 years later, Human armies continue to increase in size and sophistication.

"Two factors might explain the continuing military buildup. One is the political influence of large corporations that supply weapons and military equipment to their governments. The other is the International Coalition for Peace (ICP) to which all Human nations now belong. A peculiar feature of the ICP treaty is its requirement for all signatory nations to advance their military capability. The ICP originated in Taoso. Why it has such warlike characteristics is a mystery."

Seeing that no one had anything more to offer, Farr said, "Let's reassemble here tomorrow morning. Corr and Rhya will meet with some Humans today. Perhaps they will have some ideas for us in the morning."

News of Allon

As Allysen and two fighters trotted past a picnic area near the new military base, a Human woman waved them over.

"Hello. Do you have a moment?"

Allysen focused. The woman seemed worried, and she wanted help from Tsaeb. *Odd.* Allysen introduced her group and asked how she could help.

"I am Elaine Medlar, and this is my husband Paul. A friend of ours, Julie Snow, lived where they're building the new army base. A Tsaeb, Allon Trofeld, stopped by while we were visiting her last month. I wondered if you knew him."

"I do. What happened?"

"Well, probably nothing, but we haven't been able to reach Julie, and we're wondering if Trofeld knew anything. Would you mind asking him to give me a call?"

"I wouldn't mind, but I may not see him for a while. Tell me about your meeting with him."

"Sure... this is a long story. Julie and I taught at Saguaro Elementary. Last January, she accepted a job in the State Education office. The new job didn't start right away, and Julie decided to take some time off so she could work on her novel and visit her family. She moved into an old ranch house outside town. My husband Paul and I had dinner with her last month, and that's when we met Trofeld."

"Is the house near here?" Allysen asked.

"It was, but I think it's been torn down. It was down this road, about where the army is working on something. It was an interesting evening. The house was on a gravel road about a mile north of the city. The place was old. It had a corrugated tin roof splotched with rust, and a wrap-around porch. Inside, it felt like the ceilings were too low, and the rooms were dark. During dinner, Julie told us the Tsaeb border was a short distance farther north. After dinner, she took us out on the front porch to look at the desert. Tall Saguaro stood between round Paloverde and clusters of bristling Cholla. The air was cool, clear, and very still. It was pretty, but very quiet. After we went in, Paul said the silence was eerie. He asked Julie if she had expected it to be so quiet. She said mocking birds often sang at night, and normally you could hear owls and a cricket or two.

"There was a knock and we all jumped. Then we laughed and Julie went to the door. When Julie opened the door we could see a tall creature with fur like yours, tawny everywhere, but white on his chest and stomach. He was wearing a neat brown vest and trousers, but his chest and feet were bare. He carried a walking stick and had a box under his arm. He said his name was Allon Trofeld and he had stopped by to say hello. Trofeld said he had heard the old place was rented, and had come to welcome the newcomers to the neighborhood. He held up his box and said he had brought fruit. Julie told Trofeld she had company, and asked if he would like to come in for a moment, and Trofeld said he would be delighted to meet us.

"Trofeld placed the box on a table beside the door and leaned his stick against the wall. Julie introduced us and he explained he was descended from mountain lions and grinned, exposing very large teeth. I remember how they gleamed in that dark little room. Trofeld's walking stick was peculiar. A long straight cylinder about half his height, it had a shiny surface covered with fine markings. I asked Trofeld if he lived nearby. He said his home was just across the border. I asked what he did, and he said he furnished information for district council meetings, and traveled far too much. As he said this, his long whiskers twitched. I was going to ask about his walking stick, but Julie said she was a traveler too, and had rented the house for just a few months before starting a new job.

"Trofeld asked about her job, and then asked if she had anyone living with her. Julie said no. Then Trofeld turned his large round yellow eyes on me and asked if Paul and I had any family living with us. I told him that our two children were at home with our babysitter. I remember adding that if we weren't home by 10:30 and didn't call, the babysitter would call my mother.

"I asked Trofeld if he had a family and he said they were estranged. His whiskers twitched again as he said that. Trofeld was remarkable. He listened with understanding to our ideas about education, politics, and the economy, he told stories and jokes, and he even taught us the difference between limericks and haiku. Let's see, limerick, five lines; first, second, and fifth rhyme; third and fourth are shorter and form a rhyming couplet. Haiku: three lines; five, seven, and five syllables.

"When it was time for us to leave, we shook hands. Trofeld's hand was huge, but his fingers were short. I think he had retractable claws. When he took my hand, I had a faint sensation that needles touched my wrist. We were nearly home when I remembered my grandmother's bowl. Paul grumbled, but he turned around. I knocked, waited, and finally knocked again before the door opened. It was Trofeld, dabbing his lips with a towel. I told him I had forgotten my bowl. He volunteered to get it and asked me what color it was. I guess he could tell I was surprised he was still there. He said Julie was fixing him a bite to eat before he went home. I remember feeling nervous. Julie had just met Trofeld. Doesn't it seem odd that he answered the door?"

Allysen and the other Tsaeb did not respond.

"While Trofeld was getting the bowl, I noticed his stick was gone and his box had fallen. I put the box back on the table and looked around for the stick, but didn't see it. The next morning I had to start getting ready for spring semester, and I didn't think of Julie for days. When I did, I called and left a message about having her over for dinner. She didn't reply. I guessed she might be visiting her parents, but I tried another time, and again there was no answer."

"And you still haven't heard from her?" Allysen asked.

"No, and I've gotten worried. When I think about how quiet it was around her house that night, I wonder if Trofeld is still living nearby. If you see him, would you mind asking if he saw Julie again?"

"I will," Allysen said. "Let me have your phone number. Here's mine. Call me if you hear from Julie."

As Allysen and the fighters went on down the road, one of the fighters muttered, "It doesn't look good for Julie."

Mountainview Tour

Remington suggested they catch a city bus to the school, and he led the way to a bus stop in front of the Embassy. "This bus will take us downtown where we will transfer to a bus that goes by the school."

As they waited, Corr received calls from Allysen, Shorel, and Sims until their bus arrived with squealing brakes, creaking joints, and the scrape and clunk of its opening door. Once the three Tsaeb climbed aboard, the bus engine roared, and the big swaying box emitted a cloud of black smoke and pulled away from the curb. Before reaching what Rhya considered a good gallop, the engine went silent and the bus lurched to a screeching stop for more passengers.

Rhya's lips separated and she gripped Corr's arm as the bus drove toward a cluster of tall buildings. Yards shrank, trees and shrubs dwindled, and building size increased. Finally, only large buildings and paved lots, some with a few parked cars, lined the street. The normal background radiance of life was gone. They had reached the heart of the Human abattoir.

Corr understood Rhya's horror. *This is the inevitable consequence of sentience without Immediacy,* he thought. He remembered what Halbert Sims had once told him a story about the Human name.

"About 500 years ago, when Human ships began crossing the oceans, the Tsaeb called a global meeting to discuss the expanding problems. The Humans had not responded to the usual guidance given to young species. Moreover, the species had very little ability to understand the effects of its actions on its surroundings. Uncertain of how the world around them functions, Humans focus on their physical needs and desires. Thus, the Human birth rate always exceeds the death rate. Following a remark about the 'backward' humans, someone suggested calling them 'Danog' (Dā'-nog) which is gonad spelled backwards.

"Someone else pointed out that since Humans consider

other species less important than themselves, they might wish to call them Tsaeb (Sāb) which is beast spelled backward. Even the Danog laughed. What caused the name to stick, however, was the conference chairperson's introduction of one of the human ambassadors. I guess he was trying to be funny. He began, 'Not all species are the Tsaeb—uh, same.' Of course, that joke would have won a week's worst award in Wycliff District.

"Tsaeb liked their name and soon we all were using it. Humans didn't like their nickname, and it was dropped. By the time of the border wars 400 years later, none recalled the story. In the final treaty acceptance speeches, no Human thought to explain how: *The Tsaeb suck. Uh, that is, Tsaeb stuck.* They have a poor sense of humor."

The Tsaeb exited their bus along with most of the other passengers. Remington led the way to their next bus stop. Apart from the hiss of passing cars, and the screech and roar of the buses, they heard no sounds. The Humans clustered at bus stops did not speak. Rhya found their minds as empty as the surrounding buildings with their boarded-up lower windows and their entryways filled with dust and drifts of food wrappers. Mountainview's downtown held no soil, trees, or grass, only clumps of silent Humans standing on lifeless surfaces and shuffling on and off the creaking buses.

* * *

The Southern Plains High School principal greeted the three Tsaeb and invited them to come along on her daily visit to the library. They walked down a broad corridor with regularly spaced doors with windows. In room after room, young people sat facing an adult standing at the front of the room. Finally, Corr asked, "What are they doing?"

"These rooms contain senior classes," the principal said, nodding toward a door. "This is the Federation

History classroom."

"Are they having a party?" Rhya asked.

"Well, no. The students are listening to the teacher discuss Federation history."

"Do they do this often?" Corr asked.

"Yes. Every day."

"It must be chaotic."

"Why do you think so?"

"That many students asking questions, disagreeing, commenting, and so forth would make it hard to talk," Corr said.

"No, Mr. Syl. There is no problem. Students can't speak unless the teacher asks them to."

"Call me Corr. Does the teacher meet with each student for discussion?"

"The students can ask the teacher questions in the classroom—as long as it's one student at a time—and they can request a meeting with the teacher, but they are expected to take notes in class and remember what the teacher says. They also have assigned readings in textbooks that cover the material. I understand that the Tsaeb are all home-schooled."

"Yes. Parents, and sometimes neighbors and specialists, teach the children. It's almost all one-to-one."

"That wouldn't work here in Mountainview. Most parents work."

Rhya was thinking that this classroom system might be one of the reasons for the unusually low intelligence of Humans.

A loud, irritating buzz sounded and students flowed into the hall. Only a few seemed at all curious about the Tsaeb with their principal. One young woman, with green and blue hair, stopped, said hello to the principal, and asked if she could be of assistance. Corr said yes, introduced himself, and asked her name.

"Cory," the young woman replied with a bright smile. "Are you having a tour?" Other students stopped, forming a small cluster around the Tsaeb.

"Yes, we came to see your schooling," Corr said. "May I ask what subjects you are studying?"

"Sure. I just had Algebra, and next I have Life Sciences II."

"How old are you?"

"Sixteen. How old are you?"

"Twenty-one."

"What do you do?"

"This is Able Remington. He is an administrator at the Embassy. And this is Rhya Bright. She and I are warriors."

That riveted the teenagers' attention. A tall red-haired boy who towered almost two feet above the Tsaeb asked, "You mean like in a game?"

"No. We're real warriors," Corr said, a grin spreading across his face.

The boy leaned back a fraction of an inch and studied Corr. Another student, a young woman with rings in her ears and nose asked, "Are those sword handles?"

"Yes."

"You don't look too dangerous," another boy said.

He's probably responding to our size, Rhya thought. "Good. We just wanted to meet a few people and learn more about the school."

Meanwhile the majority of students continued to sweep past, most ignoring the group around the Tsaeb. *And so the dross floats by leaving the gold behind*, Rhya thought.

A short young woman wearing a large jacket covered with emblems stopped and after a moment said, "May I ask why you are here?"

"We're visiting the school," Corr said.

"Yes, but why? Are there any Tsaeb at this school?"

Corr focused his sensory fields on the young woman. "Do you mean Tsaeb teachers?"

"No, I mean there aren't any Tsaeb students here. We have teachers. They can tell us about Tsaeb."

Cory spoke up, "Why do you care, Rita? Are you in any

of the Tsaeb classes?"

"You mean Saving Soils or Fixing Forests? I don't have time; I plan to go to college."

Corr focused all his attention on the two girls. "Do a lot of students avoid the Tsaeb classes?"

"Just the jocks and accountants," Cory said.

Rita glared.

"Rita, do your studies truly leave no time for Tsaeb courses?"

"I just don't want to take them. You say you offer them because you want to help, but what else do you want?"

More students stopped to see the Tsaeb. A tall blond boy arrived. "Rita, what's going on? What are these Tsaeb doing here?" The boy eyed Corr and Rhya's sword hilts.

The principal intervened. "The break is just about over."

"Could we meet with students tomorrow?" Corr asked.

"Tomorrow is Saturday; students are free to do whatever they wish."

Raising his voice and projecting good will as hard as he could, Corr said, "Will all of you please join Rhya and me at the Tsaeb Embassy for lunch at noon tomorrow? We will answer your questions about the Tsaeb, the universe, and everything."

Cory nodded and several others said they would come. As the group began to disperse, Rita stepped up to Corr and, in a challenging tone, said, "I will be there."

Able thanked the principal, and as the halls drained into the classrooms, the three Tsaeb left for their appointment with the City Manager.

* * *

"We have some time before our next appointment," Able said. "Let me show you an interesting development." As they walked across a broad parking lot toward to a large structure, a small bird landed on Corr's shoulder and quietly reported on Shorel's fighter assembly. Entering through one of a row of doors, Able led Corr and Rhya to an open area filled with tables and chairs and surrounded by small food shops. He walked up to a shop with a large sign.

Tsaeb Dinette: Eat the Tsaeb Way for Health!

"This shop opened two years ago and now there are four," Able said as they stood looking at trays of nuts, vegetables, and fruits.

"I can sense toxins in all this," Rhya whispered.

"The toxins *are* a problem," Able said.

"We get more and more in the wind and rain. I wish they would just stop using the stuff. Isolating and expelling toxins every time you eat is irritating," Rhya said, frowning.

Then Able leaned close. "Think about the poor Humans; they have to rely on their automatic internal systems to handle the toxins. Often, their bodies get behind and begin adding storage cells. The added weight disfigures them, stresses their organs, and makes them susceptible to disease."

"Let's have a bite," Corr said, wanting to study the Humans scattered among the tables and in the serving lines.

Rhya nodded, "Yes, let's."

The warriors sensed that these people were more relaxed than those on the street, but still, almost none smiled.

The Tsaeb filled their trays and took seats at a table amidst others occupied by Humans. They attracted attention, but no one spoke to them. Rhya realized that she and her companions had joined in one of the mall's principal functions: people watching.

A young man wearing an apron and a big smile walked up to their table. "How is everything?"

"Fine. Do you work here?" Rhya asked.

The young man focused on Rhya and paused, transfixed by her beauty. He blinked and regained some of his composure. "Yes, I work here. May I join you?"

"Please, sit down." Corr gestured, whiskers twitching.

"This is Able Remington, Rhya Bright, and I'm Corr Syl. Have you worked here long?"

"Uh, yes... well, not here exactly. My friends and I started this business two years ago. I spend two days a week at one of the stores. My name is Allen Boyer."

"How's the business doing?" Corr asked.

"It's going well, but may I ask a question?"

"Sure."

Boyer paused and fixed his eyes on Corr. "We went to the Tsaeb Embassy to eat a few times before we started this business. We can't get all the things you eat, but we have tried to provide a similar menu. Tsaeb come by occasionally, but you are the first to buy anything. Is it because the fruits and vegetables are different? Is there anything we can do to make them more appealing?"

"Tsaeb didn't try the food because it contains high levels of toxic chemicals."

"Toxic chemicals? I don't know what you mean."

He really doesn't, Corr thought. Let's see where this goes.

"Your farmers use pesticides to protect the crops and artificial fertilizers to accelerate growth. In some places, they irrigate crops with water that has passed through a city. Some of the chemicals picked up along the way pass through the root membranes into the plants, and others adhere to surfaces. When you eat the plants most of the chemicals pass through your body, but some are stored, and some disrupt normal cell function."

"I've heard about that, but I thought the government tested for toxic materials."

"They are probably concerned only with toxicity levels that would cause immediate harm."

"But how do you know our food has the chemicals?"

"We can sense them."

"Did you choose the food in your bowl because they were safer?"

"I didn't really compare them. Rhya, Able, did you?"

"Not too much," Rhya said, "but I stayed away from the red aggregated berries with achenes imbedded in their skin, and the round fuzzy fruits."

"I think you mean strawberries and peaches," Allen said. "What do the toxins do?"

"They can cause nerve damage and cancer. Children can develop cognitive problems," Rhya said.

"Well, what can I do? Should we be washing more?"

"You can remove some of the surface accumulations, but there's not much you can do about toxins inside."

"Should we switch to organic produce?" asked Allen.

"That would help, but it won't avoid the stuff in the irrigation water. In a growing number of places, wind and rain carry the toxins to the fields and orchards. I guess you could buy from farms upstream and upwind of cities."

"What do Tsaeb do?"

"We pass all the toxins," Corr said.

Allen paused. "How—"

"Allen, I'm sorry, but we have an appointment at Town Hall," Able said.

"Could we meet some other time and talk about this some more?"

Corr said, "Your customers can't sense the toxins, and there aren't many Tsaeb in the city. Why do you care?"

Allen looked at him. "I would like to offer the best food I can."

"Organic produce will cost more. Do you think your customers will pay higher prices for a benefit they can't see?"

"I don't know without trying. If what you say is true, I don't see how we can keep serving standard produce. I'll look for more information."

"The Embassy library has a lot of material on environmental toxicity," Able said. "Also, there are monthly environmental reports that include food and water test results. You would be welcome to use them."

"Come to the Embassy and we'll give you all the help we can," Rhya said. "Corr and I will be busy for the next few days, but we'll have time after that. Send me an email next week. Use RhyaBright@gmail.com."

This young man is quick to express concern, Corr thought. He seems sincere, but will he change his mind and continue serving toxic food if it's significantly cheaper? It is very interesting that a business with a Tsaeb theme would thrive in a Human city.

* * *

After lunch, the trio caught a bus for the ride downtown to City Hall. They walked from the bus stop to a set of buildings that served as the military headquarters. As they crossed a street, Able nodded up at a device mounted on a traffic light. "See that camera? The police have begun a public surveillance program. They're placing cameras at every intersection."

"It isn't working," Corr noted, sensing no magnetic fields around the cameras. He answered a call and listened without comment.

Glancing at Corr, Able said, "Huh. I guess they haven't turned this one on yet."

Corr nodded.

"This is the site of the first army post," Able said. "The buildings in the center are the headquarters and communications center for all the units stationed in the state of Normount. The buildings to the right house the city police and the jail. The Piedmont prisoners are in that square building at right center."

Corr resisted a temptation to go to the prisoners. *Soon....*

* * *

A receptionist in the city administration building took

them to a carpeted conference room with an oak table and soft chairs, and asked them to wait. In a moment, the warriors sensed the arrival of two people behind a mirror set among photographs and posters on the wall.

Corr began asking Able about the sources of food for Mountainview, but he focused his attention on the people behind the mirror. When Johns and Lactella joined the other watchers, Corr and Rhya snapped their attention onto the bizarre pair.

There wasn't enough light coming back through the mirror for the warriors to see Johns with their eyes, but the magnetic fields projected by Johns and Lactella produced clear images and revealed some thoughts. The warriors could sense exactly where Johns was standing, and they naturally focused their eyes on that spot. Instantly alarmed, Lactella thought the warriors could see Johns through the glass. She abruptly spun and hurried from the observation gallery.

Corr and Rhya shared a glance. Both had sensed Lactella and immediately knew she was controlling Johns. They wanted very much to question the pair, but not understanding the dangers threatening the Piedmont captives and how Johns might be involved, they decided to wait. In a few minutes, a woman entered and said something had come up and the City Manager couldn't meet with them.

* * *

Lactella hurried back to Johns' office. She had felt Corr and Rhya's sensory fields, and guessed that Tsaeb could sense thoughts. She reviewed her interrogation of Marion and realized Marion had probably studied her the whole time. The police or the army must destroy the prisoners immediately. But first, she would interview a younger captive. Perhaps a child would reveal more of the true abilities of the Tsaeb. Most of all, however, she wanted to capture or kill Corr and Rhya.

Making up her mind, Lactella called General Miller, requested a young Tsaeb to interview, and said she had seen two dangerous Tsaeb at Johns' office.

"Steve, three Tsaeb came to City Hall today," Lactella said. "One is from the Embassy, but the other two were strangers and they were carrying swords. They had an appointment with me, but frankly, when I saw the swords I got spooked. Something about them seemed dangerous. Can you arrest them? I'd like to know why they wanted to see me."

"Sure," General Miller said. "Local police can arrest anyone suspected of threatening state security. Give me the names and I'll ask the Mountainview police chief to issue an arrest order."

* * *

On their return to the Embassy, Corr and Rhya found Whistol Farr and described the Johns/Lactella event.

"We've been hearing odd things about Johns, but this may be the strangest thing I've ever heard. Do you think the spider is controlling Johns?"

"Yes," Corr said. "I could sense the flow from the spider to the man." He looked at his friend. "Couldn't you, Rhya?"

"Yes, and I don't know why anyone would volunteer to carry a spider around like that."

"Maybe you should have grabbed him."

"Probably. Anyway, can you ask Sam to step up an investigation of Johns?"

"Yes."

Corr added that he needed to rest. As he walked to his room, he began reviewing the numerous reports he had received. The two fighter groups were ready for action, Farr had emissaries speaking to the Piedmont council, and the Tsaeb were inventorying farms, roads, and trails on former and current Piedmont lands. He also thought about

Allysen's tactical analysis of the new military base. Mostly he thought about what she had said about Allon.

Rhya and Able met Corr at the Embassy entrance at 4:45 that afternoon. Able had assembled gifts for the warriors to take to the Thomases. "Corr, here are the two bottles of white wine and the blueberry crème pastries you wanted."

Then Rhya held up a small package. "These are drahsalleh ball bearings. Able described some popular games Human children play and 'marbles' sounded good. These drahsalleh bearings should be perfect."

"More than perfect," Corr said, attaching his package to his pack. "They represent technology far beyond the capability of Humans. If the Thomases knew their value, they probably wouldn't let their children accept them."

"Right," said Able. "I just couldn't think of any toys we have that would appeal to kids of different ages. At least these marbles will never be shattered by a steely."

Corr and Rhya left the Embassy and walked toward the Thomas home. A light breeze cleared the air, rustling the tree leaves and shaking the blooms on flowers in the yards they passed. Both rabbits looked forward to an interesting evening. They did not anticipate the danger that would make the evening much more than just interesting.

Dinner with the Thomas Family

As they reached the Thomas home, the two rabbits looked for clues to their hosts' nature. Leaving the public sidewalk, they walked between well-trimmed boxwood hedges that separated the Thomas's curving walk from small lawns flanked by tall trees. An arched red brick entry flowed into matching brick planters bulging with daffodils, tulips, and budding irises. The polished brass hardware accenting the dark green door gave an inviting finish to the front of the home.

Howard answered their knock, and Marcie joined him as the pair entered the home. Corr noted that the Thomases were a little taller and more trim and fit than the average Human. Corr placed their health and abilities in the upper range of Mountainview Humans he had met. The two were obviously close, and seemed happy. The attitude of both Thomases felt welcoming, but Corr sensed things weren't perfect.

Corr presented his gifts, and Rhya poured the drahsalleh marbles out into her hand. "I brought some marbles for the children," Rhya said. "Shall I give them to you now or to the children later?"

"You can give them to the children," Marcie said. She motioned toward a door near the entryway. "This is our coat closet. You can leave anything you want here."

Corr guessed she had their swords in mind. Though on uncertain ground, he had plenty of other weapons. He needed to probe sensitive topics, and wanted the Thomases as relaxed as possible.

"May we leave our packs and swords here?"

"Certainly," Marcie replied.

"Let's go to the family room," Howard said, and led the way through a carpeted room with a white ceiling and green walls. Large, inviting chairs lined walls displaying photographs of landscapes and people. The rabbits memorized everything for later study.

Raised voices became silent as they walked into a

room that held a ping-pong table, a fireplace, and a compact sitting area.

Howard introduced Corr and Rhya to his family and explained how they had met.

He seated the rabbits together on a bright green loveseat that formed one side of a rectangle. A long sofa faced them across a low table containing books and a stack of coasters. Matching chairs filled the ends. Photographs covered the warm brown walls above a wainscot of golden pine. Rhya thought that despite the high ceiling and square corners, the room felt comfortable. The Thomases couldn't sense the faint fumes arising from the paint, the artificial carpet, and the chair covers. They had done well with what they had, and she wondered how much of her own environment she was unable to detect.

"Do you work at the Embassy?" asked Howard's younger brother, Allen James, who was sitting on the sofa with his wife, Millicent, and his father, Allen.

Ah, Corr thought as he felt the man's hostility. *Here's the trouble.* "Allen James, our work involves the Embassy, but we were sent here by our district council to solve a problem."

"Call me AJ."

"Would you like something to drink?" Marcie asked, with a look toward AJ. "I just made some cocoa."

Corr and Rhya said yes.

"Did you walk?" asked Howard.

"Yes. March weather has been nice."

"It has. We considered eating outdoors, but the sun sets early and it gets cool pretty quick."

The older man, introduced as Howard's father, Allen, said, "Corr and Rhya, forgive me for prying, but I believe everyone here is interested in learning more about you. Can you tell us where you live and what you do?"

Corr nodded, liking the man's direct approach. "Sure. Rhya and I live at the Wycliff District Center. Rhya is starting her internship, and I work for the district council and spend time touring the border."

Corr could see the family resemblance in the men. Tall and trim like Howard, Allen was wearing a sport jacket but no tie. Reading glasses poked out of his jacket pocket. The man had a penetrating look. Shorter, with sandy, almost blond, hair, Allen James was wearing a red shirt over blue jeans. One of his feet tapped constantly, and he wore an appraising expression. His wife wore pants, a silk shirt and scarf, a matching jacket, and a necklace and earrings. Both she and Marcie gave their full attention to their guests and the conversation. Corr liked them all, even Allen James.

"I know Wycliff District is north of us," said Howard. "How large is it?"

"The district extends north for 60 miles and it's about 30 miles wide."

"What are you interning for, Rhya?" Allen asked.

"I will be spending the next five years with a border patrol group."

"My son tells me you both carry swords. Are you soldiers?"

"We are warriors," replied Corr.

AJ asked, "Are there lots of warriors? Are you at war with someone?"

Rhya said, "There aren't many at all. We are not at war. As members of the warrior specialty we train in all aspects of combat and war, but in practice we are probably more accurately described as police officers. What is your occupation, Mr. Thomas?"

"Please call me Allen. I was a police detective until I retired last August. I guess you could say the police force is the family business. My father and grandfather were police officers, and both Howard and AJ are detectives. Are other members of your families also warriors?"

"Yes. Warriors are common in both our lineages back through many generations."

"My great-grandfather was an army officer, but I don't know about his father."

"Records in our district library go back a long way. Your family history is probably recorded there," Rhya said.

"How many warriors are there in Wycliff?" AJ asked.

"Nineteen," Corr said.

During the conversation, the rabbits studied their surroundings and the emotions broadcast by their hosts. They could sense children playing outside, and Humans in neighboring houses. Apart from AJ, everyone seemed perfectly comfortable.

"How many Tsaeb live in Wycliff District?" asked AJ.

"Just over half a million," Corr said.

"Well, I guess you couldn't be at war," Allen said. "Nineteen seems like too small a number even to police your district."

"Oh, it's more than enough," Corr said. "There isn't much crime, and the biggest job, patrolling the border, seems more like a holiday than duty. Warriors normally don't have much to do. Many other Tsaeb in the community have studied some aspects of martial arts, and all of them are able to help if a problem arises."

"All of them?"

"Yes."

"Is that because of the border?" AJ asked.

"No. It has always been that way AJ," replied Corr.

"Are you here because of border issues?"

"Yes, but our mission includes another matter as well."

"Corr," Howard said, "we all want to know about your mission, but if AJ doesn't mind, we can return to it after dinner. I believe a village lies at the heart of Wycliff. Is that the District Center?"

"Sure," Corr replied, noting a tightening of AJ's mouth. "The Center is the heart of the District. Rhya and I have rooms there."

"How many Tsaeb live there?" Marcie asked. Her coffee-brown dress was covered with flowers and leaves and it matched the drapes.

"There are 126 permanent residents," Rhya said, "but

hundreds of visitors and temporary residents are always present."

AJ's wife, Millicent, leaned forward. "Are the permanent residents the school teachers and government administrators?"

Rhya said, "A few teachers and some of the district council members live in the Center, and there are lawyers, librarians, reporters, other specialists, and interns of all those disciplines, except for the one brewer who has no intern yet." She smiled as Corr's whiskers twitched. "Where do you work, Millicent?"

"I'm an Assistant in the District Attorney's office. Do you have schools at the Center or elsewhere in Wycliff?"

"No. Families provide education. Specialists handle advanced training. Only a few live at the Center."

"Do Tsaeb come to the Center to buy food and clothes?" Millicent asked.

"The Center has stores of food and some fabrics and devices, but everything is free. Most Tsaeb make their own clothes and produce their food where they live."

"Do you trade anything with other Districts?" AJ asked.

Rhya nodded. "Mail, library materials, artwork, some foods. One district focuses on science and engineering, and another focuses on administration. Most Tsaeb paint and carve, but I don't think we have any photographers. You have many nice photographs. Did someone here make them?"

"That's Marcie," Howard said. "She's the family photographer."

"They're great," Corr said.

"Do all the Districts use the same currency?" AJ asked.

"We have no currency," Rhya said.

"I've heard that, but I don't understand how it could work. How do the Tsaeb serving in the Center or the Embassy get paid?" Howard interjected.

"No one is paid. There is nothing to purchase. Food and fiber are provided to the Center from throughout the community."

"Well, how are specialists rewarded for their service?" Howard asked.

"Tsaeb become specialists because they are interested in the specialty. Others may benefit from their efforts, but the specialist's principal reward comes from satisfying his or her personal interest," Corr replied.

Howard shook his head. "You mean no one in government service or other jobs is actually hired or paid?"

"Right. All Tsaeb choose their occupation. Most choose the traditional life of the land and become gleaners, but some choose other subjects."

"But who decides how many specialists you need?"

"No one.

"Sounds chaotic," Howard said.

"It can be. At the moment, we have too many lawyers," Corr said, his whiskers twitching. Then glancing at Millicent, he said, "Lawyers are important, but lately when a legal issue comes before the council, it can be difficult to see over all their heads. The opposite can be true as well. For instance, we currently have only one brewer."

"Sorry, but I just don't see how that system can work," AJ said.

"The land provides everything we need," Rhya said. "Everyone in the Center could return to their ancestral family homes and tend the land if they chose."

"Didn't you all choose your specialties?" Corr asked.

"Well, everyone here did, but many people do not. We can't volunteer our services, we have to get paid," Howard said. "We have to earn a living."

"Why don't all people choose their occupations?" Rhya asked to keep the topic going.

"Lots of reasons, I guess," said Howard. "But I think most young people leave home too soon. Most of my friends left home when they finished high school. Some went to college, but most found jobs, bought cars, and rented apartments. If mom and dad had let me, I would have joined them."

"Not everybody can be a cop," AJ said. "What would we do without roofers, plumbers, and garbage collectors? Society would collapse without them."

"I guess every job fills some need," Howard said.

"But really, you can't mean all Tsaeb do only what they want to do," AJ said.

"Yes, I do," Corr replied.

"But how can you? Don't some just do nothing but eat? And what do you do if there isn't enough food?"

"Ah, you see, Tsaeb follow the ideals of Immediacy and do what needs to be done. We don't want to do foolish things. It's programmed into our DNA."

AJ's brow furrowed. "What you do is programmed into your genes?"

"Sure. It's instinct. Oh, there are throwbacks. Individuals, even whole species, can show up without the Immediacy instinct." *Like you and like Allon Trofeld*, Corr thought.

"Still, you must have food shortages somewhere. You can't do what you want to when you are starving, can you?"

"In extreme situations, everyone can reduce their activity, and some can move to areas that are more productive. Many Tsaeb hibernated during the ice ages," Corr said.

"The ice ages?" said AJ. "How would you know what happened then?"

Interesting... they don't know much about Tsaeb, but only AJ is critical. "AJ, our records extend far back, long before the ice ages, to the time when our behavior wasn't so reasonable. Check with the Embassy librarian. You could trace your own ancestry back to the ice ages if you wanted." He decided not to mention those Wycliff residents born long before the ice ages.

AJ was frowning as he tried to follow that with a question.

The first to recover was Marcie. "How long have you

been married?"

Corr looked at Marcie. I can see thoughts and intentions more clearly today. Will it continue? Does this happen to everyone?

"We are not married," Rhya said. We were asked to work together, but that will end in a few days."

She doesn't have to be so firm about it, Corr thought.

"What is your specialty, Marcie?" Rhya asked.

"I teach high school English."

"Excuse me, but I still don't understand," AJ said. "Don't some Tsaeb have lots of children? Don't you always have food shortages?"

"No one chooses to have children the land will not sustain," Rhya answered. "Normally, there can be a birth only if there's been a death or if the land's productivity increases."

AJ said, "But this is nonsense. How can—"

"Well, this is fascinating," Marcie said. "I apologize for all the questions. I don't see how we can live so close and know so little about one another. AJ, can you come help me put in the table extension? And Millie, if you'll call the children in I'll put dinner on the table."

A moment later, several children ran into the room followed by a woman. "Hi Ryca," Charlotte said to Rhya.

"Charlotte," Howard said, "her name is Rhya. Corr and Rhya, this is my mother, Rebecca. You've met Charlotte and Willie. This is Robert, AJ's son," he said, motioning to a boy a little taller than Willie, "and this is Alice, Robert's sister." He pointed to a girl of about 12 with long sandy hair like her father's. She was wearing a pearl necklace and a pale blue dress.

"How do you do?" Robert said, eagerly shaking hands. "Pleased to meet you."

"Hello, Robert," Rhya said. "I'm glad to meet you, and you too, Alice. Hello, Willie. How are you, Charlotte?"

Alice stood back but the other children clustered near the Tsaeb. "Willie said you have swords. Do you sword fight a lot? Can I see your swords?" Robert asked.

"Come, children. Let's get cleaned up for dinner," said Millie. "You can ask Corr and Rhya questions after we eat."

"Can Rhya play with us?" Charlotte asked.

"After dinner, if she wants," Howard said. "Your mother will have everything on the table in five minutes."

"She'll want to, won't you, Rhya?"

"Sure," Rhya said with a grin.

"Corr and Rhya, would you like to wash up before dinner?" Howard asked. "Come this way."

Howard led the way down a carpeted hall that looked more like a photo gallery than a mere access route.

Reaching two facing doors, he said, "The guest bath is here," and indicated the door on the left. Then he opened the door on the right to a room furnished in dark stained woods. "And here is our bedroom. There's another bathroom through the door over there. Feel free to use either one."

Like everything else in the house, Corr and Rhya found the rooms, their furnishings, their colors, and the pictures on their walls interesting. Apart from faint toxicity, the Thomas home felt more pleasant than either had expected.

Perhaps I should have some pictures printed, Corr thought. My recorder surely has some good ones of friends and scenes around the valley.

During dinner, Corr tried a few jokes and soon had the Thomases laughing.

Rhya watched him and smiled. She got into the act as well, and exchanged a few knock-knock jokes with the children.

AJ laughed very little, and said little during the meal.

After dinner, Marcie and Howard cleared the table and the others went outside. Shadows were filling the yard as the sun set, but the air remained warm. Rhya and Rebecca strolled out onto the lawn. Rhya showed the marbles to Rebecca, called the children over, and offered a few to each.

"Have you played marbles?"

Only Robert and Willie had, but all of them wanted to play with this friendly furry visitor. Rhya asked where they might play.

"There's bare ground beside the house," Willie said.

Corr and the three adults watched Rhya's exchange with the children. Howard and Marcie came out, and Howard flipped on an exterior floodlight for the marble squad.

Corr said, "Excuse me for a moment." He walked toward Rhya. As he did so, his communicator clicked and began murmuring, and a small bird landed on his shoulder and delivered a message. As Corr reached Rhya and the children, Quin landed between the two battle rabbits. The children gaped at Quin, who was as tall as Charlotte. Corr spoke to Rhya in Tsaeb standard. "Stay with the children while I get the adults' reaction to the Piedmont situation. We'll be safe unless additional aircraft arrive." He looked at Quin. "Do we have 20 minutes before we need to leave?"

"Should."

Corr's face sobered with concern about the two SWAT teams approaching the Thomas home. He combined several streams of thought for an emergency review of tactics for transport vehicles. "Quin, prepare contingency defense plans and ask Farr or Sam Wharton to send two fighter units. Have someone watch the police helicopter, but check with me before disabling it. Get observers over the military hangar at the airport." He paused. "Ah, and tell Ralph we need to deal with two SWAT teams. Tell him we need door glue and patches."

"Rhya, if we have to retreat under fire, take the children into the alley. I'll follow with the adults. Do you agree the best cover lies along the rear alley to the east?"

"Yes," Rhya replied, and as Quin flew away, she turned and said, "Kids, let's go play some marbles," and started moving toward the east side of the house, followed by Rebecca and the children. "Charlotte, what's the name of your school?"

As Corr joined the adults, AJ asked, "What were those birds telling you? Is it something related to your reason for being here?"

"The birds were giving me reports. A situation is developing that might be related to our mission."

"What is your mission?"

"Rhya and I are in Mountainview because laws have been broken. Our council asked me to find out why and develop a response plan. Our response might cause further conflicts, even war, between Humans and Tsaeb. I would like to ask for your ideas about what I should do."

The three policemen, Marcie, and Millicent stared at Corr. Howard said, "I'm having a difficult time imagining that we could advise you on a situation that has the potential to start a war," Howard said.

"So you are here to get planning information?" AJ said.

"I wish our visit could be purely social, AJ, but I need to choose the best solution to the problem. I'm sorry we aren't meeting at a better time."

"Surely you realize we have no experience with military issues," Howard said. "But do tell us about your problem. I'm sure everyone would like to help you. Let's go sit."

In Howard's study, AJ spoke first. "This is wrong. We can't offer military advice to an enemy. Corr, you said you were assigned to this problem. What is your specific job?"

"AJ, we are not enemies. I want to avoid a conflict, if possible."

"Well, tell us what you do."

"I am the commander of one of our two mobile battle groups, and I serve as the principal military adviser to our council."

"That places you at the same level as our army generals. Why would you want advice from ordinary policemen, a teacher, and a lawyer?"

"I need a better understanding of Humans. I assure you, I am only interested in general attitudes, not in strategic or tactical combat information. We could go to your mayor or the army commanders, but—and please forgive me if you disagree—I've been told that your leaders often do not represent the interests of the majority of your people. Your leaders are responsible for the broken laws, but my decisions might affect everyone, not just them."

"Maybe," AJ said, "but that doesn't mean we should help you against our leaders. Our army defends our country, and our police defend our homes."

"I need to know your feelings about the crimes. Let me explain the problem, and then you can respond as you feel appropriate."

Corr described the armed incursion and the Piedmont situation.

"We want to free the Piedmont group, and we want to restore the Piedmont farm lands. The lives of the captives and many thousands of Tsaeb are threatened by unprovoked, illegal acts."

"Huh," Allen snorted. "I'm not surprised, but this is a huge problem. And I doubt your council is giving you much time."

"Not much. I have to recommend a course of action on Sunday."

"Sunday? Well, can you lay out some options?" Howard asked.

"We have discussed three. First, we could ignore the situation and hope things get better. Second, we could make a formal request for the release of the captives, and the return of the Piedmont farmlands to the Tsaeb, and if that failed, file a lawsuit in your courts. Third, we could use force to free the captives, and reclaim the Tsaeb farmlands. That option is the quickest, but it might lead to retaliation by the Federation, and that's where the possibility of war comes in."

"Corr, I don't know what to say," Allen said, glancing at Howard and AJ. "I guess it doesn't seem likely that the military would stop anything they are doing just because you asked. And I don't think you would get a fair hearing in our courts. The third option—"

AJ interrupted. "I have been around Tsaeb all my life," AJ said. "There is no way you could defeat our local military or police."

Let's push AJ a little, Corr thought. "AJ, defeating your army or police isn't the problem. My only problem is deciding whether to do it."

"Bull."

Corr said, "Millicent, you might have another view of the court system. Do you think we could win a suit?"

"Probably not. Our constitutional and statutory systems don't cover Tsaeb rights very well. If the issues are at all unclear, our judges would rule against you."

Now for the real question, Corr thought. "Everyone, just assume for a moment that the imprisoned Tsaeb are completely innocent. What, if anything, do you personally feel should be done?"

"How can we answer?" AJ said. "We don't know if any of this is true."

"AJ, the answer is the same either way," Howard said. "Civil law requires a violation or reasonable suspicion of a violation before an arrest can be made, and suspects can't be held without formal charges being approved by a judge. I don't know much about military law, but my personal opinion is that innocent people, regardless of species, should not be imprisoned." The other Thomases nodded.

Corr said, "Excuse me for a moment." He walked to the window, listened to his communicator, and spoke to a Pewee hovering just outside the glass.

"Folks, the developing situation I mentioned earlier is about to reach your doorstep. Personal opinions are what I needed, and I thank you for your comments. I would like to discuss this further with all of you, but let me ask two final questions. Howard and Marcie, why did you invite Rhya and me into your home, and why have you so freely allowed Rhya to play with your children?"

"Why, Corr... we invited you because we wanted to know more about you. There's no reason to treat you differently than anyone else we meet."

"Thank you," Corr said. "Rhya and I were delighted to be invited, and we are honored to have the opportunity to get to know you. I hope we can become friends."

Just then, Allen's phone rang. He answered and listened with widening eyes. Howard and AJ's phones also rang. In seconds, the three completed their calls and turned to stare at one another. Allen said, "We have a problem. Corr, it appears you and Rhya are about to be arrested. Everyone here will be taken with you. I don't know what caused this, but perhaps you should leave. You can—"

"Thanks, Allen, but there won't be any arrests."

"How the hell can you say that? SWAT will be here in minutes!" AJ exclaimed.

Corr said, "Actually, two SWAT teams have been dispatched, but when they arrive they will be unable to exit their vans. At this point, only one helicopter is in the air, and no planes have appeared. I will be advised if additional aircraft start to come this way. If that occurs, we might want to move your families down the alley to the east."

Corr walked back to the window and listened to a black phoebe hovering outside. "Four police patrol units are approaching. Two will be stopped, but two nearby should be arriving now."

The three police officers stared at Corr. Then there was a crash from the direction of the garage and Corr faded from view.

At the sound of the crash, Corr altered his fur to blend with the interior of the house and ran to the garage. Entering, he met two policemen rounding the Thomas's van. He thumbed open one of his harness pouches, stepped forward, and squeezed a small bulb into each man's face. He jumped back, braced himself, and broke the men's falls as they slumped forward. Then he removed restraints from their belts, bound their hands and feet, and exited through the broken side door.

Outside, Corr found a police officer beside the door, and caught a glimpse of another going around the back corner of the garage. He disabled and restrained the near officer and rushed after the other. Turning the corner, he found Rhya turning away from a bound and unconscious policeman, and the four children frozen in kneeling and standing positions beside a scatter of marbles.

An explosion shook the ground.

Rhya said, "Children, gather your marbles. Let's go into the house."

Inside, the Thomas policemen cautiously moved toward the garage. As they entered, Corr came in through the side door. Shifting to full visibility, he said, "Gentlemen, the situation is under control."

"Are, they hurt?" Howard asked, staring at the bound officers.

"No. They're just asleep."

"Are there others?" Allen asked, remembering Corr had said two police cars were approaching.

"They are also restrained and unharmed," Corr said.

"Okay," AJ said, "but what about the SWAT teams?"

Vehicles were squealing to a stop in front of the house.

"Come with me," Corr said. He led the way through the house and opened the front door. Two black police vans had parked in the front yard. Their front doors were open and their drivers lay in the grass, hands and feet bound. Quin was standing atop a van and Ralph was grinning nearby. Two rock dove perched on the vans, replacing items in their packs. Loud banging noises came from the backs of the vans.

Corr looked at AJ. "The doors of the vans are sealed shut. It will take a cutting torch to get them open."

Howard asked, "Corr, do you know what exploded?"

"The helicopter. It tried to land in the street and caught a power line. The pilot and passengers escaped before the fuel tank exploded."

During the exchanges, Corr took two calls on his communicator and listened to reports from two small messengers. He faced the Thomases. "Please forgive Rhya and me for these inconveniences. We toured a school and other parts of the city today. We didn't see any police. We could leave now, but if we do the police will arrest everyone here. That is not acceptable."

As Corr spoke, a house finch flew through the door and landed on his shoulder, spoke briefly, and left. Corr took another communicator call, "Whistol Farr, the Wycliff ambassador, offers all of you asylum in the Tsaeb Embassy. Please accept. No one can arrest you in the Embassy, and you can stay as long as you want. If you wish, we can help you begin a court action to dismiss the arrest order."

None of the Thomases spoke. In the silence, AJ's phone rang. AJ answered and listened for a moment, then closed his phone as he looked around at the group. "Dad, Howard, I'm sorry. I had no idea anyone might be arrested."

Howard frowned. "What do you mean?"

"I called the precinct after you told me you had invited Tsaeb warriors."

"Damn it, AJ! They are our *guests!*"

"I just checked in and mentioned it. I thought someone should know about Tsaeb fighters wandering around in Mountainview."

Corr said, "Much more needs to be said, but we should leave now. We can supply most things you might need at the Embassy, and we can probably return for more of your belongings in a day or two."

Howard looked at Marcie, then turned to his father. "Dad, I think Corr is right. If we stay here, we will be arrested and may have a difficult time getting released. I don't want the children placed in any kind of custody."

"Right. The arrest order specified that everyone present is a possible conspirator in a plot involving national security."

"I don't think we should go to the Tsaeb Embassy," AJ said. "We are better off arrested by our own police than locked away by the Tsaeb."

"Damn it, AJ," Allen said. "If you get arrested, you might get transferred to Army custody and not get out for a while."

"AJ, I think Allen is right," Millicent said. "I don't want the children in police custody, and I do not want to go to jail."

"Millie, we don't know what will happen to us at the Embassy."

"We know what will happen if we don't go. Besides, I believe Corr when he says he's simply trying to help us."

A field sparrow flew in, landed on Corr's shoulder, and began speaking in its small, high-pitched voice. "Did you kick the garage door apart?" it yelled as it flew out the door.

Corr grinned.

He turned to the Thomases. "No more active police are nearby, but more will come soon. With your permission, Rhya will accompany AJ, Millicent, Robert, and Alice, and members of my command group will go with Allen and Rebecca, and Howard, Marcie, and the children."

Quin and Ralph came in through the still-open front door. "Folks, this is Quin Achiptre and Ralph Mäkinen," Corr said. "Quin, meet Howard, Marcie, Willie, and Charlotte Thomas. They are going to the Embassy. Please see that they get there safely. Ralph, I would like you to accompany Allen and Rebecca Thomas to the Embassy."

All the children stared at Ralph, who was taller and broader than anyone else in the room.

Quin, Howard, Marcie, and the children headed for the van in the garage, and Corr led the others out the front door. Rhya came out with their gear and followed AJ and family to their car. Allen, Rebecca, and Ralph climbed into a blue sedan, and as Allen pulled away from the curb, Corr grinned as he heard Ralph ask from the back seat, "Do you folks like to sing?"

* * *

Police were rushing toward the Thomas home from all over the city, and another helicopter would arrive soon. Corr thought the police might stop one or all of the Thomas vehicles before they reached the Embassy. He looked up at the helicopter approaching slowly along the street looking for targets. He drew his bow and shot an arrow at an angle that caused it to glance harmlessly off the windshield. As he hoped, the helicopter darted forward to hover directly above him.

Corr turned and ran west at moderate speed toward the city limits. The helicopter stayed above him. A dove flew alongside and shouted that two army attack helicopters were approaching. Corr saw them up the street ahead and made a sharp right turn up a driveway. He ran between houses to the next street. Police cars raced toward him from the right. Corr ran left toward the looming gray walls of an electrical substation and its open gate. He ran in, followed a moment later by several police officers with drawn guns. Helicopters hovered overhead, creating a dust storm in the substation. Corr saw no other gates.

Thomases in the Embassy

Able Remington welcomed the Thomases to the Embassy and assigned them to three suites near Corr and Rhya's rooms. The suites opened into a common room with a large low table. Rhya noted that these rooms had doors and ceilings higher than hers. Whistol Farr still had to stoop when he came through the door.

"You are our guests, and we want you to be comfortable," Farr said. "All the rooms and facilities of the Embassy are open to you. You are welcome to attend all our meetings and events."

"Our phones aren't working," AJ said. "Are you blocking them?"

"I'm sorry, but your wireless phones won't work in the Embassy," Farr replied.

"Can you let us know if you hear anything about us from the police?" Allen asked.

"Certainly. Let's review the situation in the morning after breakfast."

Then he passed out small cylinders. The cylinders appeared to be made of tinted glass. "These are signaling devices. We call them nylics. Whenever you have a question or need something, just hold your nylic and speak. You will get a quick response."

Charlotte raised her nylic and looked at it closely. As she lowered it, she brushed it on her waistband and it clinked and tinkled as it bounced on the stone floor. She bent to pick it up, but it had rolled under a table. She looked at Farr with moistening eyes.

Farr knelt, fished out the nylic, and handed it to her. "It's okay, Charlotte. It didn't break." He looked at the others. "Nylics are practically indestructible, and they are simple to use. They will only work for the person who squeezes them first, and all of them will glow whenever that person is near."

"Well, thank you all for your hospitality, Mr. Farr," Millicent said. "We should get these children ready for bed now. I have to say, I'm exhausted."

Howard spoke. "Sir, has Corr Syl returned?"

"Not yet."

"Should we do something?" Howard asked.

"I'm sure he's fine," Ralph said.

Just then, Corr walked through the door.

Marcie stepped toward the small warrior rabbit. "Corr, we wondered about you. What happened?"

"Police and army helicopters started arriving, so I went through a yard into the next street. There were more police. I headed west and entered the power substation yard just ahead of them. A police car pulled up outside the substation. Two choppers were approaching, and the wind began to raise the dust."

Allen looked puzzled and then twitched and grinned.

"How did you get away?" Howard asked.

Corr shrugged. "I leaned against the wall and rested for a minute, and then I left."

Howard said, "Why didn't—"

Corr disappeared. Everyone stared at the empty space, and some realized they could see Corr's gray harness straps and sword hilts. Then he reappeared, and grinned.

"You did that at my house," Howard said. "I wasn't sure what I was seeing then. How do you do that?"

"It's a camouflage technique that warriors use. We develop fur with different colored layers. We shift and blend the layers to match the background." As he spoke, Corr changed from gray to red to blue and back to gray. "You may know about chameleons. They have skin cells of different colors. They change colors by expanding or shrinking the cells. They achieve brighter colors than we can, but we can change color much faster than they can. The gray electrical substation walls almost matched my harness and sword hilts. I just had to be careful with shadows."

Charlotte looked up at Ralph. "Can you change colors, Mr. Makin?"

Ralph grinned, slapped his arms tight to his sides, and began a spiraling color change that mimicked a spinning barber pole. After a wide-eyed moment, everyone laughed, including AJ.

* * *

A brief discussion took place in Farr's office.

"Corr, did you get to talk to the Thomases before the action started?"

"Yes, and we talked before and after dinner. They were friendly and open with us. Considering their limited mental capacity, they were impressive. I liked them." Corr glanced at Rhya. "Didn't you?"

"Yes, I liked them. With one exception, the Thomases were predisposed to trust us. They behaved very much like any Tsaeb family would."

Farr looked at Corr. "When will you have the plan ready?"

"It will be ready on Sunday."

* * *

Because of the lost helicopter, reports of the Thomas escape quickly made their way to the Mountainview Chief of Police. Different versions of the story blamed incorrect information, equipment failure, and subversion by the Thomases. All three of the City's police divisions had received the original arrest order for Corr and Rhya. The division that included Howard and Marcie Thomas's home had made the actual attempt. Now the chief gave the problem special status and assigned it to a police captain. He ordered him to find a way to arrest Corr, Rhya, and the Thomases.

The chief also spoke to General Miller about the problem. "Steve, we didn't catch your Tsaeb, and I believe the main reason is that a whole bunch of Tsaeb came in, blocked our efforts, and then removed the pair you wanted to the Embassy."

"I saw your request for the helicopters. Sorry you lost yours. I guess part of the problem is that there is no limit on Tsaeb moving in and out of the city. They can legally move in as many as they want."

"Well, can't you slow them down somehow?"

"I'll talk to Alston about this. Maybe we can set up something on Corinne Trail."

* * *

The Thomases came to the Tea Room early the next morning. They found Corr, Rhya, Quin, and Ralph surrounded by a diverse crowd of Tsaeb. Small birds were flying in and out. Charlotte hurried over and sat beside Rhya, who hugged the little girl and began a quiet exchange.

A large short-eared owl named Noah Parker was talking with Corr, and like Corr, receiving a steady stream of messages. Corr was discussing reports with Parker and posing strategic questions for general discussion. Interested Tsaeb were tossing in questions and ideas. Of course, the Thomases heard only a buzz of clicks, whistles, hums. They were completely unaware of the clouds of scents and mental interactions surrounding Corr.

Farr arrived with Wilson Smith and one of Smith's staff, a Fisher, who had volunteered to help the Thomases find their way around the Embassy.

"I'd like to introduce Nathan Jensen," Smith said, referring to the Fisher. "Nathan, this is the Thomas family," he said and introduced each person in turn.

Nathan shook hands with those he could reach.

Alice held still when the furry creature took her hand, and she continued to stare at him as he met others.

"Nathan is an education specialist. He prepares course notes for grades K-6. He has asked if he could serve as your guide while you are in the Embassy."

"Thank you, Nathan," said Rebecca. "I doubt I could find my room again without help."

"How old are you?" Alice asked the Fisher.

Nathan smiled. "I'm pretty old, Alice. How old are you."

"I'm pretty old, too," she said.

"Corr, we learned yesterday that you are the equivalent of an army general," Marcie said. "I believe it. You were the center of attention for everyone in the room as we came in."

At a nearby table a marmot grinned. "That will change as soon as he tells a joke." Marcie frowned at the scattered grins and guffaws, but then she saw Corr grinning too.

Corr stood and smiled at Marcie, "Folks, let's get something to eat before a talented heckler comes along."

Farr led the group to a table with trays, plates, and utensils. He motioned to the long food counter. "There should be something here you like." He pointed toward the far end of the counter and said, "There are some small fish and a few bugs and worms."

"Can I go look, Mom?" Robert said.

"Me too!" Willie said.

"I suppose," Millicent said.

After everyone filled their trays and took seats, Allen Thomas asked, "Corr, have there been any communications with the police department?"

"No," Corr said. "A pair of officers is stationed across the street from our front gate, but they haven't made any requests. Whistol sent a formal notice of the grant of asylum to the mayor this morning. Millie, would you like to work with some of our lawyers to prepare a motion to dismiss the arrest order?"

"Yes. When can we do that?"

"Whistol?"

"How about later this morning after you meet with Corr?"

"That will be fine."

"What is this drink, Nathan?" Howard asked. "It was labeled as coffee and the flavor resembles coffee, but it must be something else."

"Last I heard, it contained a mixture of holly berries and grains. Our food specialists tinker with these things all the time, however, and holly berries might no longer be used." The Fisher leaned a little toward Howard and sniffed. "No, it's still holly and grain. How is it?"

"Tastes fine," Howard said, taking another sip.

When everyone had finished their breakfast, Corr stood. "Rhya and I want to continue our discussion with the Thomases. Whistol, please join us. The children may go to the gymnasium with Nathan, or they may join us as well."

"I want to see the gym," Robert said.

"Me too," the others all said.

"Can you come with us, Rhya?" Charlotte asked.

"Yes," Rhya said. "But first, why don't you go with Nathan and look around the gym? I'll come after I talk with Corr and your parents."

"Okay, I guess," Charlotte said.

"I'll go to the gym too," Rebecca said. "Allen knows how I feel."

"Good. Let's assemble in the Parrot Room in 15 minutes," Corr said.

"Rebecca, children, follow me," Nathan said, and with a spin and a hop he marched out, followed by four eager children.

* * *

Corr led the adults up onto the gleaming black floor of the transformed great hall. A large pastel blue snake wound among green shrubs growing from cracks in the obsidian column.

A pedestaled, exquisitely detailed sculpture of a yellow-crowned parrot marked the entrance to the Parrot

Room, a wide, vine-embraced, oval opening between the Tea Room and the balcony/basement ramp.

Corr reviewed the border violations and the Piedmont problems. "I want to thank you for yesterday's comments. Freeing the Piedmont captives is our highest priority. Today I want to ask for your feelings about the military invasion of Tsaeb land. Here's what's happening: we have learned that your military leaders are developing a plan to take Tsaeb land north of the city. I want to know how you feel about this, and I want to know your opinions on how the people of Mountainview would react if the plan is carried out."

"We need more details," Howard said.

"Right. Let me put it this way. Assume your leaders send the army across the border to take Tsaeb land by driving away the residents."

"Corr," said Allen, "none of us would approve of using force to take Tsaeb land, but most people wouldn't feel like it was any of their business. Besides, our government might not tell anyone what's going on, and if they did, they would either blame the Tsaeb or make everything seem either harmless or beneficial."

"No one would approve of such a thing if they knew about it," Marcie said, "but even if they did know, they probably wouldn't do anything. I know for sure that my students are mainly concerned with their social lives. Many of them are interested in the Tsaeb, but their support would be weak. The same is true of their parents. Certainly a few would speak out against the military and other leaders, but I doubt they would do anything."

"I think that applies to everyone," Millicent said.

"Hmm. What would be the response if we announce the problem and take action against the army?"

"Mixed I think," Marcie said. "It sounds terrible, but most of my students wouldn't care. Adults might feel threatened, but I don't think they would know how to respond."

"Corr," Howard said, "no one knows much about our army. We often hear about threats from other countries, but nothing has ever happened, at least not in my lifetime."

"If nothing else happened, I think people would wait and see what came next," Millie said.

"I think you're right," Allen said, "but my generation is suspicious of the Tsaeb. Most of them would support our army, and they would distrust any Tsaeb statements."

Millie sighed. "Why is this happening? Is it only about the land?"

"Taking land is the primary goal," replied Corr. "But there could be other factors. It's been decades since your army had any battles to fight, and maybe they still resent the defeat that preceded the border separation. They might be motivated by a need for action and a chance to get even."

"Corr, why can't the Tsaeb just let us use some of the land?" Marcie asked. "A few years ago, Howard and I hiked around Diamond Peak. I remember that the land north of the border looked empty. What is harmed if our city expanded that way?"

"I realize that's how it looks to you, but the land isn't empty. The area you mention is home to thousands of Tsaeb. Their homes might not be visible from the trail, but they're there. Plus, the Tsaeb depend on the land for food and fiber. Reduce the land and you hurt the Tsaeb."

"But we could help the Tsaeb. Wouldn't they be more comfortable in nice tight dry houses rather than in open nests and holes in the ground?"

"Tsaeb nest sites and burrows are occupied for thousands of years, and they only move as the vegetation or the surface of the land changes. You might be amazed at the comfort and beauty of Tsaeb homes."

AJ finally spoke. "Okay, so the land is important to the Tsaeb. But if Tsaeb really are intelligent, don't they get bored just sitting around in the bushes?"

"Tsaeb do many things, but tending the land is indeed

the preferred occupation. Are you familiar with bonsai? Tsaeb gleaners treat the whole landscape like a bonsai garden. They manage the microscopic organisms in the soil, the plants, and the bugs to increase productivity, stability, and beauty.

"I still don't see why you wouldn't prefer our way of life."

"AJ, your way isn't practical. Your own scientists have shown that your way destroys soil and vegetation, pollutes the air and water, and reduces productivity. It's no secret that you won't survive if you continue using the land as you do now."

Millicent spoke up. "Streets, power, and running water are signs of progress, Corr. We all want progress. We want nice homes, and we want schools, stores, and hospitals."

"Yes," Allen said. "Even on our side of the border, most of the landscape has no houses. The amount of land we use is small in comparison to the size of the whole Earth. It would take thousands of years for much of the Earth to be affected."

"Right," Corr said. "But you see, a thousand years isn't long for soils and vegetation. We've tended them for a long time. Tsaeb civilization began forming after the dinosaurs declined. It took millions of years to develop, but Tsaeb civilization has now existed for more than 30 million years. Your lifestyle would not permit civilization to continue for even one tenth of one million years."

"Well, if it took millions of years for the Tsaeb to catch on, how can people be expected to understand?" AJ asked.

Rhya said, "AJ, Humans *are* Tsaeb. We're all just animal species. All species have to learn to get along with the others. Humans need to recognize that.

"Our historians say that long ago, wars caused massive damage and extinctions. Finally, we gained control over evolution and began to modify our impulses. We eliminated intelligent species that were dangerous to others. Some Tsaeb contend that we must use force to reduce your numbers and impacts."

After a moment, AJ said, "Do you mean the Tsaeb would... uh, kill people just because they are trying to build a better world? Are we actually doing that much damage?"

Corr said, "Yes, you are doing that much damage. The combustion wastes and other pollutants you release are beginning to affect the land. No plans have been made, but things have to change."

As the significance of what Corr was saying sank in, the Thomases quieted. AJ glared at Corr.

Marcie said, "Corr, I don't understand. There are billions of people. What would happen?"

"I guess there are lots of possibilities. I don't know them all. I'm sure there aren't any plans. There are accounts of previous events in the library and I can find someone to discuss that with you if you like," Corr said. "Shall we meet here again at 2:00?"

"But Corr," Marcie asked, "which side are you on? Do you think we should survive?"

"Yes, and most Tsaeb do. However, something will be done soon."

* * *

After everyone had gone, Rhya asked, "Why didn't you—"

"Wait," Corr said. Let's go meet our guests."

As they walked across the hall, Rhya asked, "Why didn't you mention the other leaders? Ivan Johns is involved and may be the chief motivator. Corporate leaders are involved, and there may be elected and religious leaders in on the plot too." She noticed that Corr had extended his cloak to shield them both.

"Let's keep quiet about the others for now. They'll be included, but misdirection is necessary if we have spies in the Embassy. The Parrot room isn't secure. Also, we might have a traitor among the Thomases."

South Plains High School

At noon, Corr and Rhya met Cory, Rita, and five boys, including Rita's blond boyfriend, at the Embassy entrance. The great hall awed the students, even three who had visited before. Corr and Rhya took them on a mini-tour across the hall to the Tea Room.

They paused several times to let the students study the displays. They stopped by one that included a moving water sculpture as well as places to drink. Then Corr steered them toward the central column, now an indigo pillar with twinkling stars. Occasionally, a streaking point of light followed by a shower of sparks flashed across the column.

"Who makes all this?" a boy asked.

"Tsaeb artists made most of these pieces, but some are by Mountainview Humans," Rhya replied.

"Who chooses the ones to display?" Rita asked.

"I don't know."

"They are very impressive. Is that why they are here?"

"All species like to see and display interesting objects."

"Is this whole place designed to impress people?"

"The Embassy was designed to impress in the way that any gallery or museum is designed to impress, but it also provides an important link between Humans and Tsaeb, and it provides a place to organize education and other programs," Corr said.

"It seems like the Tsaeb are always trying to sell something," said Rita.

"I suppose selling our point of view is one purpose of the Embassy," Corr said.

In the Tea Room, Rhya explained the lunch options, led the students through the lines, and guided them to a spot in the forest where they could sit together. Along the way, two large bears asked if they could join the group. Rhya welcomed them and introduced the students.

One of the bears asked why the students were visiting the Embassy. Cory, whose hair was bright green that day, said they had come to see Corr and Rhya. Then she said, "You're bears, aren't you?"

"Yes, we are black bears."

"Why are you at the Embassy?"

"We live here. Our parents are teachers."

"Are you in high school or college?" another student asked.

"Ah, I'm not sure. We will choose a specialty next year."

The students didn't understand.

"Most of the Tsaeb teachers working in Mountainview schools live at the Embassy," Corr said. "There aren't any Tsaeb schools. Young Tsaeb are taught by their parents until they are about seven. Then they choose a specialty."

"You aren't seven yet?" a boy exclaimed. "Is that in bear years or something?"

"I think years are the same for everyone, aren't they?" Andrew said, looking around at the other Tsaeb.

"You sure seem older."

"How old are you?"

"Sixteen."

"What is your specialty?"

"I don't know. I'm going to college next year. I guess I'll decide then."

"Why are you carrying swords?" a boy asked, and that question riveted the attention of the students and the bears.

"Rhya and I are specialists in combat," Corr said.

"May I see your sword?"

Rhya reached back, released her long sword in its sheath, and handed it to the boy.

He studied the intricate patterns on the scabbard and hilt, and tried to draw the sword. "It's stuck."

"I will draw it if you wish to see the blade, but you may not hold it unsheathed," Rhya said. Taking the scabbard in one hand, she drew the sword part of the way.

"It looks like glass," a student sitting beside Rhya said. "Is it strong?"

"Very," Rhya said.

"Is it some kind of plastic?"

"Yes. It's made of drahsalleh, a material harder and tougher than diamond. Watch." Rhya drew the sword, rested it between Corr's outstretched hands, stepped up, and balanced as still as a statue on one foot in the center of the blade.

"The sword is designed to resist severe stress. It could hold everyone in this room before it sagged." Corr's strength and Rhya's agility impressed the students more than the sword. "My shield and bow are also made of drahsalleh," Rhya said, patting the top of the shield.

"Who do you fight?" asked green-haired Cory.

"Wherever there is injustice, you will find us," Corr said.

"That sounds—wait—Ned Nederlander!" exclaimed a tall, redheaded boy whose pale skin contrasted with his black jacket and pants.

"Yes, and Lucky Day," Corr said, exchanging grins with the redhead and one of the other students. "Tsaeb warriors are quite a bit like your police. Tsaeb rules occasionally are broken, and our district Council asks us to arrest the rule breakers."

"Can you arrest anyone? Can you arrest Humans?" Rita asked.

"Sure, but we are unlikely to arrest any Humans unless they break the rules of the border treaty."

"But if you saw a Human robbing someone, would you stop them?"

"Sure. Wouldn't you?"

"Why are Tsaeb so mean? Why did we have to send you to live in the wilderness?" Rita asked.

"What is the border treaty?" the tall redhead asked.

Corr defeated an impulse to laugh at the barrage of questions. "A few hundred years ago, problems began to develop between Humans and the rest of the Tsaeb. About a hundred years ago, a treaty divided the entire Earth into

Human and Tsaeb lands. The treaty sets the rules for crossing the border, building embassies, and dealing with each other. Want a copy?"

"Okay."

"Mr. Syl, you said Humans and other Tsaeb. But we aren't Tsaeb," Rita said.

"Call me Corr. Humans are one of many sentient species of terrestrial mammals on Earth. Before the border treaty, they lived in mixed communities with the other species."

"I think we read about that in history, but I thought there was a problem with a bunch of angry anima...Tsaeb. What happened? What did they do?"

"There were battles and people died. Several history books describe what happened around Mountainview. You may borrow one from the Embassy library today if you want. In fact, you should. The Embassy librarian would be delighted to have someone to help."

"Sounds like our school librarian," a student said.

"Let's go to the gymnasium for a little weapons practice. You can stop in the library afterward," Rhya said.

Even larger than the Tea Room, the gymnasium contained hundreds of jogging, climbing, and training Tsaeb and Humans. Rhya led the way to the throwing room where she demonstrated some of her small cutting weapons. From the farthest point, she and Corr placed knives and stars in patterns on the self-healing wall, and then began guiding the students' attempts. They used the ancient Tsaeb warrior training mnemonics translated into English. Not as effective in English, the words and phrases gave the students a taste of the art and power that guided Tsaeb weapons use.

Several students held back, reluctant to give the others an opening to criticize their efforts, but soon the two warriors' joking but supportive style began eroding the barrier. Then, one of the boys smacked his crotch with a loaded sling. Everyone stiffened. How would the victim respond? How would the other students? When the boy began laughing at himself, the others joined in, the tension faded, and the students became a group of friends.

After all the students had stuck a blade or two, Corr left for an appointment, and Rhya invited the students to try a little archery. She took them to an equipment room and handed out bows and small tubes of arrows.

"Come with me." She took the students to an outdoor archery range beside the Embassy. She demonstrated correct form, and everyone tried a few shots. Most of the arrows missed their targets, but some stuck. Rita and her boyfriend placed all their arrows in the target.

"Rhya, show us what you can do," the tall redhead said.

Rhya reached to the side of her pack, released her bow, and shot three arrows in rapid succession toward a target far beyond the ones the students had tried. When the group approached the target, they saw the arrows in a neat circle in the center of the target.

"Wow! How did you do that?" Cory asked.

"I used my sensory fields. They let me choose the precise point I want my arrow to hit, and they let me know exactly how the intervening air will affect the arrow's flight," Rhya replied.

"Can anyone learn to shoot like that?"

"Probably, but learning to use sensory fields begins at, or even before, birth. We are trying to come up with a way to teach adults. If we do, would you want to try?"

All of the students said they would.

* * *

At 2:00, the Thomases met Corr in the Parrot Room.

AJ spoke up. "This morning, Marcie asked what you thought about us. I think we deserve to know what you are going to do."

"Right. Well, I'm not sure yet, but I don't want to hurt anyone. I'll give you the details as soon as I have something worked out."

"Yes," Marcie said. "I would like that."

"All of us would," Millie said.

AJ stood. "This is nonsense! Are we supposed to live like you? Do you expect us to stop everything, give up our homes, and go prune shrubs? You stopped a few police officers, but I can't believe you Tsaeb can stop our army. I'm leaving. Come on, Millie. The rest of you can come too if you want. Where is the gym?"

Allen looked at Corr. "I don't think you should leave, AJ."

"Why not? We should go home." AJ strode to the door, but could not open it. Turning to Corr, he shouted, "Open the door!"

Corr gazed at the red-faced policeman, "AJ, we'll try to avoid harming anyone. I want to avoid panic. Please come to the Tea Room at 6:00 this evening. I'll have more details by then."

AJ glared. He wanted to release a warning, but he decided to play along until he heard the final plan.

Disposal of the Piedmont Tsaeb

On Saturday morning, Alston Marbellet received two items of bad news. First, the Mountainview police force, even with air support from the Federation military, had failed to capture Corr, Rhya, or a single member of the Thomas family. Second, the spies sent to Juniper Mesa hadn't reported and weren't answering calls.

Shortly after submitting his weekly report, Marbellet received a terse note ordering the disposal of the Piedmont Tsaeb. "Leave no evidence of their incarceration or involvement in spying."

Marbellet directed a subordinate to schedule troop transports for Monday morning, with orders to take the Tsaeb into the canyon across the desert south of Mountainview and release them. No Tsaeb should leave the canyon.

Colonel Phillips

Corr had just left Noah Parker and was heading for his room when Farr called. Corr hesitated, but Farr sounded excited. He called Noah, and the two went to Farr's office where they found Farr, Sam Wharton, and Petra Austin sitting around a projector.

"Corr, we are speaking with Colonel Sean Phillips, assistant to the Federation Army's General Howell."

"Colonel Phillips, this is Corr Syl, our military commander."

"How do you do, Sir," Phillips said.

"Please call me Corr. What's this about?"

"General Howell asked me to call. An operation is beginning that is not acceptable to the general. He ordered me to provide a report, and request your permission to help with your defense against the operation."

Corr made a quick decision. "Colonel, we appreciate your help, but if anyone learns about this you will be charged with treason, and there may be nothing we could do to help you."

"I understand, Sir, but I agree with General Howell." He described the plan that the generals, Johns, and other leaders had developed. "When someone mentioned killing and eating Tsaeb and no one objected, General Howell decided things had gone too far."

"Will you be available to listen-in on a planning session at 6:00 tonight? Any suggestions you can make today will be appreciated."

"Yes. Is your action beginning right away?"

"Soon." Corr raised his head and spoke to Noah Parker in Tsaeb standard. "Noah, please have someone begin monitoring the colonel's family."

Colonel Phillips said, "There is one more thing: General Howell says there are Tsaeb spies working in the Embassy."

Everyone went silent.

"Are they from the group of imprisoned Piedmont Tsaeb?" Corr asked.

"No."

"Are you sure?" Wharton asked.

"Yes. General Howell said they came from International Coalition for Peace delegation in our capitol. He became suspicious when he saw a report on your long-range weapons. He checked and found a series of reports on the weapons, fighter groups, and leadership in your neighboring districts."

Wharton said, "Why would the ICP include Tsaeb? Please explain."

"I don't know anything more about them," Phillips said. "Just the basic information. The ICP central office is in Taoso. We receive military information and technology from them. I've never met any of the Tsaeb. The general believes they must represent some Human enemy of the Tsaeb."

PART FOUR: CORR'S PLAN

"He is a better planner than a comedian," said a packrat hopping off a bench.

Corr's Plan

Corr went to his room and focused all his thoughts on integrating what he had learned in Mountainview. As his plan formed, he ran simulations and reinforced the plan's structural symmetry. Everything looked good. He would turn everything over to someone else in a few days and go back to Wycliff.

At 5:00 p.m. Colonel Phillips called Corr. A crucial element of the plan and its timing had to change.

At 6:00 p.m. the Tea Room filled with Tsaeb. Colonel Phillips watched from a monitor. The Thomases were present.

Farr addressed the group. "Corr Syl was directed by the Wycliff Council to form a plan to deal with the Army incursions and to help the Piedmont Tsaeb. The entire Tsaeb civilization, through the network of Continental and District councils, has discussed and pondered the situation. Problems have increased in numerous other locations, though none more serious than here. We will be the first to take action.

"Humans violated common laws and treaty stipulations in multiple acts. First, Human farmers are using Tsaeb lands in Piedmont. To avoid starvation, 21 Tsaeb families left Piedmont to become travelers. As they passed Mountainview, the second violation occurred. The Federation Army arrested and imprisoned the families without formal charges or legal representation. The Army uses threats to family members to force prisoners to serve as spies in Wycliff and other Districts. Third, in the past month, armed military groups crossed the border into Wycliff.

"Corr Syl has prepared a plan that will free the Piedmont Tsaeb, return their lands, and stop the border violations. The District Council is reviewing the plan. Corr will give us a summary and answer questions, but first our security chief Sam Whortin has an announcement."

Sam stood and addressed the crowd. "Corr's plan

contains important elements of surprise. It may be several days before the Council responds, but from this point until action begins, no one may leave the Embassy or communicate with anyone outside without approval of the Embassy security staff. Also, Corr's plan may draw Human retaliation."

Whortin unclipped a white cap from his harness and placed it on his head. Other Tsaeb scattered around the room did the same. The caps bore the large red letters, *EDAS*. "We hope these caps worn by Embassy Defense and Security volunteers will aid our Human friends, as well as other Tsaeb, to find help in an emergency."

Corr listened to the ensuing buzz of conversation, and it occurred to him that the level of concern he was witnessing was as intense as he had ever seen. No one made a joke, even though the letters *EDAS* surely suggested humorous possibilities to most members of the crowd.

Corr stood. "The plan is quite simple. We will use force against the Human military. Tomorrow night one fighter group will take over the local military base and arrest the officers. A second group will free the Piedmont Tsaeb. These actions will be completed before morning."

"Won't the Federation step in to protect the military?"

"Perhaps, but the Continental Council will give a full report of the treaty violations to the Federation President and the Chief of the Federation Armed Forces. I do not think they will choose to go to war to defend criminal behavior, but we will see. We have fighter groups forming near all regional military bases. If the Federation responds with force, we will take the necessary actions.

"All Embassy staff not otherwise engaged must be prepared to serve as reinforcements. When we finish here, verify your unit membership. Unit organizers, verify your link associations. Beginning now, all Embassy staff not on plan duty should be prepared for action."

As Corr concluded, he sensed general approval laced with uneasiness. The uneasiness didn't surprise him. He had held back a crucial element of the plan to ensure that spies did not interfere.

"He is a better planner than a comedian," said a packrat hopping off a bench.

* * *

Later that evening, a large crowd gathered in the Tea Room. Corr didn't say much. He had realized that he could leave now. Farr's staff and members of his and Shorel's battle group could execute the plan. He wouldn't be quitting or letting anyone down. They really didn't need him. Tonight, he would give the remaining details of the plan to Whistol, and he would leave in the morning. *Perhaps I could head straight for the coast. Maybe Rhya would go with me.* He would ask.

Rhya was quiet beside Corr. She reached a decision. "Corr, I should join Athol at Boulder Court. There's no particular role for me here, and I'm sure he can use the help for the next few days. If no one minds, however, I want to come back to the Embassy next week. I want to know how the Thomases and the rest of the Humans respond to our actions."

Corr's shoulders sagged. "Are you leaving now?"

"Yes. I'll stop by my room to pick up my gear. I can reach Boulder Court in a few hours. Tomorrow, I'll help Athol prepare to execute his part of the plan. I assume our primary task will be to take the new military base. How will the remainder of the forces be deployed?"

Corr raised his mental shield. "While you go to your room, I'll get you a copy of the full plan. There are parts you haven't seen."

Corr went to the front gate with Rhya. He struggled to find a way to ask her to leave with him. "I'll walk you to the edge of the city."

As they walked, the two small creatures drew close together. Both felt a faint desire to dance in the moonlight, like the first tiny rabbits during the time of the dinosaurs.

"Corr, did you know some of the wood rats have trained plants to create moonlight shadow patterns that animate as the moon passes across the sky?"

"I have seen shadow art, but I assumed it all involved sunlight."

"I think only a few have tried moonlight. They live near my home burrow."

"Hmm... the moon-shadow stories might be unique, but the technique has undoubtedly been employed elsewhere."

"Nothing new under the moon." Rhya laughed.

"Right. Even Humans know."

After passing the crime-scene taped Thomas home and leaving the city, the two rabbits picked up the trail and stopped. Rhya turned to Corr, hugged him, shifted her fur, and disappeared into the shadows of the scrub oak spilling from the foothills onto the gentle alluvial slope. Corr sighed and crouched in the shadows alone.

* * *

When Corr returned to the Embassy, he found Whistol and laid out the rest of his plan. Resisting and then giving in to a grin, Farr said, "That sounds fine. Community service is, after all, what they are supposed to be providing. Do you want Wilson to set this up?"

"No. This is the essential part of the plan. If you don't mind spending a little time helping me list the Human statutes and Treaty articles, we can get the final draft ready for Wilson. There are counter forces at work, and we don't know how powerful they are."

"Any ideas for discovering the spies in the Embassy?"

"No. I have a deception planned for tomorrow that should help us with the military, but it won't expose the spies."

"Okay. I'll start on the statutes now."

"Whistol, before you start, I have something to tell you. I'm glad you like the plan. It's complete now. In the morning—"

Interrupted by a click from his communicator, Corr listened, jerked to his feet, snarled, and ran out of the room.

Rhya Is Trapped

Rhya held an image of Corr in her mind as she trotted along the old trail. *He seemed very tense this evening*, she thought. The steady improvements in the vegetation and soil softened her concerns. Perhaps everyone who spent much time in Mountainview became tense. As she neared Diamond Peak, Rhya sensed soldiers ahead on the trail. As she approached the soldiers, one spoke. "Stop. State your name and destination."

Ridiculous, but Rhya decided to go along. "Rhya Bright. I'm traveling to Wycliff District."

The soldier turned to another soldier and asked in a low voice, "Shall we hold this one?"

Rhya didn't wait for the reply. With a grin and "See ya," she disappeared and zipped past the soldiers. About a mile farther along she came to a large pit bordered by piles of fresh earth. Palo Verde trees with their understory of thorny tomatillo, cactus, and other shrubs pressed in on either side of the trail. Before her, a ramp entered the pit, and another ramp led out on the far side. Past its zenith, the waning moon filled the pit with dense shadows. A small blinking light rested on a pedestal near the center of the pit, midway between the ramps. Scattered objects around the light appeared to be tools. The pit was a trap. She sensed Humans off to the right, but they weren't near enough to see her or the pit.

She decided to investigate. As she inched down the ramp, she saw some sort of framework built into the sides of the pit. Her tactical senses tingled, but she decided to get a little closer to the light between the ramps to see how the trigger worked. Halfway down the ramp, she heard a snap and scraping sound. Her reflexes hurled her upward, but the trap's frame closed on her feet.

Rhya jerked as she fought to control the pain. The heavy outer bars of the trap squeezed her feet almost flat. She pushed against the top of the frame and tried to pull free. Nothing. She leaned forward, gripped the fame with both hands, and used her powerful back and shoulder muscles. Nothing. She drew her long sword, slipped it between the bars by her ankles, and probed downward for a fulcrum.

Two soldiers arrived and aimed rifles at Rhya. A minute later, more soldiers came with noose poles.

"Hello," Rhya said. "Can you help me?"

Instead of replying, the soldiers cast nooses around her. She retained her sword, but she couldn't move it. The soldiers opened the trap and pulled her onto the ground.

"Is it hurt? "

"I'll bet its leg's broken."

"Maybe. Let's get it locked up."

"Let's just shoot it," said the corporal in charge of the detail. "The lieutenant won't be back until Monday, and he won't want it if its legs are broken."

"Wait," one of the soldiers said. "What kind of animal are you?"

"I'm a rabbit," Rhya replied.

"Let's keep it," the soldier said. "People used to eat rabbits. We can lock it up and kill it for dinner tomorrow."

"Yuck, it looks too human," another soldier said.

Rhya exerted pressure against the nooses, gradually turning the razor-sharp edge of her sword toward the ropes.

"Okay, drop that knife."

"I can't drop it, ding-a-ling," Rhya said. "It's caught under your rope."

As she hoped, her reply amused the other soldiers. The corporal stepped toward her, but his noose pole pressed against his stomach and he lurched sideways. Rhya had wanted to start an exchange, but the lurch ended the opportunity.

Seething at the grins from the other soldiers, the corporal began to drag the small rabbit along a path running east from the trap. "Get moving!" he ordered.

Unable to loosen the nooses, Rhya concentrated fully

on tending to her injuries. She balanced the tension in the muscles around the broken bones, compressed injured blood vessels, and found intact vessels to increase blood flow to bruised tissues. She determined that she could stabilize the breaks and walk, even run at half-speed, if given the opportunity.

The soldiers dragged Rhya along a rough path running east toward the new Human army camp. Soon, the group reached a windowless block building with a narrow door. Inside, the soldiers added to Rhya's bonds and removed her sword.

"Let's tenderize this rabbit before we stick it in the store room," the corporal said, and he began to kick Rhya.

* * *

Corr left the trail and ran toward Rhya's position at full speed. Seeing the building ahead, he sensed both Rhya's plight and her position. He echolated his target with a short burst of high-pitched sound, leapt forward, turned while airborne, and smashed both feet into the door.

As the corporal aimed a kick at Rhya's face, the door slammed open and Corr Syl landed in the room. He took two running steps and kicked the surprised corporal on the side of his weight-bearing left leg. As the corporal fell screaming, Corr crossed the room and struck down the other soldiers. Returning to the soldier who was attempting to draw a pistol, Corr snapped the edge of his foot to the side of the soldier's head.

Corr released the nooses holding Rhya and helped her stand. He knelt to inspect her feet. "Wait."

In a moment, Ralph Mäkinen burst through the door. "Rhya's feet are injured."

Ralph bowed and knelt. "Rhya Bright, may I offer you a ride?"

"Certainly." Rhya grasped Ralph's harness and swung onto his back.

Ralph ducked through the door and, followed closely by Corr, ran full speed back to the trail, crossed it, and stopped in the shadows of a tall ironwood tree.

"Can you walk?" Corr asked.

"I have cracked bones in my feet and some deep bruising. I can walk and run at slow speeds. I want to return to the Embassy."

Corr spoke rapidly to a bat that landed on his shoulder. Then he concentrated all his sensory nets for a moment.

"Ralph, please continue carrying Rhya."

"Sure," the big wolf said. "Carrying Rhya is even more fun than bashing Human soldiers."

"Thank you," Rhya said, smiling.

At the Embassy, Rhya explained to her comrades that her injuries were not severe and she would be back to normal in the morning. Corr and Ralph took her to her room. Two healers arrived to help Rhya with the repairs.

* * *

Corr and Ralph gave Whistol Farr and Able Remington a description of the trap and the soldiers' treatment of Rhya.

"Instead of temporarily incapacitating the soldiers when we take the base, it might be wiser to imprison them," Corr said.

Farr glared. "Rhya is okay?"

"Yes. Imprisonment would be costly," Ralph said. "If you don't want to kill them, let's cripple them."

"That might work," Corr said with a grim expression.

"What is the purpose of the trap?" Remington asked.

Farr frowned. "I don't know. There's no law preventing Tsaeb from using the trail. The whole thing stinks. Perhaps we can do something to their brains. I believe Human stroke victims sometimes develop angelic attitudes. I'll find someone to research the subject. Perhaps an intense shock would do the same thing."

Final Preparations

Corr awoke early, all thoughts of travel gone. When he opened his door, he found Quin Achiptre perched on the balcony rail munching a seed cake.

"Good morning," said Quinn. "Fun night? "

"The first part was best."

"Corr, the Wycliff Council approved your plan. Sealed versions to be opened this evening are being delivered to North American border communities and Continental Councils elsewhere."

"Would you like to get something more for breakfast?"

"Sure."

"Let's see if Rhya is ready."

As the three headed for the Tea Room, Ralph, Zuberi, and Bill joined them.

Bill said, "I heard what happened. You okay?"

"I'm fine, except for feeling stupid," Rhya said.

"Oh, embarrassing mistakes are easy to forget. Ask Zuberi."

"Yeah? Well, Bill is even more intimate with embarrassment. Ask him about his cliff descent," Zuberi said, referring to the time Bill was arguing so intensely he backed off a cliff and landed in a shrub growing out of a crevice.

As Corr entered the Tea Room, conversation stopped. *Here we go*, Corr thought. He stepped onto a bench.

"The Wycliff and Continental Councils have approved the plan." The air nearly glowed as sensory fields flared and cheers filled the room. Corr studied the audience and noted the Thomases, including AJ, and several other Humans in the crowd. In a moment, Corr raised his hands and made a stunning announcement.

"The action begins tonight at 6:00." The room fell silent. "After breakfast, report to your unit leaders. In one hour, I want to see all section heads and team leaders in the Communications Center. Good luck to us all!"

Later, Corr and Farr met in Farr's office. "Corr,

everything has begun," said Farr. "We will have drafts of the initial announcements, complaints, bench warrants, and affidavits for the arrested leaders ready within the hour. Right now, you and I should read the proofs before printing begins."

"Good. First, though, I thought of another project. We should begin now to establish sterilizing facilities around the city."

Farr chuckled. "Corr, I think we should say family planning rather than sterilizing. Less ominous. I'll find someone to gather the information."

"We also need extra supplies in Piedmont. Can you find someone to gather cache inventories and request contributions from the districts?"

After the others left, Corr spoke quietly to Rhya for a few minutes. She shook her head twice, but finally nodded and walked away.

Rhya Teaches Rock Climbing

Following Corr's request, Rhya joined the Thomases as they completed a circuit of the Great Hall on their way to the Gymnasium. The adults were subdued, but not the children. Bright-eyed and energized, Charlotte ran to Rhya and hugged her. "Do you want to play in the gym?"

"Okay."

Rhya decided to work her feet a little, so she ran the track circling the gym. After 14 circuits, she returned to the group. The Thomases stared at her.

"That was incredible," Allen said.

"You were a blur, Rhya. How fast do you run?"

"Normally, I run 14 laps in less than two minutes. That's about 45 mph. I ran slower today because my foot was broken last night."

"How long is the track?" Howard asked.

"The lane I ran is 490 feet. Fourteen circuits are 1.3 miles."

"Wait," said Rebecca. "You ran on a broken foot?"

"It's mended now... just a little tender."

The Thomases all stared. Howard asked, "How did your foot heal so quickly?"

"Perhaps it was just a bone bruise. Fractures can take months to heal," Rebecca said.

"Oh, it was broken all right," Rhya said, remembering the painful impact of the trap. "There were several thin cracks caused by compression—nothing really out of place, so a few hours was sufficient to get it back to normal."

"But how?" Rebecca wondered aloud.

Rhya paused. "I focused my sensory fields and star cells on the injury, and used them to guide and accelerate healing processes."

"Mr. Farr said something about sensory fields, but I assumed they were for recognizing thoughts. Are you saying you can somehow control cells inside your body?"

"Yes."

The Thomases stared at Rhya again. Finally, Rebecca

asked, "What are sensory fields?"

"Our minds and bodies produce electromagnetic radiation. Everything we do, even moving a finger, requires a small electrical current that is surrounded by a magnetic field. A sensory field is that area in which you can sense the magnetism."

"Do all Tsaeb have sensory fields?"

"Everyone does."

"Do our doctors know about this?"

"I'm sure they do, but I don't think any know how to use the fields."

"Why not?" AJ asked.

"I don't know. Tsaeb parents teach their children to recognize and use the fields to control cellular processes and heal injuries. Those are their first lessons in Immediacy. Maybe if your doctors started early they could learn how to do it."

"Corr mentioned Immediacy. What is it?" Marcie asked.

"Belief in the importance of understanding our interactions with our surroundings. Sometimes it's called the Philosophy of Consequences."

AJ doubts everything I say, Rhya thought. I guess Corr is right.

"Rhya, are all Tsaeb as fast as you?"

"No, but some could be if they wanted to spend the time training and modifying their bodies."

Charlotte stood nearby watching a Tsaeb strolling by with a bow. "Rhya, can I hold your bow?"

"Sure. Would you like to shoot it?

"Uh-huh."

Rhya asked if the adults would mind a few more questions first. She wanted to see how they felt about the treatment she had received from the soldiers. She asked Nathan Jensen to take the children to get something to drink.

"Corr and I have both appreciated your candor. I want to ask your opinions on a new problem." As everyone listened, she described her experience with the trap and the soldiers.

Marcie said, "Oh, Rhya, I am so sorry. So that's how your foot got broken."

"Yes. But the most disturbing part of the experience was the attitude of the soldiers. They were pitiless, even though they had me bound and helpless."

"How did you get away?"

"Corr came."

"I hope he kicked their butts," Allen said.

"He did," Rhya said.

"Maybe the soldiers would have treated any captive the same way," Howard suggested. "It's certainly not the way most people would act."

"Whatever the cause, it's a terrible thing," Marcie said. "No wonder Tsaeb are concerned about our society."

"Can you think of anything that could be done to reduce the hostility?" Rhya asked.

Howard said, "At the Police Academy we learned about attitude conditioning. People naturally take sides when they join groups. In the past, cops often developed distrust for everyone except other cops. Cops can become so biased they'll break laws to protect one another. We were told to keep reminding ourselves that we are members of our society. I'll bet military training doesn't warn against the conditioning. It might actually encourage it."

Millie spoke up. "I don't see why we even have an army. I can't remember the Federation ever being at war or even having a serious conflict with anyone."

"That's not the issue here," AJ said.

But it could be, Rhya thought, remembering other such questions, and thinking about spies.

"Another possibility," Allen said, "is that people with negative attitudes might be attracted to the military, or perhaps the recruiters look for such things."

"Why don't we have screening tests?" Marcie said. "Why not discover the potential for hateful attitudes early before children grow up to become dangerous adults?"

"No," Millie said. "Attitude tests as part of a job application are fine, but I don't think we should test children. Can you imagine what an unscrupulous government would do with such information? Attitudes and beliefs are our most precious freedoms."

"We do have laws against verbal threats and threatening behavior," Allen said. "But I think what Howard said about attitude conditioning applies to everyone. We probably all have the tendency to identify with a peer group."

"Rhya, can we talk about Corr's plan?" Howard asked. "What's happening?"

"I guess the fighters are getting ready to head for the army base and the prison as soon as it gets dark."

The children were fidgeting as if they had fleas. "I have a little time. Would anyone like to try a little archery?" She helped choose arm guards, bows, and practice arrows, and led the way out to the practice yard beside the Embassy.

After everyone shot some arrows, the Thomases resumed their tour and Rhya joined Corr and Whistol Farr at a window in Farr's office.

Ten minutes later, AJ Thomas entered the archery practice yard, carried a target to the periphery wall, and climbed over.

Executing the Plan

"Good," Corr said. "When AJ warns them of tonight's attack, most of the soldiers will be called to the base and the prison. We won't have to hunt for them."

During the night of March 31 and the early morning hours of April 1, a police force composed of hundreds of Tsaeb swept into and across the military base and the city of Mountainview. As the operation unfolded, Corr and staff sat in the Embassy's Communications Center receiving reports and suggesting adjustments as situations arose. By 5:00 a.m. Monday morning, Tsaeb controlled the military base and the police stations, and they had jailed all but three of the leaders on Corr's list.

Tsaeb fighter groups blocked Human roads and trails on Tsaeb lands and delivered seven-day eviction notices to Human farmers and farm employees living on Piedmont lands. They offered to arrange moving assistance and temporary housing.

The Tsaeb prisoners received a description of the full operation. They could return home, visit the Embassy, or go wherever they wished. Supplies would reach the Piedmont caches within a few days, and hundreds of volunteers would be arriving throughout the week to help begin restoration of the lands altered by the farmers.

Marion Tummel and her daughter asked to go to the Embassy to join Arthur Tummel, the spy captured on Juniper Mesa. All 167 of the other prisoners went home. They, along with an escort of Tsaeb fighters, spent the night in a park and started home in the morning with high spirits.

* * *

Corr had kept secret until the last possible moment the planned arrests and subsequent treatment of the leaders, the elected officials, public administrators, corporate officers, and a few wealthy private citizens. These included all the individuals that the Embassy staff had determined were supporters of unrestricted growth, and thereby supported the border transgressions. Not arrested were the few conservatives who, like General Howell, favored restraint and sustainability.

Beginning with the judges, Human leaders would be required to initiate changes in key laws and start advocating quality instead of quantity. They would agree or stay in jail.

Many of the leaders could call on national support. Corr counted on the Continental Council to convince the Federation leadership that the Mountainview action would not result in deaths or injuries, and that it would not spill over into other communities. He hoped that would be enough.

The most common problem encountered by the Tsaeb arrest units was lack of respect. The judges, police chiefs, and corporate officers often stared in disbelief at the Tsaeb at their doors, and some simply slammed the door without a word. Others said they would be happy to speak with the Tsaeb at their offices in the morning. A few inspected the warrants and asked questions. In most cases, the leaders of the Mountainview community resisted arrest.

The response of the president of the Logan Construction Corporation, a regional road builder, was typical. The arresting unit that came to his home consisted of a rabbit, a warrior fox, a scaly armadillo, an ocelot, a wood rat, a northern harrier, and a pair of javelina. As they approached the house the armadillo said, "Who's going to say 'trick or treat'?"

When a man responded to the doorbell, a javelina asked his identity, presented the warrant, and asked the man to come with the unit. The rat filmed the procedure. The president listened, and then snorted and slammed the door. When he did not respond to repeated knocks and doorbell rings, the ocelot removed a small device from a pouch on his harness and cut through the triggers on the door lock and deadbolt. Then the fox, javelina, and rat entered.

They found the man standing at the foot of a staircase.

"What the hell do you think you're doing?"

"You are under arrest. Come with us, please," the javelina ordered.

"Get out. I'm calling the police."

All arresting units allowed such calls. Tsaeb controlled all police stations. Under Tsaeb supervision, dispatchers answered calls and responded as usual. They had a statement to read to callers inquiring about the arrests. They advised those callers to go with the Tsaeb peacefully.

On hearing the statement, the president said "Bullshit!" and removed a handgun from a drawer in a table by the door. Before he could raise the gun, the fox stepped forward and tapped the man's wrist, causing the gun to fall. Then the fox made several carefully-placed strikes that caused the man to fall. The fighters caught the man, lowered him to the floor, and secured his hands behind his back.

The javelina then asked, "Will you walk with us?"

When the president growled "*No!*" the other javelina stepped forward, unfurled a sheet of smooth fabric, and with the help of the rabbit, maneuvered the man onto it. The armadillo passed a band over the man's back and attached it to loops on the edges of the fabric. Then the javelina pulled the man out the door.

The man's wife saw her husband being dragged out the door and screamed as she came down the stairs. The rabbit approached and apologized for disturbing her. "Your husband is under arrest. We will not harm him. We are taking him to the central police station." He held out a packet. "Everything is explained in this document."

The unit began trotting along the sidewalk, dragging their prisoner toward the prison. The smooth sheet slid quietly along the sidewalk, but their prisoner cursed, called for help, and shouted demands. When this seemed likely to continue, the fox removed a small bulb from a pouch in his harness and squeezed it into the man's face. The man immediately quieted and his body relaxed. The group then stopped because of a shout from across the street.

An elderly man emerged from his front door holding a shotgun. "Stop right there!" he said in a loud voice. As he drew near he said, "What do you think you're doing?"

The fox walked into the street toward the man. "This man is under arrest for conspiracy to commit crimes. We have an arrest warrant." Then the fox beckoned the rabbit who approached and held out a packet.

"This doesn't make any sense," the man said, raising his weapon.

The fox snatched the gun from the man's hands, but left him standing.

A javelina said, "If you return to your home now, we won't arrest you. Please call the police. They will explain what's going on."

"Please take this," the rabbit said.

Wide-eyed, the man accepted the packet and backed toward his house. The group continued on their way to the prison.

Three arrests failed. General Miller was in Plainview at a meeting, a judge died of stroke during arrest, and Lactella/Johns was not home.

Lactella Escapes

Lactella had tormented Johns all day. The distraction from the occasional cruelty was not enough for her, and she had sent numerous jolts of venom into Johns just to watch the fear and agony surface in the surviving remnants of his personality. Normally, she knew what caused her tension—a deal that needed council approval, or a problem with a Johns family member—but in this instance, the reason for her anxiety eluded her.

At the usual 9:00 p.m. time, Lactella put Johns to bed. Unable to sleep, she had the man rise, dress, and head for his office at City Hall. As she approached the building, groups of Tsaeb were clustered near the entrances of the military headquarters and the police station. Her anxiety increased, and she drove by without slowing.

Trying to decide what to do, Lactella called Marbellet's home. The general's wife told him Marbellet had mentioned something might happen, and had gone to the base earlier in the evening. Lactella called the general's mobile phone, but he did not answer. Lactella then called police headquarters and learned that Tsaeb were arresting various leaders involved in crimes and conspiracy to commit crimes. She needed nothing more. She called and found a flight to the capitol of the Human state on Normount's eastern border.

While waiting for her flight, Lactella considered options. She assumed the Tsaeb were responding to the incursions around Diamond Peak. She also assumed that a Tsaeb attack on the Mountainview army base would provoke the Federation military. If she could make contact with those in charge, she might yet benefit.

At one of their meetings, Marbellet had mentioned visiting his son, a colonel stationed in the Federation military headquarters in Plainview, the Federation capitol. Lactella called the central military exchange in Plainview and asked to speak to Colonel Marbellet. Marbellet came on the phone immediately. Lactella had Johns explain who he was and described what he had seen and learned. She said she had information about the Tsaeb that might explain the attack.

Lactella planned her story. She would continue the claim she'd made in the earlier press release about the survey. She would describe the incursions as goodwill missions intended to increase interaction with the Tsaeb. She would also claim an interest in providing aid to the Tsaeb to improve their standard of living. If things went well, she wouldn't need to worry about getting popular approval for annexing the lower Wycliff watershed. The Federation military could give her control.

The Human Military Response

Lactella's call to Robert Marbellet came hours before the Tsaeb briefing reports reached the offices of the Federation President and the Chief of the Federation Armed Forces. When Marbellet's commanding officer failed to reach anyone at the new Mountainview base, he dispatched a paratrooper force of 122 men to determine what had happened at the base and to make any necessary corrections.

Sitting in his small windowless office, modesty masking his great wealth, William Ellison, the Chief of the Federation Armed Forces, read the briefing statements from the Tsaeb Continental Council and decided to abort the paratrooper mission. Then he hesitated and called in his Exec, Alan Horowitz.

"Al, does the Tsaeb Border Treaty give the Tsaeb the right to arrest military leaders and attack an Army base because of... uh, let's see... suspicion of conspiracy?"

"Tough one. What happened?"

"We carried arms across the border. That doesn't seem so bad, does it? These Tsaeb shut down our base, then came into Mountainview and arrested people with no military connections."

"Let me find someone in the AG's office who knows the Treaty."

The chief decided to allow the paratroopers to complete their mission while he waited to hear from the Attorney General's office. He thought about the border war, a conflict carried out in isolated battles fought with small arms. In the century since the war, the Federation military had made enormous advances. He knew of no progress by the Tsaeb and did not believe the Tsaeb could handle the modern Federation military. Perhaps it was time to demonstrate Human superiority.

Horowitz returned. "Sir, the legal staffer I spoke with says that the Treaty calls for arrests, but the presumption is that they are made by the offending side, by us in this case. He says the Tsaeb should have come to you or the president first. He advises that we thank the Tsaeb for their help and ask them to withdraw."

"Okay, we'll do that. But let's send in a serious task force. If the Tsaeb refuse, or even hesitate, we will interpret their actions as illegal and force them to comply."

The chief called Martin Toliver, the Federation President and described the AG's response. The President agreed that this could be an opportunity to begin negotiating a new Border Treaty. The chief immediately directed his staff to engage emergency protocols to overpower the Tsaeb.

The operation grew to include another paratrooper company to secure the Mountainview airport, three Special Forces units to retake the police stations and free the arrested city leadership, and two infantry battalions to garrison important points within Mountainview. The chief labeled the mission Free Mountainview. By day's end, the Tsaeb would have no choice but to disengage.

The chief ordered an interview of Colonel Marbellet. When he learned the tip had come from Johns, he asked the Military Police to locate Johns and fly him to military headquarters in Plainview.

Tsaeb were prepared. Their aerial fighters fed rocks into aircraft engines, and gassed Federation ground forces. No one died.

By noon, Mission Free Mountainview had failed. Ellison's ground forces had stopped responding and his air force had no planes in the air. Surprised and sobered by the instant Tsaeb response, Ellison called Martin Toliver.

"Mr. President, let's put the brakes on for now. Let's send the Tsaeb a note saying we thought we were supposed to take over."

"Fine, Bill. You write it. I have to explain all this to the national chamber president."

During the next few days, the upper echelon of the Federation government, military, and corporate community did little but read reports about Corr Syl's Mountainview operation.

* * *

Military police located Ivanstor Johns and flew him to Plainview. They took him to a dreary room filled with the standard gray steel furniture and told him to wait. Lactella considered abandoning Johns and finding a place to hide. After hours of waiting, and watching MPs take other people away, Lactella decided she had to do something.

Lactella Goes Deep

Lactella had despised the Tsaeb; now she began to fear them. She had to assume the Tsaeb might be looking for Johns. She needed a new identity.

Lactella left the military waiting room, took a cab downtown, bought some clothes, and took a cab to the airport. She bought a ticket for Mountainview on a local commuter airline.

The commuter planes boarded at a satellite terminal with a small staff and no security system. After handing in her boarding pass, Lactella went to the restroom, changed into new clothes, put on a ball cap bearing the emblem of a local team, and stuffed Johns' clothes and cell phone into a waste can. After a few minutes, she strolled out of the airport and took a city bus downtown. Then she made her way to the intercity bus depot. There she bought a ticket to a large city southeast of Plainview.

Lactella planned to join the homeless population. As soon as it felt safe, she would return to Plainview and find a host high in government, the military, or a large corporation.

Lactella moved Johns into a homeless shelter consisting of a small kitchen and a large room containing rows of cots and settled down to wait. Things went well until one night three men cornered Johns in an alley, beat him, and robbed him. Lactella was terrified; Johns no longer had the power and prestige necessary to protect her. The police might even arrest him for vagrancy or suspicion of a crime. The police would discover and kill Lactella.

Driven by fear, Lactella conceived a solution. She would move *inside* Johns' body. She could tap Johns' trachea for air and an artery for food. She could enter through Johns' throat and make her way to a secure site. Her present position on the back of Johns' neck placed her close to his brain, but she did not think this was necessary. She could control Johns just as well from the center of his chest. She would attach herself to tendons supporting his organs, and connect with his vascular and nervous systems.

The move went well except that the opening in Johns' esophagus would not close. After a week, ulcers formed and dysphagia developed. Lactella needed a new host. Johns could live on liquids while she searched.

Lactella loved her new position. Her control over Johns hadn't changed. She had lost nothing. She had used Johns' senses rather than her own for quite some time, and now she could get Johns a normal haircut and further improve his disguise. She wondered whether her eggs could hatch inside Johns, or perhaps in his lungs. They might need physical modifications lest they asphyxiate before learning to use Johns' system. She began thinking about heredity and the controls over form. After finding a new host she would study genetics.

Rhya and Marion

Able Remington Rhya asked to meet Marion Tummel and her family at the Embassy entrance. Now free from the Human prison, the Tummels wanted to reunite with their son, Arthur, the spy captured on Juniper Mesa.

"I'm going to supervise the Piedmont relocation camp. If the Tummels need rooms, or if there are other issues, see Ellan Marin," Able said.

Rhya showed the Tummels around the Embassy and took them to the Tea Room for lunch. They sat and chatted comfortably about their recent experiences. Rhya told them about her trap experience, and Marion described her interview with Lactella when Lactella had injected venom in Marion's neck and asked questions from within Marion's thoughts. When Marion mentioned the organic compounds accompanying the spider's neurotoxin, Rhya had an idea.

"Could the spider's secondary organics be used to alter a soldier's attitude?"

"They would create a receptive frame of mind," Marion said. "If a Tsaeb projected a positive memory into the mind of a soldier while the compounds were present, the memory might stick."

"If I can arrange to test this, would you be willing to help?"

Marion thought for a moment. "We want to go home, but this is important. I'd be willing to stay for a while to help synthesize the compounds and verify their functions." She turned to her family. "Shall we stay at the Embassy for a while?"

Marion's husband, Samuel, nodded. "Rhya, do you suppose I could use the Mountainview University library? I've been studying Human art. I'd like to check on a few things."

"Whistol Farr can probably arrange that."

Marion's mother asked, "Do you think there will be sufficient supplies for us if we return to our home?"

"Yes. The supply chain that will restock your

community stores will reach Piedmont later today."

"Then we would like to go home."

"I'll arrange rooms for those of you who are staying. Marion, I'll also ask about some lab space and a chemist."

Rhya went to the Communications Center and spoke briefly with Farr and Ellan Marin.

Ellan sent an assistant to show the Tummels to living quarters. Then she took Rhya to a lower Embassy basement level, and showed her a series of labs supervised by Elisa Loret. "Elisa has several assistants conducting tests on foods, soil, air, and water. Right now, she and her assistants are all busy with Corr's operation. Some of them could help you tomorrow. I'll send a message to Elisa. I think she'll be eager to supply materials and find chemists to help with your project."

"Thank you." Rhya went to Wilson Smith's office and explained what she wanted.

Wilson frowned, then grinned. "Hmmm... we haven't tried drugging them. Our goal with Human education is similar, but we think of what we do as a support process. You're describing forced learning. We have no experience with that, though I'm certain most of our teachers have imagined it longingly. Let me circulate a request for sensory projectors. There are some among our teaching staff, and there are undoubtedly others on Wharton's staff. As Corr's operation winds down, they may have time to help as well."

Next Rhya tracked down Sam Whortin.

"Sam, I have an idea for an experiment that might help soften the Human soldiers' attitude toward us. I need some laboratory space and a place to lock up a few soldiers."

"Well, sure. Let's see... there are some empty rooms in the basement. We'll have to change the doors if you want to hold anyone, but that won't be a problem. What are you going to do?"

Rhya explained.

"Sounds interesting. I'll have someone change a few

doors for you. Nothing like a nice dark dungeon for experimenting on brains. There are also some empty cells in the local prison. I think you should give all the leaders a good dose of correct thinking. I don't know what's in the vacated military base, but there's probably a lot of space you could use there too."

Over dinner, Rhya told Corr about her conversation with Marion and explained what she wanted to do.

"Rhya, this is the best idea yet," Corr said. "We have more than 1,000 soldiers in custody. Allysen and Ankolla are supervising the detainment, and they're getting worried they'll be stuck there. They'll deliver soldiers wherever and whenever you want."

Marion and Rhya spent the next few days assembling a team and discussing approaches to the problem. Every chemistry specialist on the Tea Room kitchen staff whipped off their aprons and hats and volunteered. Wilson Smith brought along three talented sensory projectors willing to work on the project and said others were interested.

During their first meeting, the group quickly realized they needed a much better understanding of the soldiers' hostility.

One of the sensory specialists asked, "Is the hostility something every Human has sleeping in his brain? If it is, it is genetic, and it might be impossible to control. We'll have to unravel its origins, triggers, and expressions and find out whether it varies across individuals."

Rhya called her Human psychology teacher at the Wycliff center for help to find a Human psychology specialist, particularly one interested in prejudgments involving race, gender, inter-specific intolerance, and so forth.

Synthesizing the compounds came next. Marion had retained residue from the compounds, and Rhya worried there wouldn't be enough to define the composition. She gave what Marion was able to supply to the chemists and asked them to determine whether they could synthesize the compounds.

"Both compounds are composed of biomolecules that can be classified as peptides," one of the chemists explained. "They are complex, and we have found nothing analogous to either of them." She projected a diagram on the wall. "These are fairly long chains. Production by any creature, especially a small spider, is an impressive accomplishment."

"Will they be difficult to synthesize?" Rhya asked.

"No. It appears we can use a standard solid-phase method. One problem is that the molecules will deteriorate at Human body temperatures. Extended use will require continual replacement."

"So no pills?"

"Nope. We might devise a time-release mixture, but an intravenous drip would be much simpler."

It took a week and the help of three more chemists to reproduce the first compound. The second compound required another week. Marion verified the compounds by matching them to her memory. The chemists and several other Tsaeb took injections to study.

Meanwhile a Human psychology specialist, a wood rat named Robert McLaren, devised a simple scale for sorting soldiers according to the strength of their attitudes toward Tsaeb.

"I have chosen a reasonably consistent means to score attitudes using indirect rankings of correlated objects corroborated by direct questions. The validation system uses repeated measures and a third-party assessment of a subject's opinions. The process generates a number that I call the TA Scalar."

The team nicknamed McLaren "Pusher," not because he dispensed drugs, as he thought, but because his co-workers tended to edge away when he began speaking.

On April 15, Rhya called for a meeting of the full team with Corr, Whistol Farr, and other members of the Embassy staff.

When they were all seated, she began. "We can produce enough of Compounds I and II to begin testing in two weeks. Pusher has started collecting TA Scalars for a large sample of soldiers. We'll use them to form three test groups defined by levels of intolerance for Tsaeb. We will subdivide each group into nine sets and give each set different combinations of the compounds. Our web casters will induce the same three feelings of sympathy, respect, and friendship across the groups. We'll determine dosages by the number of sessions it takes to establish a feeling that lasts for at least 21 days."

"Rhya, the whole thing seems pretty shaky," Farr said, and Wilson Smith nodded. "The soldiers' hostility might be far stronger than anything we can induce and the process itself might just make them hate us more. How did you choose the initial dosage levels? What if they are all too weak?"

"We will induce a touch of fever and nausea in the soldiers, isolate them, and tell them the drip contains antibiotics and fluids to keep them from dehydrating. We did some preliminary tests to choose the dosages. I know the whole thing isn't perfect. We're trying to implant a few memories of positive feelings about Tsaeb. Ideally, the feelings will recur whenever the subject sees or thinks about Tsaeb. Of course, the original negative attitudes might be too strong. We just have to hope we can create a better balance." She looked around the table. "Okay. Anything else? No? Then here we go."

And with that, and with the entire Tsaeb civilization watching, Rhya Bright began the first-ever effort to forcefully modify Human minds.

Two Wolverine

At the Embassy entrance a wolverine announced, "I'm here to see Corr Syl."

An EDAS capper led him to a room off the main hall where Corr was discussing the Human farm workers with Able Remington.

"You are Corr Syl?"

"Yes. Who are you?"

"I am Barth Norland," the wolverine said, moving forward with a smile and an out-stretched hand. As Corr began to stand, Barth whipped a long sword over his shoulder in a diagonal slash.

Corr snapped backward, feinted left and leapt right past the wolverine. At the door, he turned and studied his attacker as he scanned for other dangers.

The wolverine was wearing a steel helmet and a vest. In addition to a shield and a pack, he had unusually large pouches on his harness. The pouches radiated powerful waves of energy. The wolverine also had a projectile hand weapon, but he did not draw it. Instead, he pulled his shield and advanced confidently toward Corr, his movements smooth, powerful, and quick.

Corr didn't like the pouches. He drew his long sword and clamped on his shield as Barth began a series of attacks that included projectiles fired with great force from cavities in his shield. Corr blocked these and made a combination of thrusts that achieved a small wound on the wolverine's leg.

Corr retrieved his stored warrior's analysis of wolverine: Descendants of an old species, though not as old as rabbits, wolverine retained many of their species' original traits. Their numbers small, they tended to remain in cool climates. They had bad tempers.

Fortunately, Barth did not have warrior training, but even without it, he seemed dangerous. Corr considered drawing his energy weapon. He could probably hit Barth at this distance, and he didn't mind damaging the contents of the room. But he could also defeat Barth using hand weapons and not take a chance on activating the devices in Barth's pouches.

Able had frozen when Barth entered the room, and he hadn't moved since. He stepped back when Barth attacked, and he remained motionless, watching.

Rhya would arrive soon. Corr decided to draw the wolverine away. He edged out the door as he began a series of jeering taunts he hoped would trigger the wolverine's temper. "Outside, you dolt! Don't release your bowels on my floor! Are you lost? Come with me! I'll send you home!"

Barth leapt forward, making another powerful thrust.

As Corr parried, he felt a blow and a sharp pain in his side and looked down to see the point of an arrow protruding from his abdomen. Another wolverine was standing near the Embassy entrance. Surprised he had not sensed the creature, Corr leaned left to allow a second arrow to pass.

Sensory nets of the Tsaeb throughout the hall were snapping into focus on Corr and Barth. Some shifted to the second wolverine. Members of the security staff rushed toward them. Corr scanned carefully for other threats.

Able had not moved.

Corr made his decision, shifted his fur, and ran to the Embassy entrance. The wolverine there dropped his bow and jumped back, reaching for his sword. Corr did not slow. He exited the Embassy, continued across the street, and ran south through the park. As he ran, he sealed off the tissues damaged by the arrow in his side. He also started a random series of shifts in his course that, coupled with his near invisibility, would make long-distance weapons ineffective. He kept his head hunched down anyway. *Who would send such an assassin? It doesn't seem possible that the Federation would train and control Tsaeb spies or assassins.*

At a thousand yards from the Embassy Corr stopped abruptly and turned to gauge his attackers' progress. Then, pouring everything he had into running, he continued south. He also continued his scan for other dangers. When he stopped again, he saw that Barth was about 200 yards behind. *Good.* The other wolverine wasn't around.

He could defeat Barth or simply stop both attackers with his bow, but it would be safer for everyone if he led the two wolverine out of the city. Though they would have great endurance, he estimated he could maintain a safe lead for at least half an hour.

The low desert south of the city would be quite warm and would sap the Wolverines' endurance and expand Corr's advantage.

Just then, Quin flew alongside the speeding rabbit. "Hi, Corr. What's the hurry?"

Corr slowed to a stop and looked back. Numerous birds were circling above.

"How?"

"Rhya got them with her bow. "

"They're alive?"

"I don't know about the first one. The nearest one has arrows in his knee and left paw, and Ralph stomped his other paw as he passed." Quin grinned. "Unnecessary, of course—the birds had already stoned him."

* * *

As Rhya left the gym, she sensed trouble and saw Corr running. Then she focused on the wolverine near the entrance. As Corr flashed by, the wolverine drew a sword, but instead of slashing at Corr, he slowly melted to his knees and flopped face forward, the vaned shaft of Rhya's arrow protruding from the narrow slit between his helmet and his armor.

Before the wolverine completed his fall, Rhya started tracking Barth. She sent another arrow, but Barth deflected it with his shield. As she started toward the entrance, Ralph emerged from the Tea Room and raced toward the entrance. Reaching the street outside, Rhya saw Corr in the distance and Barth entering the street beyond the park. She decided to stop Barth's pursuit, but leave him alive.

Ralph smiled in admiration as Rhya placed an arrow through one of Barth's knee pits and another through a paw.

* * *

"You need to learn to call on your battle group," Quin said. "One sharp thought and we would have had them down in a minute."

"I didn't want anyone to get hurt," Corr said, still thinking of the pouches. "Besides, heading south for a little vacation seemed like a good idea."

Corr began walking back toward the Center with Quin flying tight circles overhead.

A grinning Ralph trotted up. "That was some fast running, Corr. I propose a new term for extreme speed on land: two-wolverine."

"Great," Corr said with a lopsided grin.

"Want help with that arrow?"

"That would be nice."

Ralph bent closer to look. "Hmmm, it was deflected by your harness. Any serious damage?"

"It snapped an oblique free. It's all bunched up, and I may need some help to fix it."

"Hold on," Ralph said and snapped off the rear of the arrow with his powerful fingers. He inspected the break, grasped the point, and drew the shaft out. No blood followed.

"Everything under control?"

"Yes."

"Feel like walking?"

"Yes."

Quin landed on Ralph's shoulder and the three friends walked back toward the Embassy. "Did you notice the size of that sword?" asked Corr.

"It was a Dao, wasn't it?"

Corr nodded. "First I ever saw. Who uses them?"

"I think the Asians do. Perhaps Sam knows," Ralph said.

"Or Bill and Zuberi."

They were inspecting Barth when Rhya and Sam arrived. Rhya was speaking angrily to Embassy Security Chief Whortin. "If we can't spot creatures as dangerous as these, we're pretty well screwed, aren't we?"

Sam's shield flickered on and off and he leaned away. "Rhya, who could have even imagined the appearance of Tsaeb assassins? I'm worried as hell, and will have our sensory surveillance as soon as possible."

"Humph!"

Rhya looked Corr over. "Let's ask Bill and Zuberi to come back to the Embassy. In fact, shouldn't Allysen and Ankolla join us too?"

"We need Allysen and Ankolla to supervise the soldiers. But Zuberi and Bill might as well come in."

* * *

When Bill and Zuberi arrived, they delivered a request from Allysen.

"Corr, Allysen wants to be relieved of guard duty," Bill said with a grin. "She started worrying about escapes and Ankolla is beginning to want to torture the prisoners."

Corr, Bill, and Zuberi laughed until tears streamed.

"Maybe the soldiers need a good beating," Corr said, remembering Rhya's experience. "Allysen and Ankolla should be able to leave tomorrow. Representatives from the Continental Council are negotiating with the Federation for temporary control of the local military units. When we get it, we'll set up a straw command and release the soldiers. They can dismantle the base while Rhya's group gives their minds a good greasing. Let's go over to the base and calm them down."

They found Allysen and Ankolla standing beside the front gate to the base arguing about the need for a stronger fence.

"Let it go for now," Corr said. "We should have word from the Continental Council in the morning."

"Good!" said Allysen. "I won't remain in charge of this place another day."

Ankolla left to check sentries while Corr and Allysen discussed which officers to place in charge and how to monitor the base. Allysen also described her interview with Elaine Medlar. "I could tell the woman had been frightened by Allon."

"Did Elaine say where her friend was going to teach?"

"She said it was an administrative position in the state Office of Education. Want me to dig into this?"

"No, ask Wilson Smith to make inquiries. Some of his assistants probably know people in the state office."

"Corr, I don't think we're going to find her."

"You're probably right. Bizarre, but I guess the riddle of Allon's diet is solved."

The New Mountainview

After the arrests, Corr, Rhya, and the full Embassy staff applied themselves to preparing support for new initiatives from Mountainview's leaders. They would soon know whether the leaders could truly lead.

The Human leaders received public service sentences. Corporate leadership, encouraged by tax credits, research grants, and the threat of stiffer judicial penalties, began to develop restoration projects. Congressional leaders began work on two critical projects. First, they began drafting new election laws that would limit campaign contributions, and second, they began changing the tax system to create an equitable system with rates tied to new goals. All leaders began to encourage family savings, family education, and family planning.

Politicians began using the new ideas. They gave speeches on reducing consumption, eliminating military spending, and controlling population growth. Political, religious, and corporate speakers began proclaiming the absurdity of short-term, unsustainable materialism. They praised the benefits of knowledge. A feeling akin to relief permeated the city. On the streets, people began to relax, occasionally to smile, and some even paused to chat.

* * *

Following the attack, Corr and Sam began collating information to see whether they could determine the origin of the wolverine. Trained and confident, the pair must have a home base.

The surviving wolverine would give nothing to interrogators. The assassin's mental shield became monolithic when probed. Normally a shield did not block its user—otherwise the user would become blind to its surroundings—but under stress, the wolverine's shield blocked all senses, outbound as well as inbound.

Impressive, Corr thought. This is an ideal technique for

spies and assassins.

Sam expected to pierce the shield eventually. "It has to be done carefully so we don't destroy his memories."

Corr found explosive devices and weapons in the wolverines' pouches, but nothing he found bore indications of origin. He sensed he was overlooking something, and devoted a thoughtstream to the problem. He was confident he would find an answer.

* * *

Two unlikely friends visited Corr one day in June. While leaving the gym, he met the South Plains High School students, Cory and Rita.

"Mr. Syl, Rita and I agree with the ideas on sustainable populations," Cory said.

"Yes," said Rita. "We each received the new IUD implants and have formed a pact to adopt or have only one child if we ever have families."

"Please call me Corr. Do you think other students will go along?"

"Oh, they all will now," Rita said. "We'll make them."

The young women's decision reflected a social revolution occurring in Mountainview. In their speeches, elected leaders began replacing misdirection with honesty and reason. They encouraged independence and discouraged ignorance. Creativity and entrepreneurial energy exploded. Backyard gardens, small manufacturers, local services, and family-owned retail enterprises of all types proliferated. The Normount Corporation Commission received so many business filings it fell behind for the first time in its history.

One Christian evangelist joined the revolution and switched the emphasis of his sermons from isolation and materialism to tolerance and generosity. When his congregation began growing, other church leaders began to follow suit. Messages changed, and humanism began to rise.

Architects, engineers, and builders began creating compact, efficient designs. They studied the utopian experiments of the 19th century, the 20th-century planning experience, even the arcology ideas of Paolo Soleri. They also reviewed the rich source of ideas for alternate habitations in fiction and fantasy going back hundreds of years.

Certain outsiders observing the changes found the lack of cultural inertia or resistance to the new ideas frightening. Power could be lost so easily. Morgan Silverleaf later wrote that the brightest Humans had promoted a culture of ignorance and self-interest. Whereas before they must use deceit and repetition to reinforce their arguments, they now found that honesty and reason required no repetition. Illogical goals such growth in an already crowded society evaporated like frost in morning sunshine.

They began discussing ways to start shrinking the population. Overnight, they became statesmen.

Not everyone could adjust. City Planner Albert Morton signed the affidavit that stipulated the new goals, but after a few weeks he decided he would not change. His training and aspirations required growth. He applied for positions in other cities and soon moved his family away from Mountainview.

* * *

Rhya began talking with some of Wilson Smith's teachers about a new use for Lactella's venom. She proposed that Human limited mental ability was more functional than physical, and that with the secondary compounds from the venom, she could change the functions.

"We might implant memories of thought sequences just as we implanted emotions. Perhaps we can give them a simultaneous thinking experience that will persist. Let's see if we can't double IQs using the same procedures we applied to the soldiers."

Again, she had no trouble finding help, and soon had a team setting up an experiment. A call for Human volunteers produced a sufficient number and, within days, the first experiments began. Team members implanted experiences, and measured the results. Rhya and the others agreed that they would expand the treatments if the abilities persisted for at least 14 days. On the last day they tested the volunteers. In about half of the subjects, the new abilities had already faded away.

Both Wilson Smith and Whistol Farr recommended terminating the experiment. Farr said, "Rhya, the techniques will probably fade away in all the volunteers. Human brains just aren't capable of heightened awareness."

Rhya listened, but before she would give up she wanted to talk with the volunteers to see whether she could get any ideas about the failures. Twenty-eight Humans had taken the treatment. Sixteen had lost most of the new ability. Rhya interviewed all the failures and began on the successes. At first, she saw no differences; then, suddenly, she realized how the two groups differed. Volunteers who had jobs that enabled them to benefit from the techniques remained smarter. *Well, there you have it,* she thought. *Practice makes perfect.*

Rhya explained what she had found to Smith and Farr. Thereafter, she met no resistance expanding the experiment into a regular program. Corr Syl and everyone else delighted in the results of Rhya's experiment. They believed she had found the solution to the Human problem.

* * *

Piedmont flourished. Marion and her family returned to their home and helped with the restoration of roads, trails, and farms. Most of the Human farm workers joined in the effort in return for the right to develop small family farms in the area.

The future couldn't have looked brighter.

* * *

The Thomas children often used the gym, and the adults sometimes had lunch with Corr and Rhya.

One day about a month after the arrests, Marcie said, "Rhya, we would like to invite you and Corr to another dinner with the family. Are you free next Saturday?"

"Sure. What's the occasion?"

Marcie grinned. "Howard wants it to be a surprise."

On Saturday, just as they had done weeks earlier though it seemed like ages, Corr and Rhya walked to the Thomas home.

This time, Charlotte and Marcie met them at the door. Though unnecessary, Corr and Rhya placed their swords and packs in the hall closet where they had been placed last time.

"Everyone's in the backyard," Marcie said.

"Come and see our playhouse," Charlotte said, taking Rhya's hand. Soon both Rhya and Corr were chasing screaming children through doors and windows of a tiny version of the standard Human home.

After dinner, Howard made his announcement. "Rhya, I would like to make a request."

"Just a moment," AJ said. "First let me say that I wish to apologize for my earlier behavior. I'm afraid that the anti-Tsaeb attitude common in the police academy rubbed off on me. I was a fool to have behaved as I did, and I am sorry."

"Thank you, AJ," Corr said. "I'm very glad things worked out."

"We all are," Howard said. "Corr, we all wish to volunteer for the Tsaeb training program. We did some investigating and talked it over, and we believe it's a great opportunity."

* * *

Corr and Rhya spent all their time involved with day-to-day operations. Corr was in charge of a monitoring web, carefully observing the activities of the judiciary, police, and city leaders. Rhya was in charge of another web that monitored the progress of the drug-treated military personnel and the new techniques program. Corr felt happy around Rhya, but he was itching to get away from all the duties, preferably with her.

A day came when everyone could see that the reformation of Mountainview would not stop. Wilson Smith and other Embassy staff were signing up growing numbers of Humans who wanted to undergo drug-assisted training. Rhya, Corr, and Corr's battle group made plans to go home.

One afternoon, Corr decided to mend a loose pad under a harness strap. He and Rhya crossed the street to the park and sat under a tree while Corr worked on the pad.

"I guess a two-wolverine run is hard on equipment," Corr said.

"Hmm?" Rhya murmured, busily cleaning her own harness.

"Ralph said the speed of my flight from the wolverine deserved its own name: two wolverines."

Both rabbits chuckled and Corr winced with the memory of the impact of the Wolverine's arrow. "Damned Ralph," he said, holding his side. That set them both laughing, Corr hunched forward and Rhya leaning back on her hands.

In the midst of her laughter, Rhya gasped, "It should be a special retreat code for warriors: Two-wolverine! Two-wolverine!"

Corr rolled onto his back laughing, gripping his stomach.

Rhya laughed harder, but managed to wheeze, "Sorry."

Zuberi and Bill walked up, and Bill said, "What's so funny?"

Rhya sat up wiping her tears. "Hi, Zubilly," she said and started chortling again.

Corr's face contorted as he pulled up his knees and rolled onto his side.

Zuberi began chuckling, and Bill joined in.

"What is it?" Zuberi asked.

"Two-wolverine speed," Corr gasped, sitting up and wiping his eyes.

"What's that?"

That evening, Corr and Rhya walked through the park holding hands and talking about what they wanted to do. "Let's go to the ocean," Corr said.

Rhya didn't agree right then, but Corr felt sure she would join him.

* * *

On Friday, Corr suggested a return to Golden Court, the pub they'd visited when they'd first come to Mountainview. Rhya didn't want to go, but Ralph said they should. He wanted to see some bare legs and gold shorts. Perhaps he could do a little entertaining. The only empty table at the Golden Court was in the shadows beyond the dance floor. *Perfect,* Rhya thought.

Three young women at the next table began alternating their interest in the dancers with glances at the Tsaeb. A gold-clad young woman arrived and asked whether they wished to order drinks.

"Three glasses of beer," Corr responded.

"We have several brands on tap. Any preferences?"

"Dark will be fine, Miss," Ralph said.

"Coming right up," the young woman said with a smile.

As they took their first sips the dance ended and tables nearby filled with the warm bodies of young dancers.

In a moment, the band resumed. Corr prodded Rhya. "Let's dance."

The music had a good strong beat, and after a few half-steps while they studied the other dancers, they began similar movements. Soon after Corr and Rhya returned to their table, a young man Rhya asked to dance. Young women at the next table asked Corr and Ralph to dance.

Between dances, Corr began telling jokes. The space around their table filled with chairs and standing Humans. Soon the dancers became an audience roaring with laughter. Rhya rolled her eyes at Ralph, but she couldn't resist laughing along with the young Humans. She grinned as she wondered whether Corr would become a stand-up comedian in Human nightclubs.

PART FIVE: LI'S WAR

Treachery is trust violated. Trust based on false belief leads to grief. Trust earned with deceit leads to contempt.

Li's Assassins

The old General Li taught his son a great deal about the conduct of battles and war. Aaron learned rapidly, and the general could tell that one day he would be an excellent field commander. But battlefield knowledge would not be enough.

During the Border War, General Li's armies had lost every battle with the Tsaeb. Tsaeb commanders concentrated the right strength in the right place at the right time to defeat Human advances. They faded into the landscape when the Human armies achieved an advantage. They could not be lured into a trap, they appeared in unexpected places, they broke supply lines, they captured scouts, and they never let the Human soldiers rest. Tsaeb commanders were military geniuses more capable than anyone Li could set against them.

He finally realized that even the great ability of the Tsaeb leaders could be a weakness, and reasoned that these lords of war were probably district council members during peacetime. The war was over before his spies could verify the origin of the leaders.

The general never met the Tsaeb commanders or even heard their names. In surrender, he met only diplomats. The general burned with the insult. Of course, the Tsaeb leaders weren't disrespectful. They had simply returned to their normal lives—most as gleaners, and a few as printers, storeroom managers, and librarians. District counselors and other volunteers interested in setting up peace agreements came to meet the general.

* * *

The old general taught his son that defeating the Tsaeb required eliminating their leaders. The two began developing spy and assassin networks composed of Tsaeb misfits. The networks became Aaron Li's chief responsibility. By the time the Mountainview events occurred, he had infiltrators in place around the globe, and he had an army of more than 10,000 highly trained killers.

Misfit Tsaeb made excellent assassins. They tended toward the lower end of Tsaeb intelligence, but their capabilities exceeded those of any Human. They could use sensory webs, and they could manipulate their physiology to heal injuries and increase their strength and speed.

Li's training facilities in Shⓔnzo province developed loyalty as well as warcraft. He invented and supported a Tsaeb organization called the Organization for Fair Treatment for All (OFTA) that claimed to defend the rights of the unfortunate. Misfits who responded to promises of power and revenge became righteous crusaders.

As the assassin force grew, Li gave control to Ya Zhōu. Zhōu developed special units to search for likely Tsaeb to recruit, and he encouraged reproduction. The slow response surprised Zhōu and Li, who knew nothing of the powerful genes and memes that influenced Tsaeb reproduction. There were offspring, however, and Zhōu saw to it that children learned early the necessity of destroying Tsaeb civilization.

Children learned to honor their leaders and uphold military codes of behavior. Some became the bright young leaders of Li's covert forces. The schools did not teach Immediacy. They channeled the normal Tsaeb tendency toward responsible behavior into loyalty to their superiors and support for OFTA.

Halen

A Polar Bear named Halen commanded Zhōu's assassins. Halen would have developed to an excellent level five under normal circumstances, but he lost his parents before completing his education. The icy surface of the polar bears' home had thinned, and large fissures opened more and more frequently. One of those had swallowed Halen's parents.

Halen's training had not advanced to Immediacy or its derivative concept, Equivalency, the set of rules for dealing with others. He had no rules against killing sentient beings. Too young to survive by himself, Halen was lying on the ice, almost too weak to move, when a friendly sea bird stopped to investigate. Thereafter, Halen simply called for help whenever he became hungry. He killed only to survive, but satisfying his hunger reinforced the act of killing. Halen became contemptuous of his benefactors. He began to view their trusting altruism as naïve stupidity. He began to look forward to killing, and eventually came to kill for recreation as well as for food.

The council of the district in which Halen lived finally realized they had a monster in their midst and ordered his death. Wounded and pursued by a Tsaeb warrior, Halen had chanced upon one of Zhōu's training details. The leader of the detail recognized the bear's value and flew him away to safety and anonymity.

As Halen progressed through Zhōu's assassin training program, he matured into a ferocious fighter and a brilliant organizer. Within a few years, he became the leader of Zhōu's army of assassins.

Learning of the bear's desire to kill and his willingness to eat his fellow Tsaeb, Zhōu gave Halen responsibility for culling unfit recruits in return for Halen's promise of absolute secrecy. New recruits, banished for lack of ability or commitment, learned too late the supreme cost of failure. Zhōu had a special room provided for Halen's exit briefings. The room had a secret window from which Zhōu often watched Halen play with, and kill, his victims. Halen knew about the window, and often enhanced his performance for Zhōu's enjoyment. Zhōu invited Aaron Li to view Halen's kills. Li attended only once.

* * *

Zhōu established three spy networks: a Human network included officials at the highest levels of government and provided reports on troops, arms, and political movements; a network of Tsaeb assassins filled several roles, including infiltration and reporting from within Tsaeb communities. The assassins sought positions in the seven Continental Centers and many of the largest Tsaeb embassies; the third, smallest network included the best students of the Tsaeb assassin's school. Ya Zhōu developed it in secret, and kept it hidden from Li.

* * *

Li and Zhōu knew the Tsaeb council had approved Corr Syl's plan before Corr did. Li could have ordered Corr's assassination, but he decided to watch to see what would happen. The broad scope of the attack amazed him. The arrest of the Mountainview leaders came as a complete surprise. As subsequent parts of the plan unfolded and the arrested and released leaders began advocating sweeping changes, Li saw that Mountainview hadn't just lost a battle, it had lost its soul. He must intervene.

First Li sent the wolverine to kill Corr. When they failed, he decided that sending only two assassins for Corr had been a mistake, but one that could be rectified. He learned of Rhya's intervention with the assassins and her work with the spider venom, and he decided to kill two birds with one stone. Li directed Halen to prepare a foolproof plan for a double assassination.

The Continental Council Request

The North American Tsaeb Council described the Mountainview operation to other continental councils and exchanged views on the need for a global version. They proposed inviting Corr and Rhya to come to the center on Brushy Mountain to prepare a global plan.

As the changes in Mountainview began to manifest, the proposal for a global plan gained support. Finally, the seven continental councils unanimously adopted a resolution to put the global resources of the Tsaeb behind a project led by Corr and Rhya.

The resolution placed Corr in charge of developing a general plan and found volunteers to help organize fighters and resources. The resolution also gave Rhya responsibility for refining the attitude-adjustment techniques and supervising regional coordinators directing local operations. Corr and Rhya would have residence and research facilities for as many family and staff as they wished. They would have unlimited travel and communications support. The leaders of the Tsaeb civilization were asking the two rabbits to save the Human species.

Of course, the councils could not order Corr and Rhya to do anything. The North American Council sent requests to each rabbit. It did not occur to any members of the seven continental councils that either rabbit might refuse. Spies sent copies of the invitations to Li and Zhōu.

After receiving the invitation, Corr sat quietly for a while, and then went looking for Rhya. "Rhya, a remarkable request just came from the Continental Council."

"I think I have the same thing. They want me to expand the Human training projects," Rhya said.

"To the whole planet?"

"Yes. You too?"

"Yep."

"You won't go, will you?"

"Remember when we talked about going hiking,

perhaps making a trip to the ocean?"

"Yes."

"That's what I want to do. I'm not ready to become an administrator. Besides, don't you think there must be a lot of specialists in organization and administration who could do a better job? I want to return to Wycliff. Will you go with me?"

Rhya thought for a moment, then sighed and looked up. "I *would* like to go home for a visit, but I have to accept their offer."

Corr nodded.

"Corr, let's take some time to write detailed accounts of what we did. We can write instruction manuals with examples and potential alternatives. That will enable the continental councils to get the project started."

"Good idea."

During lunch, they told Farr about the requests and their decisions.

"Corr, I hope you'll reconsider. Replacing you may not be as easy as you think. Nevertheless, things here seem to be unfolding properly. It looks like Mountainview is improving. I don't see why you shouldn't go home. You know, many Tsaeb and Humans appreciate what you did here. We should hold a farewell party."

Rhya said, "Hmm, Whistol. Good idea. Let's invite some Humans too... maybe even a few of the leaders."

"Ah, yes—a perfect way to celebrate the beginning of the reformation!"

News of the party sparked excitement across Mountainview. The mayor and other city leaders offered to help with food and entertainment. Farr and the Embassy staff decided to hold the party in the park across the street and let the Embassy buildings serve as a resource facility. Organizers agreed to hold the party on Saturday, July 20.

Li Responds

From his quiet office in Taoso, Li saw the changes in Mountainview as a form of warfare by the Tsaeb. When he read Corr and Rhya's invitation to the North American Council headquarters, he knew the moment for which he had spent a lifetime preparing had come.

Aaron Li employed a secret team of professional war strategists charged with preparing for war with the Tsaeb. Their constantly evolving global battle plan included all members of the ICP. Li selected a plan and had Ya Zhou send out envoys. National commands would conduct the offensive, but target priorities, overall coordination, and timing would come from Li. The initial strike would include all seven continental councils, all 49 embassies, and more than half of the 4200 Tsaeb districts.

Halen's assassins would execute the first stage of Li's war. They would make surprise attacks on the continental councils, embassies, and 400 of the district centers. The assassins would eliminate the Tsaeb leaders. They would complete their assignments and pull back before the full attack. Li asked Halen to lead the Mountainview Embassy attack.

"I want you to take charge of the Mountainview operation. Send me the heads of Corr Syl and Rhya Bright. I will pickle them to use as a warning to Tsaeb leaders. In return, I will give you their community of Wycliff—a private larder for your use."

The big bear smiled. "As you wish."

It only remained to choose the date for the attack.

* * *

When Li learned of the upcoming Mountainview celebration, he decided to launch the Human offensive on the night of the party. At 11:00 p.m., teams of assassins would enter Tsaeb district centers, embassies, and continental centers to eliminate leaders. At midnight, an aerial bombardment would strike the centers and embassies. As the dust settled, paratrooper teams would land and hold the targets until an occupation force arrived.

There would be one exception: an advance team of assassins led by Halen would find and kill Corr and Rhya. Halen's team would enter the Mountainview Embassy just ahead of the assassins assigned to hunt and kill Whistol Farr, Sam Whortin, the other section chiefs, and any members of Corr's mobile command group who happened to be present. Li's infiltrators in the embassies and district centers would help the assassin teams destroy long-range weapons and communications systems. Later, the infiltrators would serve as interim administrators within the Tsaeb districts.

Eliminating Tsaeb leaders would give the advantage to the Human armies. To help restrain any survivors of the assassin attack, the Human occupation forces would capture and imprison all Tsaeb found near the Embassies and centers.

* * *

While Ya Zhōu was having the plan delivered to ICP members, Li reviewed the overall situation. He wanted a better understanding of what had prompted the Tsaeb to take action in Mountainview. He knew about the Piedmont prisoners, and he knew about the military forays across the border, but he didn't know the reasons. He made inquiries, and he learned about Ivan Johns.

Li guessed there was something special about Johns that had prompted him to enlist corporate and military aid to expand his city into Tsaeb lands. When he learned that Johns had evaded the Tsaeb arrests, he ordered him found and brought to Xi'ou.

Li's reports on Mountainview seemed odd. Tsaeb domination should have left the city's residents depressed or defiant, but his reports indicated neither.

Li visited Mountainview a week before the party. Pedestrians filled the sidewalks, but the streets carried few vehicles. Many streets were blocked, and some had been stripped of pavement to the bare ground. Li puzzled over this until he passed a blocked street and saw hundreds of people removing the pavement. Had they gone crazy? He stopped his limousine and stepped out onto the sidewalk. The work force included men, women, and children. Laughter was common, and small children were darting about. As Li watched, people walking by smiling and even said hello to the tall old man in the blood-red silk cloak and felt slippers.

Li abruptly ducked into his limousine and made a hurried trip home.

Corr and Rhya's Reports

During the weeks leading up to the party, Corr and Rhya worked on comprehensive reports of their actions in Mountainview. They did everything together, but they sensed things were changing. They didn't smile as often as they had in the past.

The rabbits spent their evenings in the Tea Room. As party time approached, the Embassy population swelled as volunteers helping with party preparations appeared and stayed, and families of Wycliff District residents began to arrive. Dinnertime became a major event.

The two rabbits developed a version of Corr's plan that could be applied anywhere. They included information packets, sample bench warrants, and visual records of arrests. They made changes and recommendations based on Mountainview experience, and they included a full account of Rhya's operation, including an analysis of the compounds, complete sets of personality tests, and results of dosage applications.

"Rhya, we need a more general complaint against the leaders. Here in Mountainview, we had criminal acts that justified the arrests. Other districts and embassies will not have such obvious crimes by their local Human leaders," Corr said.

"How about paying them?" Rhya asked.

"Maybe, but it would take much larger bribes than Wilson used. It wouldn't be a hundred percent effective, and those who refused to participate would criticize and sow doubt."

"What about environmental pollution? That's at the heart of the problem. Maybe other districts can claim they are threatened by environmental degradation from chemicals originating in Human cities and towns and call that a treaty violation."

Corr pondered. "I don't know how you get the Humans to accept that. Let's ask Elisa Loret if she has any ideas."

Elisa Loret directed them to a specialist in a new field

of Human science called ecological services. They learned that the concept of environmental valuation was well developed and already familiar to the Humans.

"That gives us a measurable basis for civil suits and orders to desist," Rhya said.

Corr and Rhya discussed the issue with Farr and an Embassy lawyer.

The lawyer said, "The districts won't be able to win such cases in Human courts. They will have to use district council rulings. Humans will ignore such rulings, but the rulings give the Tsaeb the necessary standing to issue citations. To issue arrest warrants you need something stronger."

"Well, if the Humans ignore the citations we can issue warrants, can't we?" asked Corr.

"Yes, but arresting and holding leaders will require something stronger," the lawyer replied.

"A similar issue is the loss of species," Rhya said. "Couldn't we argue that it is criminal to kill other species, especially if extinction occurs?"

"Okay, let's combine those ideas," Corr said. "The Humans are causing deaths and localized breaks in ecosystem processes whenever they build something. Their cities and industries release toxic pollutants. Those acts cause harm. Let's start the report by saying that the first step is for continental councils to issue complaints to regional Human governments. The complaints can call for immediate halts to the criminal activities of releasing pollutants. If the Humans ignore the complaints, almost a certainty, arrests can follow."

"Would you like me to call for a team of lawyers to draft complaints, citations, and follow-up arrest orders?" Farr said.

"Yes," Rhya said. "But it might be best to get this started at the Continental Center."

Finally, the rabbits wrote summaries of their reports and gave the reports to Farr to review. At last, a few days before the party, the rabbits produced a final report to send to the Continental Center. As they took a final look through the report, Corr brought up a question.

"One thing bothers me—where is Johns? It may sound histrionic, but there really is evil loose in the world. He might not be the only one. Perhaps we should include a chapter on him. If we insist, the Continental Council would probably start a search."

"We can do it tonight. Shall we go down for some food?"

"Yes," Corr said, and issued a challenge. "Last one there...."

And with that, the two laughing gray streaks launched themselves along the balcony and down the stairs.

The Party

Visitors filled the Embassy and the grounds on the day of the party. Though there was room for all to sleep within the Great Hall, many had chosen to sleep outside under the full, leafy trees beneath a bright, gibbous moon. In the clear air at sunrise, Corr and Rhya were sitting on the bench outside the Embassy entrance marveling at all the activity in the park.

The party officially began at noon. Welcoming speeches were brief and heavily applauded. Whistol Farr spoke about the contributions Corr and Rhya had made to the future of Mountainview. Arden Aquila thanked Corr for his service to the community. Then, to the amusement of everyone except Corr and Rhya, Wild Bill described the subtle maneuvers Corr had undertaken to place Rhya in his group for the journey south from Juniper Mesa, and Ralph Mäkinen defined Two-Wolverine Speed.

Finally, facing a delighted crowd, Corr and Rhya thanked everyone for coming, and wished them all a fabulous day.

Later in the day, Jonas Miller, Halbert Sims, and an unfamiliar warrior joined Corr and Rhya.

"Great party," Halbert said, after introducing the other warrior and describing her as a friend.

"We're heading back to the Center, and I wanted to congratulate you before we left. You have done very well," Sims said. "I am proud to have served as your teacher, Corr.
"

"Yes, you both did a great job," Miller said. "I'm leaving, too. I'll travel with Halbert, but I don't plan to stop at the Center. Rhya, come see me when you have some time."

Following an afternoon of conversation and entertainment, volunteers set up a long line of tables and partiers helped bring food from the Embassy. In the long line moving past the tables, the Humans were just another Tsaeb species.

After dinner, a Wycliff DJ took over the sound system

with a few sweet melodies, but soon he had everyone dancing wildly with his selections. Thus, on a fine day in the middle of summer, Humans and Tsaeb ate, danced, and sang together, differences forgotten. Everything was perfect.

After a few dances, Rhya and Corr's battle group gathered beside the Embassy entrance. The warriors were headed for home. They planned to make a leisurely trip, camping that night just north of the border and resting another night near Ralph's home. Corr and Rhya would stay one more day to say farewell to the visitors from other districts and from the Continental Center.

At 10:00 p.m., Whistol Farr, Arden Aquila, and the Mountainview mayor took the stage, invited everyone to come to the Embassy for brunch in the morning, and wished everyone a good night. A warm sense of brotherhood filled the hearts of the thousands of members within hundreds of species in the park. For them all the future had become a brighter, more beautiful place. Like everyone else, the large polar bear wandering through the park found the mood quite delightful.

Rhya Falls

At midnight, Rhya and Corr were standing on the balcony outside their rooms gazing over a peaceful scene. Sleeping partiers covered the floor of the Great Hall. As the two warriors' tactical senses began throbbing, they scanned the inside of the building intensely.

"Rhya, let's take a look around outside."

As they walked across the hall, a small crowd of Humans emerged from the entry tunnel and stopped in a tight group before the entrance. Corr sensed terror. There were Tsaeb among them, including a large white creature. Then the Tsaeb and some of the Humans moved back into the entrance tunnel.

The white giant boomed, "Hello folks! Look here!"

Corr shouted, *"Get down! Bomb!"*

The sudden huge blast sent thousands of bits of shrapnel ripping through the hall.

Howard and Marcie Thomas had gone to the Tea Room looking for Corr and Rhya when pieces of shrapnel ricocheted around the room. The total silence that followed soon filled with the cries of injured and frightened occupants of the Great Hall.

Howard crept up to the door and peered in. Shrapnel had smashed the parrot statue off to his right, and beyond it, in the midst of the hall, Corr stood and walked briskly toward the central column carrying a lifeless body.

* * *

Several bits of shrapnel had struck Rhya. Shielded by a stone bench, Corr had suffered only a shallow groove in his left shoulder. The Humans at the entrance all died, and many Tsaeb throughout the hall were dead or injured. Eyes closed, body unmoving, Rhya fought to survive. Her right femur was broken. There was an entry wound under her rib cage, a ragged exit wound on her right side, and another wound on her left temple. Corr determined her heartbeat and respiration were acceptable, then turned his full attention to the Tsaeb at the entrance.

A group of armored Tsaeb poured into the Great Hall. The large white individual was a polar bear. The bear was scanning the hall, and his thoughts held images of Corr and Rhya. Corr scooped up Rhya, moved out of sight behind the column, and began running toward the wall near the alcove where the balcony ledge passed through the floor and became a ramp to lower levels.

The ramp entrance would be visible to the intruders. When Corr reached the wall and had to leave the cover of the column, he slowed, shielding Rhya as well as he could. He shifted his fur and walked toward the ramp. Halfway there the bear spotted him. With silent intensity, the assassins ran toward him. Corr responded with a burst of speed.

Howard saw Corr change course for the ramp, realized he was carrying Rhya, and saw another Tsaeb with a drawn sword running to intercept Corr. Howard shouted, but so many shouts were filling the air he doubted Corr heard him. The Tsaeb coming up behind Corr was closing rapidly. Desperate, Howard yanked off a shoe and, with another shout, hurled it as hard as he could. The Tsaeb ducked, but barely slowed.

This time Corr heard Howard. He glanced back and saw his pursuer. As he reached the ramp entrance, two more Tsaeb leapt toward him. Corr barely slowed. Holding Rhya with one arm, he drew his long sword, ducked a thrust by the Tsaeb running up behind him, and spun to cut all three.

Running down the ramp, Corr switched more of his attention to the tunnel ahead.

The Tsaeb Response

Corr's battle group headed north and camped near the Center Cache after leaving the party. They were sitting around a camp light chatting with local residents when Bill jumped up and Quin landed.

Quin cried, "Bill, can you sense Corr?"

After a moment Bill said, "It's faint. What's happened?"

"There was a bomb blast inside the Embassy. Many are hurt."

Ralph dashed away with Allysen and Ankolla close behind.

A nighthawk called, "The Plainview fleet of eight heavies is in the air, and troops are boarding transport planes. Our aerial spotters stopped no bombers."

"All right," Quin said. "Let's see... Bill, Zuberi, let's make sure Shorel, Sims, and Aquila know." He turned to a small swift perched nearby. "Peter, get help to survey the area around the center and the Embassy for any foreign Tsaeb. They might be wearing steel helmets and body armor."

"Will the centers be destroyed?"

"No worries. The embassies and district centers might be harmed by nuclear weapons, but the Humans have none of those ready for use. We know of nothing stronger than their 900-pound chemical bombs. Those produce massive overpressure and heat, but apart from shrapnel that might fly up to two miles, the bombs cannot harm our drahsalleh-coated structures."

Quin paused and thought for a moment. "Okay, here's what we'll do. First, we'll make sure Sam, Whistol, and the council get the long-range weapons ready. Then, we'll begin forming two crisis armies, weapons only. Sims needs to lead a Force-2 group of 2,058 fighters into the District Center. Call on residents north of the center. We'll call up a Force-4 group from residents near here. I want you two to get them inside the Embassy by 5:00 a.m. We'll ask Shorel to form a Force-4 group equipped for a three- to four-day deployment to the Embassy. We can expect large forces to approach the Embassy on the highways. Tsaeb and Humans must be warned to either get inside the Embassy and district center by 6:00 a.m., or to move beyond the blast zone. Damn. That will be hard for the Mountainview Humans. Our long-range weapons had better work."

Zuberi said, "Bill can start assembling the force. I'll get the sleeping gas reserves from the cache."

Quin looked around. "Right. Other ideas? Okay, we have to hope Ralph, Allysen, and Ankolla can help Corr and Rhya stabilize the situation at the Embassy. I'm going to assemble and lead a Force-1 group of aerial fighters to the Mountainview airport."

In the Tunnels

As he carried Rhya down the basement ramp, Corr searched his memory for a safe place to stop and tend Rhya's wounds. The head wound had limited her internal defenses. She had controlled some of the bleeding, but not enough. Without help, she would die soon.

After two more circuits, the ramp would curl into a tightening spiral that ended in a corridor around a massive platform supporting the central column of the Great Hall. Crevices radiated from the corridor into the surrounding rock. One crevice—but Corr did not know which one—led to a hidden exit in a large jumble of boulders northeast of the Embassy.

As he entered the tightening spiral, Corr decided to slow his pursuers. He laid Rhya beside the wall, drew both swords, reoriented his fur, and ran silently at full speed back up the ramp. He encountered and killed two rabbits without having to slow. A moment later, he ran into a string of five. Thrusting and slashing he managed to kill them all, but in the process he lost his momentum. Knowing the remaining ten attackers would have sensed the attacks, he ran back to Rhya, picked her up, and continued into the spiral while using various aerosols to mask his and Rhya's scent.

At the column foundation, Corr found rough-hewn passages forking left and right. Seeing nothing to help him choose, he ran left a few dozen paces noting several wide crevices. Then he ran back to the fork and ran right. He immediately found a rough opening that led away from the column base. He sent a pulse of sound into it, and from the echoes, determined the opening would become too narrow to pass. He ran on and found two openings close together. Echoes inconclusive, he ran on past a few more crevices, released faint scents, and returned. He ran a few paces down the second tunnel, allowed a scent of blood to escape and returned. Then, suppressing everything, including his breath, he ran down the first tunnel.

Often scrambling over rock falls, Corr hurried along in the dark. After a hundred yards, the tunnel branched. Corr left clues in both branches, then in full suppression ran down the left branch. He used the same strategy several times, alternating left and right. He soon realized he had gone too far to be on the path to the emergency exit. Rhya was running out of time.

He decided to stop and tend to Rhya's injuries until the intruders brought the fight to him. In full suppression, he entered the next tunnel branching to the right. After a hundred feet, he gently laid Rhya on a flat shelf of rock and began studying her injuries.

"Corr," Rhya said softly. "Leave me and go. They need you in the Embassy."

"Let's rest awhile first," Corr said.

Corr used his sensory fields to explore Rhya's wounds. Her skull was fractured, and it appeared that one or more pieces of shrapnel had disintegrated and scattered throughout her body. It had damaged her liver, her aorta, and her small and large intestines. Rhya's automatic defenses had sealed most of the major artery damage, but the aorta and many smaller veins were still leaking. The greatest immediate danger came from a hematoma forming beneath the skull fracture. The pressure would soon begin causing brain damage, and it would end Rhya's ability to limit the aortal bleeding.

Corr held Rhya close and began using his sensory fields to seal off damaged vessels feeding the hematoma. He had to concentrate everything on the work. Once he got enough of the bleeding stopped, he would begin the task of constructing a lymph conduit to drain the hematoma. The hematoma continued to grow. With a last scan of his surroundings, Corr gave up all his defenses and added the nets of his automatic warning system to the job of repairing injuries. Gradually his mind's connection to his external senses faded as he fought to save Rhya.

* * *

When Halen reached the base of the central column, he sent assassins in both directions. Soon they returned and reported the rabbits must have gone into a crevice. Halen could smell fresh blood. He divided his group into teams of two to search the crevices. Meeting Corr in a narrow tunnel would be dangerous, so he warned the teams to call for reinforcements when they found the two rabbits. Halen established his command post at the base of the column platform and exhorted his assassins to work fast.

* * *

The assassins holding the Humans at the Embassy entrance did not survive very long. Sam Whortin had flooded the tunnel with gas, but when that only affected the Humans, he shifted to swords. He and several members of EDAS used a secret door in the entry tunnel and caught the assassins by surprise. They wounded and captured one assassin, and they killed two.

As they finished, a group of at least 50 Tsaeb came running up the tunnel and began attacking Sam's team. Sam sent a call for help and began a slow retreat up the tunnel. More fighters joined him. Soon, hundreds of Embassy staff and guests joined the battle.

Unable to defeat the intruders while they held the tunnel entrance, and taking continuous losses, Sam called Whistol Farr. "Whistol, the stuff Rhya used to brainwash the soldiers—is there any left?"

"Yes, I think so. Why?"

"Maybe we can spray it into the tunnel and knock these bastards out."

"How much do you want?"

"We can use a pressure washer. Bring five gallons."

Farr returned in minutes with two sealed one-quart canisters. "This is all we have."

"It'll have to do. Let's try mixing the stuff."

"Able, ask the systems operator to close the upper vents so air pressure will build up in the hall and create a breeze down the tunnel."

EDAS fighters placed the pressure-washer at the side of the entrance and placed the siphon in the bucket. Sam signaled an emergency retreat. "Okay, Whistol, let's see how these guys like this fog."

The fog wilted the Tsaeb assassins like lettuce leaves licked by flame. Sam learned later that he had used a thousand times the quantity of Lactella's compounds needed to knock out the intruders.

"Good," said Sam. "Now, let's go hunting downstairs."

* * *

Halen was waiting to hear from the crevice searchers when he heard rapid footsteps. One of the sentries he had left at the ramp entrance ran up. "Our second team is down."

Halen thought for a moment. "Set two proximity bombs on the floor across from one another 50 feet inside the entrance. Place two more bombs high on the wall across from one another a hundred feet farther down the tunnel. Set all the bombs for a five-second delay. When the Embassy security force approaches, let yourself be seen, then run back here."

The first set of bombs wiped out most of Sam's security force. Sam and three others leading the way had run past the explosions and were unharmed. Sam returned to the main hall to assemble a new force. Messengers from Quin arrived and explained that three warriors would arrive soon, and urged Sam to prepare the long-range weapons. Sam decided to do that and let the warriors handle the tunnel.

* * *

Ralph detected an odd scent lingering in the Embassy entry tunnel. He held his breath, ran to the hall and beheld a tragic scene. A cluster of Sam's EDAS caps lay at the basement ramp entrance, and he ran to them. Learning that Corr, Rhya, and their pursuers had gone down the tunnel, he dashed in. A guard shouted after him, "Watch out for the bombs and the polar bear!

Ralph spotted and disabled the second set of bombs and sprinted on down the tunnel. He sensed a powerful presence ahead and guessed it was the bear. Hoping the bear carried a Dao like the wolverine, he prepared his attack plan. Running silently and invisibly at full speed, he spun through the tightening spirals of the ramp.

Sensing Ralph's approach, Halen whipped out his sword and swept it in a smooth diagonal arc down from his right to his left, but Ralph had dropped to the floor in a slide that took him between Halen's legs. As he passed, Ralph thrust his short sword into the bear's groin. Rising and turning as he slammed into the base of the pillar, he swept his long sword through a smooth arc, decapitating the bear. He whipped around, turning his attention to the tunnels. He paused for a moment, then trotted into the right-hand opening. He passed the first tunnel and paused for a second when he reached the two openings close together. Then he entered the first tunnel.

Trotting along the path Corr had taken, Ralph met and killed two intruders and hurried on. After a few minutes, he entered the chamber and found Corr and Rhya.

Corr looked up. "Ralph?"

"It's a rescue, old boy," Ralph whispered. He gathered the two rabbits in his arms and ran back through the tunnels and up the ramp. Reaching the hall, he shouted for help and soon had several powerful minds assisting Corr.

In a few minutes, Corr relaxed his concentration and stood. He looked at Ralph, grinned, and abruptly sat down. "Whew. Thanks, Ralph. What's going on?"

"I don't know." He bent to study the bloody furrow across Corr's shoulder. "Let's get Sam to give us an update."

"Did you see the big polar bear?"

"Yes. He was a head taller than me." Ralph grinned.

* * *

Like waves of a single storm striking a rocky cliff, the Human attack made little impression on Tsaeb civilization. Only 22 Federation bombers evaded the Tsaeb long-range weapons and no Tsaeb structures were seriously damaged. Tsaeb fighters overran and destroyed most troop transports en route. The bombs killed many Humans around the bombed embassies and destroyed huge areas of vegetation and soil around the bombed district centers.

Almost 14,000 Tsaeb died in battles with Li's spies and assassins—many of them were members of district and continental councils—but Human casualties exceeded one million. Many soldiers died on their way to battles, but many more civilians living near the bombed Tsaeb embassies died. Had all the Human bombers reached their targets, millions more innocent Humans would have died.

Even the least-involved citizens felt outrage at their leaders' criminal lack of concern for their people. Tsaeb leaders now had everything they needed to apply Corr Syl's plan worldwide. A global assembly of councils agreed unanimously to ask Corr and Rhya to come immediately to Brushy Mountain and launch their plans.

Ya Zhōu

Li sat in his dark study reading the mind-numbing reports. Only in Asia and Australia did the Human military remain in control. The Tsaeb had taken everything else. In one week, the Tsaeb had annulled decades of planning and had destroyed almost all Human forces. As Li scanned through the sheaf of bleak reports, he noticed that his agents had arrested Ivan Johns. With no clear purpose in mind, he requested Johns brought in.

Lactella was terrified. Johns had been arrested by a military unit wearing strange uniforms, then flown a great distance and locked in a small room. Now, guards handcuffed and shackled him and brought him to stand in a shadowy room occupied only by an old man flipping through a stack of papers. Standing there in the heavy silence of Li's workroom, Lactella's thoughts vibrated about like web-tethered moths. She realized that facing her across a small table was probably the most powerful figure she had ever encountered.

At last, Li raised his gaze and studied Johns for a moment. He sensed there was something wrong with the man. He asked a few questions about Johns' origins and occupation, but his interest quickly faded. Nodding at something Johns said, Li turned his attention to the garden outside his window.

Lactella began disengaging from Johns' system.

Li's thoughts filled with scenes from Mountainview. Those people had been happy. Recently defeated by the Tsaeb, they should have been at least as unhappy as city dwellers normally were. They were immersed in crowds of strangers, noise, and smoke. They faced a daily struggle to acquire money for food, water, and safety. They lived with increasing poverty, crime, pollution, and uncertainty. And now, an enemy had taken over their government. Struck by a thought that caused him to jerk his head, Li suddenly understood why the people in Mountainview were happy. They had accepted the Tsaeb way of life. And suddenly Li saw it: the enemy of the Humans was not the Tsaeb. It was Humans.

Lactella locked Johns' muscles, tore into his esophagus, and began dragging her swollen abdomen up John's narrow throat.

Li took a new look into his past. Pride had fueled his father's hatred of the Tsaeb. Suddenly, a bright light of comprehension illuminated many things clearly for the first time, and he saw what he must do. He didn't notice the thin black legs in the corners of Johns' mouth or the eight glittering black eyes peering from between his parted lips.

Li thought of his granddaughter and smiled. She would love the Tsaeb. Thinking of Mountainview, he wrote a note to his wife, telling her that he had finally found the perfect spot for a vacation, and that she should take their daughter and granddaughter and leave immediately for the city of Mountainview. He and some of the household staff would join her in four days. Li suggested that upon her arrival, she should ask for a local celebrity named Corr Syl. He beckoned a young man who appeared and bowed. Li asked him to deliver the note to his wife and accompany her to the airport.

When the young man appeared, Lactella froze and began searching the shadows behind Li.

Li flipped open a recorder. *Where is Ya?* First, he would order his forces to suspend operations and call for a truce. Then he would request a meeting with the Tsaeb central council in Europe. Finally, he would invite Tsaeb into the lands he controlled. Once a powerful enemy, Li would now become a powerful friend. He glanced out the window. The sun was shining, and abruptly he was weary of his dark study. Today he would walk in the garden. Aaron Li smiled.

Lactella was poised to slip out of Johns' mouth, slide to the floor, and approach Li under the desk when a door opened and Ya Zhōu walked up behind Li.

A father's hatred had not influenced Ya Zhōu. He had known all along that the Tsaeb had good intentions and that Human developments led toward a bad end. But Zhōu delighted in power and wealth, and he feared he would lose both if the Tsaeb ever gained control. He had hoped fervently that Li's strategy would work, but since it hadn't, he intended to hang on to what power remained. Aaron Li had failed. Ya Zhōu's time had come.

Zhōu withdrew a small device from his robe, stepped forward, and laid a comradely hand on Li's shoulder. As the most powerful man on Earth sagged back in his chair, Zhōu looked up and said, "All out."

Appearing out of the shadows, three women bowed and left.

Alone now with his friend and mentor and an unmoving Ivanstor Johns , Zhōu pushed Li onto the floor, rolled him onto his back, and drew a gleaming dagger. With no more than a slight hesitation, Zhōu plunged the dagger up through Li's diaphragm into his heart. Then Zhōu clasped Li's hands around the dagger, rolled Li over, and lifted his chest onto a footstool. As blood spread around the body, Zhōu walked to a cabinet and returned with a long sword. He chopped downward on Li's neck and then sawed with the sword until Li's head fell to the floor. Zhōu picked up Li's recorder, replaced the tape, and called loudly for assistance.

When the guards returned, Zhou ordered, "Place this man in the disposal cell and have the cell emptied in the morning." As the guards pulled a petrified Johns away, Lactella retreated down her host's bleeding throat, her mind blank with terror, a scream pressing on her throat.

Corr's Decision

Two weeks after Li's war ended, Corr, Rhya, and Corr's battle group met for dinner in the Tea Room. The war had changed many things.

As soon as a new Mountainview ambassador volunteered, Whistol Farr would go to Brushy Mountain to replace the assassinated Chairman of the Continental Council. Farr had asked Able Remington to take over the position of Executive Administrator for the North American Council.

Corr's battle group would soon be making their last trip together. Ralph had accepted a request from Duncan Mäkinen for warrior training. Allysen had received and accepted a similar request from Lila Bright. Ankolla would remain with Allysen and assist with Lila's training. Zuberi and Bill would serve on the Wycliff Council, and Quin was joining Athol's battle group. Rhya, who was now fully recovered, had agreed to go to Brushy Mountain and help implement a global version of her Human treatments. She and Able Remington were leaving for Brushy Mountain in the morning.

Corr Syl no longer knew what he wanted. The attack by the assassins that had nearly killed Rhya, and then the surprise attack by the Human armies, had changed things. His highest duty was to go to Brushy Mountain and help solve the Human problem—but there was his plan.

"Corr, have you decided?" asked Ralph.

"No. I have something to do first."

* * *

In the shadowless light of early dawn, Corr came within striking distance of his childhood friend, the mountain lion, Allon Trofeld. The lion was kneeling at the edge of a live oak thicket. Leaves had covered the dry ground. There were no tracks or other signs of the lion's presence. He was hunting. He did not know that his every move was monitored and that every potential victim and been warned away. The rabbit studied his friend. *Is he shaking?* Sorrow overcame Corr as he remembered all those times in their childhood when he had failed to understand his friend's need. *But the deaths, and poor Lisa....* Corr let his mind fill with the memories and the sadness. After a moment, he sent some of the memories away to a shadowy valley in his memory world. He accelerated his reactions, released his scent and sensory webs, and allowed his fur to reflect light.

His auburn eyes intense, arms loose at his sides, hilts of crossed swords rising above his shoulders, the warrior spoke. "Hello, Allon."

The big cat twitched, turned his round yellow eyes on the small rabbit, and purred, "Ah, Corr the warrior. It's been a long time. Are you here for breakfast?" Then, without drawing a breath, the great cat leapt toward the rabbit swinging his stick.

Corr initiated an ancient combat technique. He sprang forward to meet the attack. As he slammed into the wide chest, he grabbed Trofeld's vest, kicked sideways, and swung onto the broad neck. As Trofeld tucked his head and dropped his shoulder to make a crushing roll, Corr drove his short sword between the lion's atlas and second cervical vertebrae, snapping the dens, and driving the blade down into the spinal cord. He jumped clear as Trofeld's roll became a sprawl. Then Corr dove in, plunged his sword beneath the rib cage, and severed the descending aorta.

Trofeld thrashed as latent nerve impulses and spasms shook his body. When they passed, Corr approached and knelt beside his friend. After a moment Trofeld whispered, "Thank you, Corr. Regret finally becomes the greatest emotion."

"Goodbye, Allon."

Then, as if he'd remembered a joke, a faint smile appeared on cat's face. His body relaxed and his eyes dulled.

Corr remained beside Allon until the harvesters came; then he rose and inventoried Allon's possessions. He found letters addressed to Allon's mother and father and to himself. Corr's contained three sentences: *Good luck on Brushy Mountain. Oh, you, a comedian? Forget about it.*

Corr smiled with moist eyes.

Corr tucked the letters in his pack and picked up the stick. He stared at it for a moment and then dropped it beside the body, He nodded to the harvesters and trotted away.

That night, Corr reflected on his life before this eventful year. Memories of his childhood goals were precious, but no longer compelling. He felt relieved. With Allon's passing, Corr's distaste for responsibility had evaporated; duty had become desire. He looked up at a sky marred by jet trails and the lingering stain of Mountainview's glare. It was time to go to Brushy Mountain.

But first, Corr would go to the Wycliff District Center. He wanted to thank Aquila for appointing him Agent of the council, and then formally resign that position. He also wanted to make a farewell visit to the Tavern.

In the morning, he would adjust his ivy a last time and leave for Brushy Mountain. He thought about Alex Maypole and the rock-paper-scissors contests. He realized he now knew how to pierce the squirrel's shield and anticipate his throws, but he felt no desire to do so. He would go late to the morning match, and afterward have breakfast with Alex, Tau, and his other friends. He wanted to tell his new story about Ralph and the polar bear.

The End

Appendix A. Origin of the Tsaeb Civilization

The Tsaeb are the descendants of intelligent creatures who evolved far in the past and whose physical and cultural evolution gave them mastery of their bodies and Earth's natural systems.

Billions of years after the Earth formed, the first living, self-replicating organisms appeared. Evolution progressed, and after another billion years, complex organisms became common. Among these, mutations and the random process of evolution produced an occasional species with extra connections and tissue within their brains. Not needed to operate muscles or sensory apparatus, the extra tissue added memory, emotion, and insight.

Intelligence first appeared in the seas, but it was during the long age of the dinosaurs that sentient creatures invented complex social and physical systems. In those times, intelligence was not great. The early intelligent beings had only a partial understanding of the world around them. They could only be certain of their immediate sensations and their emotions, their appetites, and their desires. Sparks of genus flared, but did not last. Conflict and war were incessant.

After great natural catastrophes ended the dinosaurs, sentient mammal species proliferated. What had been rare genius among the dinosaurs became common. Mammals mastered genetics, ended disease and senescence, and reshaped their bodies. They devised machines and weapons of great power. In spite of their expanded intelligence, mammals, like dinosaurs, were ruled by their fears and desires. The dinosaurs were never at peace, but in the new age of the mammals, war became far more destructive. The mammals' first ten million years spanned the Paleocene epoch of Earth's geologic history. It was an Age of War.

In dark times near the end of the Paleocene, the mammals brought the Earth itself to the edge of existence. Species numbers and needs increased rapidly. Massive industries poisoned the soil, the water, and the air, and global temperature rose. Weeds and fires covered the land, and the stability and productivity of Earth's biosphere plummeted. Battles over dwindling resources became ever more devastating. As each great species faced the finality of extinction, the risk of a doomsday act of desperation or vengeance enveloped Earth like a dark shroud.

Natural forces caused the dinosaur extinction. Sentient self-indulgence, like a great river approaching a falls, carried the mammals toward their apocalypse. But on the eve of oblivion, like crocus blossoms peeping through January snow, wisdom began to appear. Some mammals sought and achieved control of fear and desire. They crossed the threshold to sapience.

Descendants of some of the eldest mammals, the cottontail rabbits, were first. They defined the goals, disciplines, and traditions that transmuted sentience into sapience. These small creatures began the revolution in a time of great physical hardship and danger. Individual survival required strength, endurance, and knowledge of defense, combat, and war. The warrior specialty emerged as a global guild unified by knowledge and purpose. Sapient warriors from species of the land, air, and sea became Earth's greatest power.

Going beyond one's fears and appetites to sapience requires a high degree of intelligence, self-discipline, and foresight. Warriors recognized these traits and unified them in an ethical system they called Immediacy. It is a simple fact that the consequences of one's actions are most evident in one's immediate vicinity. Immediacy, the philosophy of consequences, strives for balance in all conditions, concepts, and creatures.

Like the fertile layer of ash left by a firestorm, sapience and Immediacy covered the Earth. The warriors fought many battles with individuals and species that did not accept Immediacy. By the end of the twenty-million year Eocene epoch of Earth's geologic history, a sapient civilization following Immediacy covered the globe. But as you know, dangerous individuals and species appear from time to time, and civilization needs its defenders.

History of the Tsaeb. Introduction.
Morgan Silverleaf, Librarian of Wycliff District

APPENDIX B. PEOPLE & PLACES

Human characters belong to a single species, *Homo sapiens*. They have all the variability in stature, coloring, and facial features found on our Earth.

Tsaeb characters include numerous intelligent species of mammals, birds, reptiles, and arthropods. Mammals and reptiles have evolved toward similar forms, but they retain some of their original features, especially their coloration and skin covering. Birds and spiders retain their original forms though many have hands, and some are larger than their progenitors.

People

Name: Role

Aaron Li: The hidden power of Human nation of Taoso

Able Remington: Chief assistant to Whistol Farr

Adisa Lin: Visited Piedmont and Embassy

Alan Horowitz: Executive Assistant to William Ellison, Chief of Federation Armed Forces

Allen James Thomas: Detective married to Millicent

Albert Morton: Mountainview City Planner

Alexander Maypole: Corr Syl's nemesis

Alice Thomas: Daughter of AJ and Millicent

Allen Boyer: Owner of the Tsaeb Diner

Allen Thomas: Father of Howard and Allen James ('AJ')

Allon Trofeld: Corr Syl's friend and convicted murderer

Allysen Olykden: Warrior in Corr Syl's battle group

Alston Marbellet: Air Force Lieutenant General

Ankolla Siran: Warrior in Corr Syl's battle group

Arden Aquila: Chairman of the Wycliff District council

Arthur Tummel: Captured on Juniper Mesa, son of Marion

Athol Shorel: Leader of Wycliff's first battle group

Bataar (William) Lee (Wilder): Warrior in Corr Syl's battle group

Charlotte Thomas: Daughter of Howard and Marcie

Corinne Ellis: First student to greet Corr and Rhya

Corr Syl: Warrior, leader of new battle group

Duncan Mäkinen: Human boy adopted by Mäkinen family

Ellan Marin: Diplomat and Aide to Whistol Farr

Elsa Loret: Liaison to Mountainview government

Halbert Sims: Warrior andCorr Syl's teacher

Halen: Aaron Li's chief spy commander

Howard Thomas: Detective married to Marcie

Illia: Corr's friend, the Rock Squirrel leader

Ivanstor Johns: Mountainview City Manager

Jonas Miller: Wycliff warrior who taught Rhya Bright

Lactella : Mentally-gifted black widow spider

Lila Bright: Human girl adopted by Rhya Bright's uncle

Lisa Roman: Attacked by Allon Trofeld

Marcie Thomas: Teacher married to Howard

Marion Tummel: Interviewed by Lactella and Mother of Arthur

Martin Toliver: Federation president

Millicent Thomas: Assistant District Attorney married to AJ
Morgan Silverleaf: Head Librarian for Wycliff District
Nathan Jensen: Fisher who guided Thomases in Embassy
Noah Parker: Assisted Corr Syl
Petra Austin: Embassy liaison with Human Colonel Phillips
Quin Achiptre: Warrior in Corr Syl's battle group
Ralph Mäkinen: Warrior in Corr Syl's battle group
Rebecca Thomas: Mother of Howard and AJ
Rhya Bright: Warrior in training
Rita Anderson: Conservative high school student
Robert McLaren: Psychologist developed soldier attitude scale
Robert Marbellet: Air Force colonel
Robert Thomas: Son of AJ and Millicent
Sakura James: Diplomat and Aide to Whistol Farr
Sam Whortin: Embassy security chief
Sampson Howell: Army general .
Sean Phillips: Army colonel Assistant to general Howell
Stephen Miller: Army Engineers General
Tau Korhonen: Wycliff Counselor
Whistol Farr: Ambassador to Mountainview
William Ellison: Chief of the Federation Armed Forces
William (Willie) Thomas: Son of Howard and Marcie
Wilson Smith: Head of Embassy Public Affairs and Education
Ya Zhōu: Aaron Li's cousin, friend, and chief assistant
Zuberi Taxus: Warrior in Corr Syl's battle group

Places

A border separates Earth's two civilizations, the Tsaeb and the Human. Tsaeb lands are divided into a hierarchy of continental and district councils. Human lands are divided into 90 nations with thousands of states and state subdivisions. Humans have no jurisdiction over any oceans except for areas east of Asia and Australia.

Place: Description

Border: Separates Human and Tsaeb lands. Established by treaty following the late 1800's Tsaeb defeat of the Humans

Boulder Court: Fighter assembly point W of the Corinne Trail

Juniper Mesa: Uplands on SE edge of Wycliff, 5 mi N of the border

Continental Center: North American Tsaeb admin center on Brushy Mtn. in Ozarks

Corinne Trail: Ancient north-south path through Wycliff District, follows White River, passes west of Diamond Peak, enters Mountainview from northwest

Diamond Peak: Tall volcanic remnant between border and Mountainview

Embassy: Tsaeb Embassy in Mountainview, Human capital city of Federation state of Normount

Federation: 25 states occupying parts of North and Central America

Gray Hills: Volcanic range forming E border of Wycliff District

Jones Creek: Tributary to White River comes from Gray Hills in E

Mountainview: Capitol of Human state of Normount, population 2,000,000

Normount: Human state, Capitol is Mountainview

Oriven District: Wycliff District's western neighbor

Piedmont: Small Tsaeb community southeast of Mountainview

Plainview: Federation capitol

Redfield District: Wycliff District's E neighbor

Sand River Bend: Fighter assembly point E of the Corinne Trail

Sand River: Runs south past Juniper Mesa

Sawtooth Mt: Mountain home of the Piedmont community

Sentinel Spire: Tall lava capped butte near Juniper Mesa

Shēnzo: Aaron Li's home province and seat of power in E Asia

Silverril District: Wycliff's NE neighbor

Taoso: The oldest Human nation; home of Aaron Li and Ya Zhōu
Traveler's Notch: Natural alcove in base of Sentinel Spire near
    Juniper Mesa
White River: Principal river running S. through Wycliff District
Wycliff Center: Administrative Center for Wycliff District
Wycliff District: Corr Syl's home, 1800 mi^2; half a million sapient
    residents
Wycliff Embassy: Located in NE suburbs of Mountainview
Xi'ou: The capital of Shⱬnzo, Aaron Li's home province

Now that you have finished my book, won't you please consider writing a review? Reviews are the best way readers discover great new books. I would truly appreciate it.

Acknowledgements

My incredible wife Denise, suggested I write a novel, and she spent hours reviewing early drafts. Dr. Michael P. Randall and Professor Joseph E. Rubi read my early atrocities and gave valuable tips for transitioning from academic to creative writing. Members of Professional Writers of Prescott, Prescott Writers Workshop, and Prescott Writing Adventures also shared ideas and methods. I found useful writing advice on hundreds of Internet blogs and writer's groups. Most influential were the thousands of authors who have written about writing and who illuminated techniques with their stories. I especially liked the methods books by Roy Peter Clark (*Writing Tools*) and Nancy Kress (*Dynamic Characters*). Joe DiBuduo and Yoly Fivas generously contributed helpful suggestions.

CONNECT WITH GARRY ROGERS

If you liked Corr Syl the Warrior, go to GarryRogers.com to read more about the Tsaeb and check the progress on *Corr Syl the Terrible*.

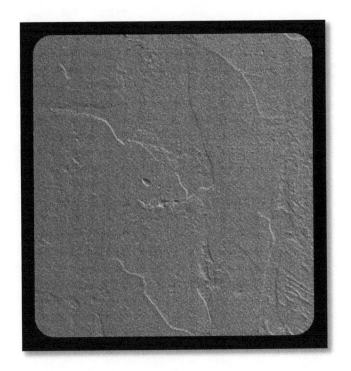

Made in the USA
Charleston, SC
01 March 2014